MW00478920

Coming Home

Coming Home

A Texas Sisters Novel

Audrey Wick

TULE
PUBLISHING

Coming Home
Copyright © 2018 Audrey Wick
Tule Publishing First Printing, June 2018

The Tule Publishing Group, LLC

ALL RIGHTS RESERVED

First Publication by Tule Publishing Group 2018

No part of this book may be used or reproduced in any manner
whatsoever without written permission except in the case of brief
quotations embodied in critical articles and reviews.

This is a work of fiction. Names, characters, places, and incidents are
products of the author's imagination or are used fictitiously. Any
resemblance to actual events, locales, organizations, or persons, living or
dead, is entirely coincidental.

ISBN: 978-1-949068-52-8

Dedication

This book is dedicated to my parents, siblings, and extended family who make where I live feel like home.

Acknowledgements

Home can have different meanings to different people. To me, home is as much about people as it is about place. And no matter where I am, I am grateful to be surrounded by people who make me feel the love of home.

My parents and siblings have been wonderfully supportive of my writing. Extended family also helped create a welcome atmosphere for my first book.

I am indebted to Dr. Julie Ardery and Bill Bishop, who planned a homecoming for *Finding True North*. Artwork and support by Suzanne Batchelder and scene guidance from Eric Batchelder helped me get ready for Book Two. And Georgina Hudspeth helped adorn me with beautiful handmade book jewelry.

Beth Wiseman and Elaine Thomas, your encouragement fueled me through edits.

Karen Rock, Joanne Rock, and Catherine Mann, years ago you cheered me on and stayed in touch through my debut publication, giving me models of publishing success.

Amanda Gifford and Melissa Smith, your forever friendships and the ways you champion creativity are gifts. Yvette Janecek and Adam Klein, your thoughtfulness exists in quiet gestures that I will remember always.

Many early readers, bloggers, librarians, book enthusiasts, friends, and fellow Tule authors helped me launch the series, along with guidance from my agent Barbara Collins Rosenberg.

The group of Meghan, Michelle, Sinclair, Lee, Monti, Marlene, and Jane at Tule Publishing, thank you for believing in this story and believing in the Texas Sisters series.

Brian and Luke, our trips to New Mexico are precious memories, and I know we'll have more adventures in the future. Still, it's always good to come home.

Chapter One

M ALLORY FREDRICK CROSSED her legs and swung her right foot into a rocking motion, trying to calm the nerves that had plagued her for a week. Iker, the human resources director, clicked absently through a set of electronic forms, the computer screen illuminating his face in odd patterns of a white-washed glow. "This is not a situation I've encountered before."

"That makes two of us." Mallory's stomach felt as empty as her nearby classroom.

"We've got some options." Iker's directorial tone was mechanical, as if he delivered lines like this any time there was an emergency incident regarding a faculty member. Still, his lack of emotion coupled with little eye contact left Mallory unconvinced. She continued to swing her foot, settling into a rhythm to expend some of the frustration that had mounted between the time she discovered the threat, her meetings with the college's police department, and now human resources.

Because this meeting with Iker involved her future and her paycheck, it was even more intimidating than her time with the Santa Fe College police chief.

Iker reviewed the faculty handbook, a document Mallory

herself had referenced multiple times over the last week. Policies, protocol, and procedure were in place to protect both students and faculty, but even these rules didn't quite cover Mallory's situation. Because when it came to social media use by college students, that was a rather gray area to enforce in regard to conduct.

Iker read words Mallory had nearly committed to memory. This was nothing new.

And some of what Iker was saying didn't even apply, an argument the chief had made. That was why Mallory's student, Jesse Sands, had been slapped with a misdemeanor instead of a felony—even though a fine line had been walked.

Interpreting Mallory's frustration, Iker admitted, "The college may need to look into updating a few of these policies."

Mallory didn't even try to camouflage the tartness in her reply. "Glad I could be the one to bring that to light."

Every bit of continued reference to Jesse and his incident sickened Mallory further, exacerbating her stress because of the viral way the student's words lurched beyond Mallory's control. Successfully, Jesse had managed to threaten, humiliate, and shame Mallory while muddying the waters of college enforcement through public posting on social media.

Using her name.

For anyone with an Internet connection to see.

He posted a loose threat that he would "get her" followed by a series of expletives about the college. He added a violent meme that wasn't of Mallory, but anyone who didn't know better could have assumed it was.

This, according to the police, fell under the definition of threat on a public official because of her teaching position, though the student's exact words didn't cross into felony territory.

Mallory had sensed Jesse was upset before the posting. Her experience as an educator told her as much. He had been coming late to class and was on the brink of academic probation if his grades didn't improve, but when he failed his last assignment, that was when the online posting hit.

So Jesse Sands had been pulled from class, slapped with a year's suspension, and escorted off campus. But by the time he stepped off the curb of Santa Fe College property, his words had already cut like a deep injury. Mallory's confidence was shaken, her safety stirred in a way she had never experienced in five years of teaching full-time at a college and in a department she loved.

Mallory took a week off to personally regroup, and the police chief assured her she would be safe when she returned to campus for December-finals week. She had timidly resumed a routine of shuffling from the faculty parking lot to her office to the classroom, but she felt uneasy. Her eyes scanned her surroundings at all times, and she didn't step anywhere she would be alone even though she felt that way. Colleagues offered sympathetic glances and basic apologetic comments for what had happened to her, but there was little meaningful conversation. Maybe people didn't want to get involved. Students even eyed her with suspicion. She could only imagine what sensational gossip was swirling around the hallways. The unease was palpable, like a suffocating fog she couldn't escape as she marched through an end-of-the-semester routine that should have otherwise been certain and celebratory.

"I'll talk with the chief about his recommendations for bringing some updates to the attention of the college's board." Iker scribbled a reminder on a nearby sheet of paper, though Mallory had little confidence that updates would be timely. After all, any changes were too late to affect her.

The damage had already been done.

Iker spun a slim printed stack of papers in Mallory's direction so she could read them. "You had asked about options for the spring semester given this semester's . . . setbacks."

The clinical word choice punched Mallory in the gut, a further blow of humiliation that proved even human resources was ill-equipped to handle nuances of emotional ramifications from a student they only knew by name and collegiate identification number.

Not like Mallory.

She'd had fourteen weeks to get to know Jesse, seeing him every Monday, Wednesday, and Friday. She taught his first-year composition course and was a sideline cheerleader for his progress just as she was with all of her students. Jesse had a face, a personality. But, here, he was a statistic, not a person.

"Yes, my *setbacks*"—Mallory emphasized the word— "have been challenging this semester."

Iker forced a curt smile before continuing. "And we want

you to know the college continues to support you. We want you to feel safe."

That feeling had escaped her for a week. The two little words of "get her" kept ringing in her ears, lassoing around her and constricting her movement through routine days. She had never been one to look over her shoulder in fear. But, now, doing so was the only way to know if he'd be following her with malicious intent. News stories of college attacks and violence had always seemed so foreign to Mallory.

Not anymore.

Was this how it all started? And, if so, how would it stop?

Mallory could control her own actions, but she couldn't control Jesse's. That was what scared her the most.

"We've done what we are able to do within the limitations of our student conduct guidelines and New Mexico state law to make sure Jesse doesn't bother you."

But you haven't done enough. Mallory wanted to bite back. That was the point. Jesse had been removed from view, but his virtual comments were indelibly stamped into her psyche. "Our hands are a bit tied because Mr. Sands—"

"Jesse," Mallory corrected, not wanting to honor him with any ounce of respect. He certainly hadn't given any to Mallory through his actions.

"Jesse," Iker continued, keeping his voice in grayscale, "didn't cross the line into a felony. He didn't say how or when he would carry out the threat, so while we take this very seriously, there's only so much we can do in accordance with—"

"Guidelines. Got it." Mallory already had all the legalese explained to her by the chief. Jesse hadn't erred far enough for the legal system to kick-in with serious protection when it came to her well-being. That was the worst of the situation, this helpless limbo of a problem being addressed but not with the level of seriousness it warranted.

No students were caught in the net of Jesse's online threat, so the college deemed it appropriate for Mallory to step back into the classroom to administer end-of-semester exams. But it felt foreign to do so. There were plenty of students she enjoyed in the course, and she tried to focus on them. Yet she had no sureness in standing before a classroom of students who had likely heard, read, or seen those words and that image online. Her confidence had been knocked back to a level of rookie teaching, not to mention the hit to her self-worth.

How does a person regain footing when her sense of safety has been rocked?

"You have a five-course teaching load for the spring semester." Iker's look forward was an attempt to minimize the focus on this fall semester, but anxious thoughts of all those new responsibilities—and new students—sliced further into Mallory's nerves. "All faculty have a three-week holiday break now that final exams are complete."

Mallory nodded. She knew the routine well, but three weeks seemed much shorter now than it had ever seemed to her before.

"So that should be plenty of time for you to rest, regroup, and refocus." Iker stiffened his jaw as he poised his pencil atop the header of the first page of papers that sat between him and Mallory, the words "Faculty Contract" teasing with Mallory's subconscious. Most full-time instructors were thrilled to sign contracts guaranteeing their continued employment at the college each year, though seeing the words now were more like a contract to imprisonment. How could she snap out of feeling this way?

Iker shifted his pencil, removed the page, and pointed to the header of a new one. "As you can see," he continued, "the college does have a sabbatical policy in special cases."

Mallory had studied the language of that in the faculty handbook, and the policy seemed to be from another era. It was an underused and rarely discussed option that involved a three-ring circus of hoops through which to jump if a faculty member at the college wanted to make it work. Still, she was thankful for an opportunity to discuss it, halting the rhythm of her foot as she focused on what Iker would reveal. "Go on."

"I spoke with your dean prior to our meeting." He shuffled past the page to yet another. "And she provided this letter of support for your use of a sabbatical." He slid the letter closer to Mallory.

Uncrossing her legs, she leaned in and saw the unmistakable signature of Dean Vanguard beneath two brief paragraphs authorizing spring semester release. Mallory read through the lines with surprise and an eagerness to understand the specifics. Her dean had mentioned nothing to her personally. "This says that my contract would be prorated."

Mallory knew the meaning of the word, but wanted to be sure she understood the application through the context here. "But what exactly does that entail?"

Iker drew his hand away from the letter, righting his posture as he clarified. "That means you can choose a sabbatical this spring with no penalty. Your five classes will be redistributed to available faculty. None of those classes will be cancelled."

For her future students' sake, that detail made her blow out a breath in relief. After all, her challenges were not their fault. "That's good to hear."

"The liberal arts department has a willing pool of adjuncts as well as a few full-timers who are agreeable to taking overloads. Dean Vanguard is confident those classes can be covered with simple changes to the instructor of record." Mallory knew that was, indeed, an easy process which involved a quick software update from "Professor Fredrick" to a different instructor's name.

"That's great news." It was the first bit of pleasant surprise Mallory had heard all week. But there was more to understand about the change. "So, then, what happens to my contract? And my spring pay?"

Iker straightened his posture. "That's where we're in new territory."

As Mallory suspected.

Iker seemed to choose his words with care. "If you accept the spring sabbatical, you remain an employee of the college for insurance purposes." Mallory could sense the blow coming before Iker said it. "But your contract will expire at the end of the spring, and you will receive no paycheck after this month."

So that was why Santa Fe sabbaticals were not used. They were in name only. No perks. No pay. And Mallory's worst fear. "Is there any guarantee of a future contract?"

"There's never a guarantee." Iker's words were delivered as finitely as the end-of-semester student averages Mallory had inked just hours prior. "The board will have final approval of all faculty jobs for next fall. You may be offered a contract again, but that's all dependent on state funding and enrollment numbers."

There was always that fear. Her job was safe but only one year at a time. Plenty of adjunct faculty were gunning for full-time employment, so Mallory had a reputation to uphold if she wanted to remain competitive. And if she stepped out of the picture—even for one semester—there was no telling what her future might hold.

Her eyes fell to her lap, dejection and contemplation swirling in a nauseous internal cocktail of a choice to be made. She thumbed her band of bangle bracelets, reminders of trips to the Santa Fe Plaza. She loved to shop directly from artisan jewelers selling their stunning wares of turquoise, tiger's eye, and sterling-silver bobbles every weekend. The bright colors of the American Southwest spoke to her, and her personal collection of jewelry was her biggest splurge. Each, however, carried special meaning of a particular event, celebration, or occasion that happened in the town that had provided her with her first full-time teaching job and charmed her with personality she had grown to love. The tinkling of silver against silver was the only sound in the otherwise silent office.

Mallory didn't lift her eyes as she mustered a shred of confidence to ask, "When do I have to choose?"

Iker leaned forward, willing Mallory's eyes to look at him. "Mallory . . ." He spoke as if he were comforting a child who needed a simple explanation. "That's why we're here."

Mallory kept her hand on her bracelets but met Iker's gaze, puzzled by his statement.

Reading her confusion, Iker leveled the news. "You have to decide today. Will you teach in the spring, or will you take an unpaid sabbatical?"

And so that was how Mallory would mark this day. This was the exact moment Santa Fe suddenly stopped being her home.

MALLORY COLLAPSED ONTO the well-worn futon in her apartment's living room, its padding flattened from years of use. Her Persian cat, Bella, mewed near the base before jumping into her lap with physical force that matched the figurative force she had been dealt by human resources.

Instinctively, Mallory reached behind Bella's right ear but couldn't bring herself to offer more than an obligatory scratch. Iker's insistence that she make a decision about the spring before she left the HR office placed her on a trajectory of temporary unemployment that she hadn't foreseen. For years, her heart had been in teaching. But, in the few short moments it took her to sign the sabbatical paperwork, that same heart was drier than the Chihuahuan Desert.

Mallory closed her eyes and leaned her head back, hoping the stress that had built behind her eyes wouldn't turn into tears. She focused on deep breathing and relaxation, letting Bella's small movements be her only distraction. That cat always seemed to be without a care in the world.

Must be nice. Mallory envied her beloved pet's freedom. What were a cat's biggest daily decisions? Surely they paled in comparison to Mallory's.

Wild thoughts and random questions of her spring joblessness weren't eased by a few moments of solitude. But how could she combat the emptiness of purpose that was staring her in the face? The sensation was so alien.

"Bella!" Mallory squealed, her eyes popping open.

The cat's front paws sank into Mallory's torso as she begged for attention. The feline didn't care what had happened to Mallory during the day. Her entitlement for affection knew no bounds. Mallory bit her lip as she studied her only companion for the moment. She nuzzled Bella's chin as the cat relaxed against Mallory's chest, completely engulfing her in a show of love that made the waterworks begin. Her eyes pooled with tears. And as Bella revved her purring to the volume of a coffee maker, emotion cascaded down Mallory's cheeks. The progress she had been making in her professional life had crashed to a halt, leaving her with nothing but a tear-stained face and a loneliness like she had never before experienced. Even Bella's nudges and cuddles couldn't shake them from Mallory.

She dabbed at her eyes with the back of her hand before looking around her apartment, mentally tallying the bills that were coming due now that month's end was upon her. Electricity. Internet. Cable. Insurance. Water and sewage.

Rent.

She sniffled with a sharp intake of realization. Her last paycheck would cover those bills, but there would be no more money coming in after that.

Nothing until . . . August? And that paycheck would only be guaranteed if she was offered a new contract.

And Iker had made no promises about that.

How could she afford to pay for over half a year's living expenses with no paycheck?

Bella mewed a hunger cry.

"And you'll need food too, baby." She tried to verbally assuage her pet's fears as well as her own. Financially, the next few months would be tough. But showing up to work every day and placing herself in what could be harm's way didn't make sense. Her safety had to take priority. "I'll find a way."

Bella made eye contact as she lifted her head toward Mallory whose fingers massaged in a series of firm strokes between Bella's ears. Then a buzzing of her phone atop the nearby coffee table interrupted their bonding. Mallory lunged with one hand as Bella adjusted to the sudden movement with light clawing against Mallory's sweater. Both grumbled at the change, Mallory redirecting her attention from Bella to the caller.

Her younger sister's greeting on the other end of the line from Texas was the bright spot Mallory's day had lacked. "How did you know I needed to talk?" Mallory tilted her head to hold the phone as she bent toward a familiar voice.

To Paige's credit, she listened calmly as Mallory filled her in on every fearful and uncomfortable detail of the last two weeks. Perhaps Mallory should have been miffed that her younger sister was the voice of maturity and reason, which was the sibling role Mallory had always played. Instead, Mallory was grateful for the reversal. Patient and rational, Paige articulated the choices Mallory had and verbally weighed their pros and cons.

The apartment complex didn't allow subletting, so that option was off the table. "How much would it cost to break your lease?"

Mallory had a vague idea and relayed it.

"That's just a fraction of what rent would be for the next six months." Mallory nodded with shared agreement that Paige couldn't see. But as if she sensed it, Paige then added, "So save yourself that money. And other expenses." She paused just long enough so Mallory understood the seriousness of her offer. "Come stay with me in Texas through the spring."

But saving rent and moving in with her younger sister wasn't that simple. Paige was recently engaged. Her fiancé, Everett, was adapting to the role of stepfather for Paige's young son, Nathan. And they lived twelve hours away.

It was a home. But it wasn't Mallory's.

Neither, though, is this. She looked absently at the walls of her apartment, which suddenly felt smaller. She inhaled air that suddenly tasted staler. Even Bella seemed to turn up her nose at some indistinct change.

Santa Fe wasn't feeling like home.

"A change of scenery would be nice, wouldn't it?" Paige urged.

Mallory couldn't argue with that. "But what about Everett?" Her sister was planning a summer wedding. "I don't want to cramp any of your plans with him."

"He's not living here," Paige reminded her sister. "It's just me and Nathan at the house. Everett's staying with his parents, and he's still on the road a lot."

"To Amarillo?"

"There and back and there again. He'll finish up with the job transition before the wedding, but there's a lot he's trying to get straight."

Mallory admired Everett's work ethic and the care he took of his aging parents. He was also so good to her sister, so Mallory certainly didn't want to be a burden to their romance and their limited time together.

But Paige was still powering the Talk Train down the tracks. "Besides," she added, "Nathan would love some quality time with his aunt. He's going to be out of the toddler stage soon. A preschooler this year, if you can believe it."

Mallory smiled at the very mention of her only nephew, whom she didn't visit often enough. Seeing more of Nathan would be fun. But it wasn't just Mallory who would need to come to Texas. "And Bella?"

Paige countered with another cheery reply. "Nathan will love her. He's really gentle with animals. Plus the extra bedroom you've used before is just as you left it. I haven't done anything but vacuum in there. It's yours if you want it."

Mallory twisted her wrist, studying the coils of jewelry. On the one hand, her sister was coming to her rescue with an offer that seemed too good to resist. But on the other hand, would running away solve anything?

Her palms were sweaty just thinking about the continued stress under which she would live if she stayed in Santa Fe. Her world was rocked, and she couldn't breathe here. But Paige was giving her a place—albeit temporary—where she could.

So Mallory made up her mind for accepting Paige's lifeline. As she clicked off the call, she turned to Bella and announced, "Looks like we're going to Texas."

Chapter Two

MALLORY HADN'T BEEN to Texas in over a year. The last time she stayed with Paige, it was under emergency circumstances. Paige needed Mallory when Nathan was hospitalized with appendicitis, and Mallory stepped up to help her sister, who was essentially operating as a single mother during that time. That was also when Paige reconnected with Everett, a blast-from-the-past turned fiancé. Mallory couldn't be happier for her sister.

Paige's life was perfect.

Mallory's was a disaster.

She padded into the kitchen to boil a kettle of water. Thumbing through the assortment of tea bags in the pantry, she decided on a green tea and lemon balm blend. Something had to calm her nerves enough to focus on the next task for the evening, which was research.

She needed to access her bank account, set cancel dates for several of the apartment services, check into storage options for her furniture, and compare costs of moving companies. There was no way she could box, load, haul, and organize in less than two weeks' time before the end of the month.

And the holidays were upcoming.

The college's fall semester ended the third week in December, so Mallory had calendar closure but little else. She muttered a phrase that expressed anything but seasonal cheer.

She poured herself a steaming cup of green tea, flipped to a clean page in her journal so she could take notes, tucked a pencil behind her ear, and started tapping away at the keyboard. She made notes as she navigated from one window to the next, moving along not only in matters she needed to accomplish but adding ones that hadn't originally crossed her mind.

Forward the mail.

Inform the credit card company.

Request a rebate for two prepaid services that were being cancelled.

She also notified the medical insurance company of a change of address. Luckily, that incentive hadn't been slapped away from her by Santa Fe College with the acceptance of a sabbatical. She assuaged further fear with a telephone call to the twenty-four-hour customer service line. "And will my policy still be valid in Texas?"

The voice on the other end of the line confirmed with an answer as sharp as a vaccine needle prick. "As long as your primary care physician is in network."

Mallory breathed a sigh of relief followed by another long drink of warm tea as she hung up the phone. Bella mewed from her perch on the front windowsill looking out into the apartment parking lot.

"Good reminder," Mallory muttered, as if she knew exactly what Bella was signaling. "I should probably call the vet in the morning." She turned to a new page in the journal and put that task at the top of a to-do list for the following day.

Silently, Mallory hoped she wouldn't need to use any vet in the near future. Bella was up-to-date on her shots, but any medical expense at this juncture would be an especially hard financial hit.

"Stay well, Bella," she willed aloud.

The cat lifted her paw, licked between her toes, and expressed nothing but oblivion to the tornado of technical activity that Mallory's day was generating.

The final task for the evening was selecting a moving service. Paige's offer was for a place to stay, not a way to get there. Her sister had room at her house in Texas to hold some things, and given Mallory's uncertainty of the future, taking her up on that offer would be a safe option. But she also had big furniture and housewares that would require a storage unit. That was where a professional's help would be needed.

Digital listings for moving services all looked the same, so like the spin of a roulette wheel, she let her luck ride as she chose one at random.

Four Guys.

It could well have been the name of a jazz band or a pizza parlor, but they were Santa Fe movers who advertised "no job too big or too small." She studied their cartoon logo. *So could I just pay for two guys?* She needed manual labor, but maybe they'd be negotiable on rates. She shrugged, willing to give it a shot with a late-evening phone call since, after all, they didn't advertise any sort of hours.

Mallory punched the numbers on her cell then tapped her pencil on the edge of the table as she waited for what she presumed was going to be an automated message.

The husky, smooth voice who answered was decidedly not a machine. "Alec here." The words tumbled so fast that Mallory fumbled with her own to reply.

"Oh, um . . ." She switched ears with her phone. "I'm trying to, well . . . my name is Mallory—"

"Hi, Mallory." Alec's buttery voice on the other end of the line slipped into her ear, teasing her focus. "What can I do for you?"

So much. She bit back anxiety for the barrage of answers she could have given if this conversation were going to veer into telephone psychiatry.

Alec, perhaps adept at fielding calls from emotional customers, filled Mallory's silence. "Need a mover?"

"Yes!" She practically spit the word as if she were holding it in her cheeks.

Alec's cool laugh washed over her as he assured in a steady delivery, "Well, you've got me."

And something about those words flipped a switch in Mallory. Because, aside from Paige, she didn't really have anyone. Not in Santa Fe, at least. Tears welled in the corners of her eyes and a lump formed in her throat as she squeaked a "thank you" reply that sounded more like a kitten's voice than a human's.

Alec didn't miss a beat. "I suspect there's a little bit of

stress on you with the whole moving process. So, don't worry. Four Guys will take care of you." Then he added more definitively, "At least this one will."

And the torrent of emotion Mallory had kept in check all day came pouring out in soft sobs. She hunched her shoulders and curled into the phone, clutching it like a lifeline of human understanding. Four Guys was going to help her move, and one guy was going to make all the difference.

ALEC O'DONNELL LISTENED to the starts and stops of the female caller's voice as she communicated through sobs. A woman crying was not at the top of his list of most pleasant sounds. It had to be right up there with the grizzly sound of a bandage ripping from skin or the awful grinding noise of dental office equipment.

If anyone had told him he would play armchair psychiatrist in his choice to start a moving company, he would have laughed. He had formed the group with three friends during college, a casual way to make extra money that had turned into a lucrative venture. When they got their act together and registered an actual company—as opposed to just pocketing cash for helping fellow college students with loading and unloading items via pickup truck—that was when they decided this could be a career.

Choosing jobs, setting their own hours, and not having to dress in business suits or punch a time clock were real advantages to their Four Guys venture.

Handling crying women over the phone, however, was never a part of the job any of them had anticipated.

Breakups, divorces, spontaneous adventures—female callers were typically the ones who needed the most help, and many needed it quickly. So Four Guys made it a point to handle the whole process. They could assess, box, load, drive, unload, and pretty much help with anything else requested by a client during a move.

Brokering conversations between ex-lovers, following a divorce decree for the splitting of assets, or moving furnishings to more than one household were routine occurrences. So were some things that others might have considered a little less routine.

Dog sitting? Been there.

Draining and refilling a saltwater aquarium? Done that. Twice.

Bubble Wrapping an entire collection of porcelain circus figurines? Nailed it. Though that had actually taken two of the four guys at once.

Alec was used to accepting the challenge of a customer's request and finding a way to make it happen. He suspected from the sobs on the other end of the line that this was a breakup situation. "Will you need a storage unit?"

"Yes." The voice of the woman named Mallory sounded so far away, so helpless. Alec wanted to make this as easy for her as possible. "I've got a couple of really great possibilities. Two units we work with give unadvertised discounts to us, so we'll have you covered there and keep the cost low."

Lines like that always worked wonders for putting customers at ease. But if it did so to Mallory, she didn't let on.

"So is everything going into storage? Or are you headed to another location?"

"Texas." The syllables sagged with the weight of emotion that only Mallory knew.

But if Alec was going to agree to this job, he needed to know more.

He tried to keep things light as he chided, "Now that's a big state, sweetheart." He hadn't planned for that pet name to slide from his lips, but when it did, he couldn't take it back.

The unexpected word hung in the air between them, teasing either one of them to say something about it. Alec knew from working with enough women that even a single slip of the tongue was enough to ruin a bid.

He didn't want that.

Alec wanted Mallory to speak because he needed to make sure he had control of his lips before he opened his mouth again.

Mallory cleared her throat and used Alec's own word in a spunky reply. "This sweetheart knows it's a big state."

A woman with wit. That was Alec's weakness.

Mallory clarified her destination. "A little outside of San Antonio."

Alec refocused on the task and conjured a mental map of interstates and highways from New Mexico that connected into the heart of Texas.

"Less than half an hour east of it. A town called Seguin."

Alec had never heard of it. If any of the other guys had, they weren't around to ask. Tavis was home with his wife waiting for their new baby to arrive any day. Greg and Rory had a ski trip with their wives and kids in Taos. Alec was staying close to home for Christmas and agreed to man the phones because none of them had expected any big jobs.

But as he fished for more information from Mallory, he was sensing that this could turn into one. Especially when she added the one piece of furniture that was his worst nightmare.

"There's a piano." Mallory revealed it with far less fanfare than he was feeling at the thought. "It's an antique. My grandmother's."

"I'll be sure to take extra special care of it." Though Alec didn't even yet know how. That was certainly a job for more than one guy. "And when do you want it moved?"

"This week. I've got to be out by the end of the month."

That immediacy deflated him. He was sure Greg and Rory had already left for Taos, but Tavis was in town. Maybe he could steal away for a few hours to help. "Any other surprises?"

Mallory was silent on the other end of the phone, which wasn't a good sign. He filled the void with a practical cue. "Just wanting to be informed."

Tiffany lamps?

A family of ferrets?

Relocation of a greenhouse?

Alec mentally prepared for the worst. "Hit me with it."

Mallory's even reply wasn't what he expected. "I left my

job today."

Alec's chest tightened. He could hear the pain and heart-break in her voice. "Well then." He was going to have to keep this fragile one from completely falling apart. "Sounds like you could use a change of scenery. Lucky for you, Texas winters are absolutely gorgeous."

MALLORY HAD GONE to bed shortly after the phone call with Alec, laden with a heart of uncertainty, a head full of worry, and a stomach full of green tea. She hadn't even bothered to eat dinner because she had no appetite for it.

She hadn't exactly been let go; Iker assured her that her full-time position would be held in her absence and her office would not be used by anyone else. But she needed to make a decision about the following academic year by mid spring so her name could be in the pool for fall contracts. The board extended those over summer, and even though there was no guarantee, she did have five years of employ-ment history behind her. Yet without a paycheck and without a teaching schedule for the upcoming semester, she was in an odd professional limbo. And when she told Alec over the phone she had left her job, it was the easiest way to simplify her complicated circumstances.

Now, she was in new territory.

The morning after her last class for the semester was usu-ally one of long rest. With grades inked, paperwork complete, and her office closed for winter break, she could sleep in and relish the peace brought by the end of an academic term. But today and for the coming days there would be absolutely no tranquility. She had work to do.

Sorting, organizing, and packing were the orders of the day. The last time she moved was when she had landed the job in Santa Fe, her first teaching gig with full-time employment. She was so proud.

And she was so unattached.

She had rented this apartment and furnished it with no more than a carload of possessions and a pickup bed of cheap furniture: twin sleeper, one bookshelf, and a futon. Over the years of being at Santa Fe, she had upgraded her furniture and found her niche in décor. A handcrafted wood dining table and coffee table anchored the combination living and dining room. Gorgeous hammered silver vases and dishes adorned their tops along with corner accents of dried lavender branches looped together artfully with twine. Her two Mexican Equipale leather armchairs were her favorite pieces. She also upgraded her bedroom last year to a four-poster full-size bed with solid wood headboard.

Her possessions were treasures to her, and she could save them in a storage unit. She was not worried about that, but the question of cost for moving was unclear. Alec was coming by this morning for an appraisal, and he was also bringing boxes and other packing supplies. She could take care of some things by herself but was grateful that he could deliver the supplies to speed the process.

Then there was the piano.

She had described it to Alec over the phone, an upright piano from the 1940s. It wasn't as bulky as a grand piano and didn't even take up as much room as her bed, but it still required careful consideration for moving.

"Grandma would turn over in her grave if she knew I was going to have to put this into storage." She apologized aloud to her grandmother even though the only set of ears to hear the words belonged to Bella. The cat paused in the shadow of Mallory's stance as she eyed the piano, rubbing her tail against Mallory's black leggings. Bella's fur tickled Mallory's bare feet, and she wiggled her crimson-colored toenails in response.

"You'll miss this spot too, won't you, Bella?" She lowered herself onto the smooth wood of the pull-out bench and tapped the surface as Bella jumped next to her. Bella would often curl atop the bench for a lazy afternoon nap when she wanted a place to stretch her long feline limbs. She'd miss that spot for sure. "And what else are you going to miss?" Mallory looked around the apartment, now realizing there were little things like this that would carve an absence inside of her.

As if she could stand her insides being any hollower.

But Bella didn't seem to notice. Mallory stroked the rich fur across her backbone as Bella responded with a purr. That was the only sound until competition from the doorbell seized Bella's voice. She stiffened her hind legs, stilled her body, and raised her head in the direction of the sound.

"Must be Four Guys." *Or at least one of them.*

Mallory stood and made her way to the door. Alec had,

after all, said he'd be coming alone to drop off the moving supplies and make an appraisal. She rose up on tiptoes to peer through the peephole.

Half of Alec O'Donnell was shielded from her view thanks to a stack of folded cardboard boxes and a tube of Bubble Wrap. A roll of packing tape was looped through his fingers, but Mallory was able to spy some impressive bronzed forearms, taut from the angle at which he was holding the moving supplies. The confident set of his shoulders filled the space even with the door between them. She judged he must be at least six inches greater in height than she was, maybe more.

He shifted his weight, and the early morning desert sun played with highlights against his hazelnut hair, making some strands reflect blond. It also accented the golden stubble of hair growth on his cheeks, though even that couldn't mask the matching deep dimples on each side of his otherwise chiseled face. He was hard work and Hollywood rolled into one.

I ordered that? Mallory lowered her heels back onto the floor, reestablishing her balance and catching her breath. Alec O'Donnell was nothing like the cartoon image of his face from the Four Guys logo. If the trio of others ranked half as hot as Alec, Mallory wondered why they didn't opt for an actual photo.

Marketing 101. Show off the assets.

Oh boy. In her leggings and oversized sweater, Mallory suddenly felt underdressed for meeting Alec face-to-face. She smoothed the hem of her sweater, finger-combed her blondish-brown tresses, and bit her lips to force a little color into them. Then she placed her hand on the door and inhaled sharply to welcome Alec into her apartment, unsure of what she'd feel when nothing physical separated them.

"YOU MUST BE Mallory." Alec greeted with a nod of his head instead of a handshake since his arms were full.

The lean woman opened the door with a fresh face and a smile. "Mallory Fredrick." Though she didn't make a move to usher him in. She stayed protectively behind the threshold, with one hand on the jamb as if she could slam the door in his face at any moment.

"I'm Alec," he clarified, just to make sure she didn't. "And I've got a Saturday delivery for you," he joked, raising the stack of boxes and Bubble Wrap an inch higher like the moving supplies were take-out pizza boxes.

Mallory shook her head, as if suddenly aware he was in need of a place to put everything down. "Of course." She swung the door open, gesturing for him to come inside. "Just on the floor is fine for now. Unless you see—"

A flash of pewter streaked past them and bolted outside. "What the—"

"Bella!" Mallory dove to the side of Alec, brushing against him as he sidestepped the commotion that had just disappeared from his feet. "Bella!" She screamed again, loud enough for at least the nearest quadrant of neighbors to hear.

The family-friendly design of the complex and its kept nature with manicured landscaping and pristine sidewalks made Alec suspect there weren't generally too many noise disturbances. Even the potted plants flanking her front entrance added to the balance of the place. Mallory disappeared around one and out of his line of sight, so he bent to place the boxes against the entry wall before he stepped back outside to see where Mallory—and that thing—had gone.

Ferret?

Lap dog?

Chinchilla?

Whatever it was, it was fast. And so was Mallory. That was good, especially if that thing was going to be part of the move. He mentally questioned why Four Guys didn't charge more when animals were involved. They could slow a project worse than any human.

Alec closed the door behind him in case there was a second critter inside, though he didn't shut it all the way. "Need some help over there?" Mallory was just beyond the edge of her apartment, near a sprouting sago palm. She had crouched low, coaxing an animal from behind the plant with an outstretched arm.

"She's okay. Just got to grab her out, and these fronds are so pokey." She strained toward the base as if it were a giant Venus flytrap. The billows of her loosely-woven sweater stretched with her movement, her black-legged bottom half steady beneath her. Her outfit was monochromatic, but a series of bright necklace strands swung and jangled, making a soothing noise, sweet like a siren's call. Her crimson-toed bare feet firm against the concrete provided another pop of unexpected cuteness.

Alec shook his head to force away thoughts of attraction. *I'm here to help her move.*

And he had brought donut holes.

Mallory had sounded so emotional on the phone that food seemed appropriate. Some of the other guys perked clients with muffins, cookies, or even coffee. Those little services seemed to go a long way, especially in securing a job after an estimate.

But donut holes? Did any woman like them as much as men? Or young children? The choice of confectionary goods now seemed juvenile. He glanced back at the plain white bakery bag placed on the floor next to the Bubble Wrap. Maybe he could run back to the truck with them and scrap the idea altogether.

Or just eat them himself.

He was overanalyzing, a habit he long held. He pinched the bridge of his nose and shook his head to refocus. Still, a nagging tingle lingered, and it wasn't just in his head. It started when he came face-to-face with Mallory, and it fanned from inside his chest. Flush with this feeling he couldn't identify, Alec was glad when Mallory made a move. She sat back on her heels, victoriously holding the retrieved fur ball.

A cat.

Why did it have to be a cat?

Cat hair was one of Alec's moving pet peeves.

"Meet Bella." Mallory placed her fingers beneath one of

Bella's paws and jerked it up and down, forcing the cat to wave at him.

"Hi." He gulped. The cat did not look amused.

Mallory steadied herself to stand as she championed a smile, a sweet one that set her face alight. "She just got spooked. And she's probably hungry." She tiptoed across the cement to the threshold of the apartment with Bella cradled in her arms. That cat would smell the donut holes in no time.

"And you?" Alec stepped backward into the apartment, holding the door for them both.

"I could eat."

He shut the door behind them in a single, calm move, hoping control of his body would help him retain control of his words. "If you haven't had breakfast . . . well, I . . ." His tongue twisted with the same churn as his insides. "I brought something." He reached for the bag and held it out to her. "Consider it a complementary part of the moving estimate this morning."

Mallory bent at the waist, Bella sliding from her lean arms. The necklaces jangled before Mallory stood and only quieted when she rested her palm across her chest, sandwiching the strands. All fell silent.

"It's not much of a delivery. Just a little something Tavis hooked me on." He rotated the bag. "Donut holes?"

Mallory's silence broke as she groaned what could only be described as the cutest expression of hunger Alec had ever heard.

The donut holes were a winner.

And as Alec caught a glimpse of Mallory savoring glaze remnants left on her fingers a few minutes later—her cheeks drawing in as her eyes lit from the sugar rush—he had to agree that the food was a winner. But so was working this job.

Chapter Three

I N MANY WAYS, an impromptu move was easier than a planned one over several months' time. Mallory could make a list of items to do, and she could cross them off.

Quickly.

That was exactly the pace at which her life was progressing ever since she sat in Iker's office. The week before that, when she was reacting to Jesse's threat and still trying to hold together a professional demeanor in her classroom, her whole world moved in slow motion. But now she was living at lightning speed—making decisions, completing phone calls, and racing toward a temporary move to Seguin.

Through her years in college, she had learned to measure her life by semesters. Every milestone and holiday was either during her teaching time or in between while on breaks. She tried to keep the same pattern as she envisioned her life during the spring bunking with her younger sister.

It's only for a semester. At least that was what she could tell herself.

Thinking long-term was hard in crisis mode. And that was how Mallory had been dealing. Her academic world was rocked, and she was in crisis management. She had to appear strong, even though she felt so very weak.

But as she thought about Paige, Mallory drew strength.

The two of them had always been close, and they also had a pleasant relationship with their parents. But they each made lives in different areas, only triangulating once or twice a year. Their mom and dad retired to Angel Fire, on a small property they purchased with sweeping views of the Sangre de Cristo Mountains in northern New Mexico. The elevation was gorgeous, and even Mallory loved the surprisingly European feel of the cool, well-kept town. But her parents didn't need a grown daughter at their doorstep, nor did she need to chance snowed-in mountain passes this time of year. Angel Fire didn't feel like a sanctuary from Santa Fe. Seguin, however, would provide distance and comfort.

And this move to Texas wasn't like hers to Santa Fe. When she first interviewed for and accepted the full-time position at Santa Fe College, she had done everything on her own. She took pride in that, and she took pride in each of the milestones she reached at the college, from technology certification to new class assignments. She even had plans to approach Dean Vanguard about new section development for a sophomore-level literature course, but that conversation couldn't happen now.

"I'm on sabbatical." She mumbled the words to herself, needing a constant reminder. Turning her brain *OFF* when it came to work-related matters wasn't even a switch she knew how to operate.

Her life had been her work.

Had been.

Had.

Even thinking in past tense was difficult.

Which was why the present was easier. And the present was, indeed, flying by.

Alec had given a storage estimate at a nearby facility that seemed sensible. The biggest draws were zero money down on the unit and the ability to pay month-by-month, which was perfect since she wasn't exactly sure at what point she would be retrieving her stuff. This arrangement gave her breathing room.

She needed Alec's muscle with the heaviest boxes and the furniture moving, and his estimate for doing so was incredibly reasonable. He left Mallory's apartment after leaving directions to the storage unit, with a promise to return with one of his entrepreneurial partners when she was ready to move the furniture.

"Just call, and I'll be ready," Alec assured with a smile.

He almost seemed too dependable to be true.

Mallory walked him out and locked the door behind him. She now had a full day to take care of most everything else herself. Kitchenware, linens, décor, and everything else deemed nonessential for the equivalent of one semester away got packed.

But Mallory had hard decisions to make with her attire.

And with her jewelry.

Sorting those took most of the morning. During a break, she telephoned her sister. "Remind me of Texas winters?" She swung open her closet door with one hand as she held her phone in conversation with Paige in the other. Alec had mentioned the season, so weather was on her mind.

Or maybe it was just Alec who had been on her mind.

Her head had been cloudy with worry for so long that it was hard to think straight. But rather than articulate anything about her one guy hunk, Mallory focused on picking Paige's brain in regard to meteorology. "January's worse with rain and wind than December, right?"

"You act like this is some foreign place," Paige chided into her ear.

"It might as well be," Mallory leveled. "Santa Fe sits at elevation. Over seven thousand feet. You're at—what? Probably not more than two hundred?"

Paige's incredulous reply shrieked through the line. "Five hundred!"

"You sure about that?" That could hardly be called elevation. Hills and mountains were not synonymous.

"Absolutely. I confirmed it during last year's hurricane season."

Mallory groaned at the thought of a natural disaster on top of her personal one. "Don't tell me."

"Stop worrying. Hurricane season is in the late summer. And you'll be gone by then."

"Ouch." Mallory voiced the pain from her sister's verbal jab. "Planning much?"

"Oh, come on." Paige softened her voice. "You know what I mean." She added pep to her words, sounding effervescent that was more fizzle than fizz. "You'll have a whole different outlook by then."

"It's not about *outlook*." Mallory took offense at that.

"Look, Mal," Paige tried again. "Come to Texas. Stay.

Regroup and refocus."

Easier said than done. Although she had made the decision, the process of going through with it didn't come easy.

"When you're ready for a next step, you'll know."

Mallory hoped it would be that simple. By going to Texas, she hoped to escape Jesse and feel safe again.

"And in the meantime," Paige resumed the bubbliness of her earlier comments, "I can borrow your clothes, right?"

Just like my kid sister. She smiled, knowing how much Paige adored sneaking into Mallory's closet as a preteen to play dress up. During their later teen years, Mallory would green-light Paige to borrow something special for a celebratory event or school occasion. "I actually have a stack of clothes I'm putting to the side for you."

Paige squealed her delight into the phone. "My wardrobe totally needs an overhaul."

"Don't get too excited." Though it was too late. "My storage unit is limited, and I may want some of these things back." Decisions were happening so fast. She could part with some pieces, but she was on the fence about others. Still, looking at the accumulation of clothes and having to box, label, and critter-proof garments was a daunting task. Donating some things to charity and some to Paige would make it easier than hauling and loading everything, only to reload and haul it all over again at a later date. And she wasn't entirely sure what she would need or want to wear in Texas. She was used to professional attire every day of the week, but wool slacks and silk blouses weren't exactly the most practical pieces for where she was headed.

Paige brushed off the possibility of Mallory reneging her castoff clothes, teasing, "You know this is the only reason I invited you, right? So I could get a spring wardrobe makeover?"

Mallory pressed back on Paige's questions with ones of her own. "What about sisterly love? Care and compassion? Concern for my well-being?"

Paige completely ignored them, continuing her dramatization with "And you are bringing jewelry, right?"

That's crossing the line. No one touched Mallory's prized jewelry collection. "Hands off, Sis."

"A girl can dream."

She heard the wistfulness in Paige's voice, a wistfulness that matched her own. True, Mallory had amazing jewelry and a fashionable wardrobe. But Paige had a son, a home, a steady job, an upcoming wedding. From where Mallory stood, her little sister had it all together.

If Mallory could just get that—any piece of that sense of togetherness—the trip would be worth it. Because, right now, Mallory was heading southeast, but aside from that, she didn't have much sense of direction.

LATER THAT EVENING, Alec ran the tap in his bathroom sink until the water warmed to his liking. He placed a washcloth beneath, soaked it, and then wrung the excess moisture. He rolled the cloth, leaned forward, and lay the heated fabric against his neck. Using his hands to steady his support against the counter, he let the warmth transfer into his muscles in an effort to melt some of his fatigue.

Self-employment was a dream in so many ways. He and the guys were in charge of their hours, their jobs, and their workload. They got paid what they earned, with no middleman siphoning their profits. Those were the perks.

But there were certainly times where one guy bore the brunt of the workload, which was the story of his life today. After Mallory's morning bid, he answered two other afternoon calls for antique loading and unloading for a couple of businesses in the plaza. Those were quick, profit-generating calls. Yet they took a toll on his body. If he could choose, he'd much prefer calls like Mallory's.

He thought back to her. She hadn't fully explained her urgency, other than to say she was without a job. She did make it clear she needed to be out of the apartment by the month's end, which was fast approaching. Alec had gotten her settled with the packing supplies, but she was wavering on a few things. For instance, she wasn't keen about putting the piano into storage.

Still, he was glad to have gotten her a self-storage unit at all, given the tight supply this time of year around Santa Fe. Mallory seemed so pleased with that, and she embraced the boxes and packing supplies with an eagerness like that of a child with a new toy. He smiled as he thought about the grateful look on her face when he exited her apartment. The job of a mover might not solicit the same amount of respect given to public servants, first responders, or medical professionals, but Alec had always taken pride in how he was able to assist others when it mattered most to them. That was the biggest perk of his job—truly helping people when they needed it.

Alec cocked his neck and removed the towel, snapping it open. He righted his posture and rolled his shoulders, satisfied by the temporary release of the strain in his upper body. He folded the towel and placed it neatly at the corner of the bathroom sink. Loose and relaxed, he decided now was the best time to check up on Mallory with a phone call.

He cut the lights of the bathroom before retrieving his cell phone from the living room. He thumbed through his contacts, a lengthy list of clients from year to year that he never deleted. Perhaps it was an unconventional badge of honor to scroll through names of all those for whom he had worked—the Cravens, the Giffords, the Herrings, the Schultzes. So many as he reminisced. He skipped over Mallory's name and came back, recalling its placement with her last name as "Fredrick." Over the years, remembering first and last names together was becoming increasingly difficult.

Good thing he had technology.

He punched Mallory's name and waited for her answer, which didn't take long. "Hi, it's Alec. Just calling to check on you."

"That's a nice surprise." Her voice registered the same tone of appreciation she had expressed when he left her apartment. "I've already made two trips to the storage unit."

A workhorse! "That's great." Progress was always what

Alec wanted to hear. When clients were productive, he could worry less and plan more efficiently.

"Little by little. It's not easy work. But manual labor is the best solution for avoiding extra holiday pounds."

"Come now." Alec imagined Mallory's lean arms and shapely legs muscling their way through packing and stacking boxes. "You don't need to worry about extra pounds." Yet as he said it, a rush of internal heat flooded his chest. It tightened from the swirl of visualizing Mallory and hearing her voice.

And that didn't happen with his clients.

That shouldn't happen.

Clients could be so fragile, and he thought that of Mallory when he first talked to her over the phone. But when he met her in person, there was daintiness but also a palpable energy. He sensed tenacity in her eyes and saw it in her movements. She was a woman determined.

Which made it all the more quizzical to him that a woman with warmth in her voice and fire in her moves could have left her job.

Mallory picked up where Alec stopped. "Normally the holidays are when I add my winter weight. Eggnog, fruitcake, cookies, and hot cocoa are not exactly friendly to my waistline."

Winter weight? This girl? Hardly. Alec really shouldn't have started talking about weight and waists.

He said as much with a dismissive, "Sorry. I didn't mean to imply—"

But Mallory wouldn't let him stick his foot in his mouth.

"No problem. You've toured my apartment and will be getting up close and personal with my things. I won't hold you to perfect small talk."

She had a way of putting him at ease. "That's a good thing . . . because I wanted to ask about the piano."

Mallory mimicked the sound of low notes descending on the instrument's keys. "That's the biggest mesquite thorn in my side at the moment."

Alec smiled to himself at her Southern twist to the familiar adage. And her humor. The banter between them created a fondness he couldn't deny, making her feel less like a client and more like . . .

She's my client. One who is moving out of state. Alec wouldn't let himself go there. Mallory was paying him to do a job. That was that.

He cleared his throat to swallow his daydream and got back to business. "So I spoke with Tavis, and he can help me move the piano into your storage unit if we do it in the next two days."

"Storage?" Mallory halted him by cutting in further with, "That's an antique, and it's not going there. I thought about it, but I can't do that. Not to the piano, and certainly not to my grandmother."

"Okay. If you sell it, I can't—"

"Nope." Mallory was firm. "Not going to do that either. My grandmother—"

Alec knew how stories that started like this ended . . .

"Had a dying wish for this piano to stay in my family."

Now it was Alec's turn to be the one taking orders.

"What's your plan with it?"

"It's coming with me. To Texas."

Silence hung between them on the line as Alec thought about that.

Cat, piano, and a jobless New Mexico transplant headed southeast. What a trio, like a bad country and western song. But Mallory had plans to make this a trip for four. "Can you help me get it there?"

Alec gulped. A road trip wasn't exactly his idea of holiday merriment.

Yet Alec O'Donnell was a mover. Hauling stuff and taking orders was what he did. And saying "no" to a dead grandmother's wishes, a fussy feline, and this girl who had a hold on him in ways he didn't understand was not an option.

When Alec gave his affirmative reply, he was certain Mallory's shriek of excitement could be heard far outside the walls of her apartment. Maybe even all the way in Texas.

Chapter Four

MALLORY WAS ELATED Alec was going to help her move her grandmother's piano to Paige's home. When she was lamenting what to do with it to her sister over the phone, Paige jumped at the chance to house it. She babbled about Nathan taking lessons someday, about maybe even Mallory teaching him a few simple chords.

Right.

Because teaching "Hot Cross Buns" to a four-year-old would fill the void of not being able to teach her passion to college students.

She really had to bite her tongue on that one.

But Paige was insistent, swapping in to Mallory's role as older sister, at least for the moment. She swore she was not trying to poach the antique, nor would she saddle her with an immediate dismissal of it whenever Mallory moved again.

Relegating the beautiful piece to a darkened self-storage unit would bring shame to their grandmother and tension from their retired parents. At least this was Paige's MO.

So it was decided.

Once Alec agreed, the previously unfussy road trip just became more so. A piano couldn't be moved by one person.

Paige told Mallory to come down from the mountains—

and her high horse—and make sure Alec was going to do the job for a reasonable cost. So when he called to check in, the opportunity presented itself for her to ask for a specific price.

And she agreed to it.

Just a week prior, Mallory had been curled in her bed in the fetal position, scared for her safety and nervous about her future at work. But with a hefty to-do list and a new deadline of getting her apartment cleared by the end of the month, she could somehow breathe again.

Not fully.

But at least she was standing and not knocked down.

Plus, she had Alec as an anchor during this transitional time. When he called to check on her the following day, he also asked about progress of everyday items. "So, would you say you're about at twenty-five percent packed? Or more like half done?"

Mallory glanced around her apartment, a veritable tornado of activity with doors swung open, cupboards ransacked, and Bubble Wrap cradling chair legs, picture frame edges, candle holders, and her now unhinged ornamental lighting. Her living area was a cross between something apocalyptic and otherworldly. "Let's say half. There's just some cumbersome stuff. How did I even get so many things?"

"Years of accumulation?" Alec's banter over the phone was a helpful distraction to the current state of her personal space.

"I haven't been in Santa Fe that long." Though even as Mallory said as much, she remembered how, little by little, she had picked up an item here and there around the city at various boutiques, galleries, festivals, and craft fairs that resulted in everything she now owned.

"Not long? Tell me about it." Alec prompted Mallory into sharing more about her life moving to the state.

She told him how long she had been in Santa Fe, what she enjoyed most about the climate, and how it was ultimately the college which attracted her. But Mallory's career pain was still raw, so she was vague about her actual employment there.

Aside from that, telling guys she was an English professor was usually a complete turnoff. They invariably countered with the predictable, *"Oh, better watch what I say"* or *"I'm sure you're going to correct my grammar,"* which Mallory never did. Why was it that some men were intimidated by intellect? Enough guys had made those type of comments that Mallory usually just said she was employed at a college and left people to think she worked in recruiting or enrollment. They never asked many questions when she gave her generic answer and moved on to asking them about their careers.

But this wasn't a conversation between two people who were on a date. *Keep telling yourself that, Mal.*

After a few minutes of back-and-forth conversation that didn't hit anywhere near the barometer of awkward that plagued her last few dates, Alec asked about her moving supplies. "Are the boxes doing the trick? Remember that you can always return the unused ones for credit."

Right. Back to business. Who was she fooling in thinking—even for a moment—that this was a conversation anywhere outside of the for-hire range? With her world turned upside down, her perceptions of everything seemed to be off. She replied with a brusque, "Perfectly fine."

"And the Bubble Wrap and tape?"

The evidence of their use was all around her, boxes she needed to take to the unit caving in around her from the kitchen to the foyer to one wall in the living room. "Doing their jobs."

"Good."

Mallory, though, was nearly out of tape. Perhaps double-securing the box bottoms wasn't the wisest use of her supplies. "Maybe too good."

"How's that?"

"Well, I went a little overboard with the tape . . . and I even boxed up more than I should have done at this point."

"What do you mean?"

Mallory wasn't going to waste the time or the tape and slice back into boxes for a few items she needed. In her fervor to pack the kitchen, for instance, she had boxed every pot, pan, dish, cup, and storage container. There were a few rogue Tupperware lids and a plastic spoon left in the utensil drawer.

"I had forgotten I would need to eat," she admitted sheepishly.

"So that just means you'll have to eat out."

She would have found humor in Alec's comeback had she not immediately felt the fear that had spiraled her into this position. She wasn't in any mood to go out and possibly put herself in harm's way by being seen.

By Jesse.

Or any of her other students, really. Surely news traveled fast and, as was often the case in college, traveled dishonestly.

Santa Fe was a populated area, and the chance of running into any specific individual on a single outing was slim. But Jesse Sands had made a promise.

A threat.

With Jesse suspended, would he be lurking for her elsewhere? If she were seen in public, might he somehow be alerted? Mallory hated thinking like this, but there was so much about this kid she didn't know. So aside from driving to a self-storage unit, she wanted to completely avoid the public.

Just in case.

She wasn't ready to risk what she was trying to rebuild. "I don't want to eat out."

"Understood." Alec's one-word response showed he was listening, but he couldn't have actually comprehended. "It's just that eating out—"

Maybe he wasn't really listening. "I'm not going out by myself." *There.* She sounded fragile and perhaps even ridiculous, but she wasn't budging.

Alec cleared his throat on the other end of the line. "That's not what I meant."

This conversation was making her uncomfortable with flashbacks she didn't know how to stop. She stumbled through a series of "Trust me" and "It's complicated" excuses that sounded much more pathetic than Mallory would have liked. Her words were nose-diving now, just as her confidence had done during the last two weeks.

Alec broke in, and that was when he tried again. But his words were not at all what she expected. "I'd like to have dinner with you, Mallory."

Oh.

Mallory swallowed her shock.

This was—an invitation.

A date?

MALLORY HAD DATED during the five years she had been in Santa Fe, but there was only one semi-serious guy, a mortgage broker at the bank where she kept her savings and checking accounts. Joaquin was personable, kind, outgoing, and fun. His wardrobe was a bonus; the man looked impeccable in a suit. But, ultimately, after several months, the relationship had simply run its course. There wasn't much of a spark, just mutual respect for each other as people and their focus on careers. Parting had been amicable.

A few times, Mallory was asked out by someone connected to the college, and on a couple of occasions, she agreed. But her teaching responsibilities always came first. A common misconception about teaching was that she only "worked" when she was in the classroom.

Wrong.

There were lectures to prepare, essays to grade, paperwork to complete, student conferences to hold. Then there was the weekly grind of creating quizzes, running copies, updating technology components, managing emails. Monthly surprises cropped up like committee work, textbook project assignments, curriculum revision plans, and other various departmental matters.

So when Mallory did date, it was always with the understanding that a guy would slide into her routine but not rock it.

Now, she had no routine. And Alec held silent on the other end of the line, waiting for her to respond to his dinner invitation.

With something.

Anything.

"That's a, um, really nice thing to ask." The response tripped on her tongue. At times like this when she fought with phrases, she was certain people questioned her skills as an English professor.

Alec picked up her slack, echoing a few of her words. "It'd be a really nice thing to do."

True, Alec seemed nice enough. But she was leaving. To another state. Of all people, Alec knew that. "It's just that—"

"You're moving." He laughed. "I know."

Right.

His words were nonchalant. "You have to eat. I have to eat."

"You make it sound so simple."

"Eating usually is."

Mallory, though, had gone without much of an appetite these last couple of weeks that meals weren't as simple—or nearly as enjoyable—as they should have been. If only Alec knew what a hard time she had been having . . .

"You don't have anything in your kitchen," he reminded Mallory. "No way to cook. And, frankly, I've been busy and haven't done much of that on my end either. So I would like to eat a good meal. And I'd like some company while doing it."

It still sounded simple. How did Alec do that? On her end, life was so complicated, yet this request was plain. Sensible. Reasonable. As if to address Mallory's unspoken hesitation, Alec baited her with, "That's all. Just food. No pressure."

She didn't have to let herself get reeled in by him, but she also privately admitted a decent meal sounded great. So when she accepted with a "yes," the word leapt from a place of hunger. "But I've got so much work to do," she added, a line she frequently had used in past dating circumstances when it came to work preparations, though here it was for packing.

"You've hired me for some of that, you know."

"I know." Mallory rolled her shoulders, readjusting the phone. What she wouldn't admit to Alec was her real hesitation for leaving the apartment. At least staying inside kept her from having to be publicly seen. She also didn't want to add how much she dreaded venturing out and risking a run-in with the one student who was the impetus for her sabbatical.

So Mallory saved face by letting Alec think her desire for privacy was connected to the move.

"No problem," he breezed. "I'll bring something over."

This guy had an answer for everything.

"Any preference for takeout?"

So not only would this be a date, but it would be a private one. Just Alec. And Mallory. Alone in a half-packed apartment. At least she could admit she had never accepted a date like this before.

ALEC CLICKED OFF the call with Mallory and leaned back to let the cushions of his couch embrace him. He hadn't planned to ask about dinner. The offer just arose organically, so Alec went with it. That was how most of his interactions with Mallory had progressed, and talking with her hardly even seemed like work.

The ease of interacting with Mallory was a pleasant surprise. He could handle this job on his own, without full teamwork from the other guys. That was certainly a holiday blessing in its own right since Tavis and his wife were crawling the walls waiting for their baby's arrival, and Greg and Rory had their hands full with kiddos of their own. Alec thumbed through his phone messages where he read a text check-in from Greg and slid through pictures sent by Rory. There was over a foot of fresh powder on the ground in Taos, a blanket of pure white snow covering fir trees that framed idyllic mountain views in each happy shot sent to Alec. The kids looked ecstatic, with wide smiles eclipsing their faces. Seeing their happiness at a white Christmas brought a smile to Alec. He remembered a few of those from his childhood.

Back when he had a family.

With both parents deceased, his immediate family felt far emptier around the holidays. He had one sibling he saw enough of and an extended family because of her, but he felt the absence of his bachelorhood. There was no one in his household with whom to share special traditions or wake up beside on these cold winter mornings.

Just him.

His friends had their families, and his sister had hers. He was the outsider when it came to fitting in there. He was alone.

And, as he anticipated a holiday by himself, he had to admit he was also feeling lonely.

Nonetheless, Alec wasn't the type to cast a shadow. He left encouraging digital responses to Greg and Rory's messages, reminding them to spoil the kiddos with lots of snowball fights and hot chocolate. Then, he switched his attention to deciding on dinner.

The impromptu outreach to Mallory wasn't typical of how Four Guys wooed their customers, but he wanted to do something for her even though he couldn't put his finger on why. Was it because he took care of his clients? Sure. But he did that with donut holes, not evening meal delivery to a sexy single. There was something else. Was it because she had hinted at an interest in more than packing supplies? Maybe.

Armchair analysis of the actions of the opposite sex were tough enough, but they were nearly impossible with an empty stomach. A deep growl of hunger reminded Alec he needed to make good on his promise for dinner. His fingers did the work in finding a couple of local dishes from one of the plaza cafes. With a few clicks, his selections were ordered. Alec would enjoy *chili rellenos* and hoped Mallory would too.

But more than that, Alec didn't want her enjoyment to stop with the food. He wanted his own version of wide-grinned enthusiasm like he had seen in the guys' pictures from Taos.

However, he didn't want it courtesy of Mother Nature. He wanted it from Mallory.

Chapter Five

THE SPICY SMELL of *chili* teased the air that preceded Alec as he made his entrance into Mallory's apartment. "Dinner is served." He held a plastic bag in one hand and palmed two Styrofoam cups of sweet tea in the other.

"That's quite a delivery."

Alec launched into his best radio voice as he echoed the words and gave a comedic plug for Four Guys's "Service, smiles, and great taste in cuisine."

Mallory couldn't help but laugh at his playfulness. "No doubt about that." She beamed and held open the door.

This was now the second time Alec had been inside her apartment, though between their phone calls, it felt like they had spent more time together. So she was relaxed in conversation with Alec. She intended to get his expert opinion on storage options for some of her paperwork and books. The unit she rented wasn't climate controlled, which was far cheaper than ones which were. Yet she had some hesitation about merely boxing some of her particularly precious papers from college along with other documentation she might need that she wasn't comfortable keeping in her work office. So she would use the evening to ask about that.

But as Alec brushed past her, her attention was drawn

decidedly to him. Alec's elbow grazed near her chest, sending a tingle of heat her way. The combination of warm food and Alec's inviting presence filled the room. She wasn't used to having a man in her home, certainly not one as good-looking, hard-working, and electric as Alec O'Donnell.

He flashed a dimpled grin. "It's good to see you," he acknowledged in a lowered voice that sounded yummier than the food he was delivering. His voice was butter, and his words made Mallory melt.

What is happening to me?

As she closed the door behind him, she squeezed the knob and counted down by three seconds with her lips pursed so she wouldn't drool. She suddenly had an appetite for much more than dinner.

Alec broke her private concentration. "Where shall I put this?"

She fought for composure as she spun to face the source of her axis tilt. "There on the kitchen counter is fine." She gestured toward the efficiency-sized area that was framed with an open, chest-high countertop to make it feel bigger than it was. Off to the side was her rounded wood dining table that could hold four, but she only had two chairs. Seeing the setting for a couple made her realize this impromptu dinner might be more intimate than she intended.

Not that Mallory had the best track record of late with reading people or sensing their intent.

When will I stop thinking about those events? Daily, Mallory fought with a replay of mental images all tied to her forced sabbatical. As hard as she tried to shut her brain from reliving the student threat and rehashing the college's response, she couldn't. She was caught in a feedback loop of thought which she could only hope a move to Texas would solve.

Alec snapped Mallory back to his presence with his words. "I hope you like everything I ordered." Alec hoisted the bag onto the counter, his bicep tensing beneath his tight, long-sleeve T-shirt as his did. That got Mallory's attention, as did his next movement. As he reached to place the drinks adjacent to the food, the hem of the cottony fabric caught on the back waistband of his dark-washed jeans, giving Mallory full view of a posterior arc that was every bit of perfect.

"Yummy," she murmured.

Alec heard but didn't acknowledge her double entendre. "I hope you like it." He rattled off the menu.

Fresh hatch green *chilis* grown in New Mexico were stuffed with gooey *asadero* cheese before being fried with a thin, crispy coating. A drizzle of intensely flavored red *chile* sauce rounded out the richness of the dish that was an explosion of Christmas colors on a plate. A side of *posolo* with pork added to the meal while a sharable size of chips with salsa gave them reason to start munching. Crispy, fried *sopaipillas* in bite-sized triangles with honey for dipping topped off the meal.

"This is divine." Mallory inhaled the exciting combination of spicy-sweet smells. She would enjoy the meal, and she was already quite enjoying the company of a man, especially one whose very presence was warmer than their entrees. "I haven't had a meal this perfect in far too long."

"You've been busy." Alec stood back from the table so she could take in the meal while he balled the take-out bag between his ample palms. His size and assuredness with everything from moving to meal delivery made Mallory glad she had chosen Four Guys.

And that only this one guy had shown. Alec was all she needed.

"Trash?" He prompted of the softball-sized waste he held.

"Let me take that." She tossed it into the garbage under the sink while Alec readied the napkins and plastic utensils that had been sent with the takeout. As she snuck a peak at Alec from her view in the kitchen, she admired the way the light from the fixture above created a shine like a spotlight. The illumination highlighted streaks of blond in his hair, brightening his face and making him practically glow. His thick locks, warm body, velvety voice, and strong movements would have been satisfaction enough, if not for the food too.

Mallory couldn't stare the whole evening like he was some car-lot Cadillac. She pivoted back into her dining area. "We can eat here." She stepped toward the table, steadying herself by holding onto the back of one of the chairs. "If that's all right."

"It's all right with me." He rolled up his sleeves, started carrying the containers two by two, and repeated with a wink in Mallory's direction, "*This* is all right with me."

Somehow, this stranger of a man didn't feel like one. He was inviting, polished, and full of kindness that extended beyond his work. When he finished setting the food, Alec slid back Mallory's chair and gestured for her to have a seat. Then this luxury make and model of a man welcomed her into the first relaxing evening she had experienced in weeks.

MALLORY AND ALEC had an enjoyable meal where time flew because there was so much to taste, which led to so much to say about New Mexican cuisine. Alec explained he was a native of the state and as such could speak to the finer points of dishes' characteristics. Mallory was a convert to the unique flavors she had grown to love during her time in Santa Fe, though she admitted her heart was with Tex-Mex.

"Queso," she admitted point-blank. "Cheese dip makes everything better."

"Touché." He conceded with a nod of his head and a lifting of his Styrofoam cup. Mallory raised hers in kind for a mock clink before they both drew a long drink from their straws. "Is there good Tex-Mex food where you are headed?"

Mallory swallowed her gulp of sweet tea. "There's good Tex-Mex food all over that state."

Alec reached for a chip, biting the crisp edge in a clean break. "I remember saying it's a big state."

Mallory grabbed a chip of her own. "That tells you there's a lot of food."

Conversation with Alec was easy, and the more they talked, the more Mallory wanted to dig a bit. Steering the conversation away from food, she focused on Alec. "So, tell me something about your life before Four Guys."

Alec finished his bite and leaned back in his chair. "What do you want to know?"

Mallory kicked back in her own chair, wiping salt from her fingers. "Anything, really. Tell me about life before owning a moving company. Or life in Santa Fe when you were younger."

"Am I old?" he teased. Alec cocked his head with his cute cheek dimples on full display as he paused in conversation.

"Hardly." She laughed.

"When I was a teenager, I used to think that being in my thirties was going to feel so old." Alec stared thoughtfully.

Mallory nodded as he spoke, knowing exactly what he meant. Her college students would say as much, as if somehow that marker of hitting thirty was middle-aged in their minds.

Alec continued his honest assessment. "But I'm thirty-three, and I have to say that I wouldn't trade being this age for any other age. I really like life in this decade."

"I'm not far behind you." Mallory folded the napkin, placed it on the table, and raised one of her hands as if she were taking an oath. "I turned thirty-two this year."

Alec raised an eyebrow, presumably surprised at their similarity in age. "You don't look a day over twenty-five."

Mallory was sure her cheeks blushed from the compliment, but she couldn't help prompting him to "Keep layering on the charm."

Alec didn't miss a beat. "You're young. Personable. Attractive."

That last word made Mallory's throat catch, and she had to reach for a sip of her tea to choke back a verbal reaction. If her cheeks weren't flushed before, they certainly were now.

His compliments continued. "You're polished. You're professional. And it sounds like you had a steady job at the college."

Mallory's outward redness suddenly felt blue. *If only you knew . . .* She hadn't told Alec she was a professor and now wasn't the time to correct any misinterpretation that she was a faculty member and not a staff member. Doing so would not only come across as pretentious, but she'd have to explain why she was a professor without a teaching schedule for the upcoming spring. Explaining all of that was just too heavy of a conversation at the moment. "Yes," she said instead, "working at the college was a steady gig."

"I remember that about my mother." Alec kept his gaze on some invisible space above where Mallory sat. "She had a steady job in education. She was a teacher."

"Oh?" Mallory's interior focus now shifted to Alec.

His voice was solid, though his tone was low as he explained that she worked at a Santa Fe public high school. "As an English teacher." The similarity sucker punched Mallory, though she tried to keep cool as Alec continued talking about his mother's work. "She taught several different grades throughout the years, but she really liked juniors. You know, transformative ages and being able to make a difference."

"I can imagine." Though Mallory could do more than that. For a moment, she let herself think she'd step back into a classroom tomorrow, doing the job she loved.

"She was really good at it too." Alec paused and smiled at what seemed like memories only he knew. There was a slight hint of pain in his voice as he repeated quietly, "Really good."

Mallory wanted to be sensitive to whatever memories Alec was processing. "It takes a special person to be a teacher."

He lowered his gaze to Mallory's. "You're right about that. That's what we all thought about her." And then Alec revealed more to his mom's past than Mallory had expected to hear. "The whole family was reminded of that two years ago during her funeral."

"Oh, Alec," Mallory began, unsure if she should reach out and squeeze his hand or stop the conversation altogether. She didn't intend to have Alec relive any pain by taking the conversation in this direction. "I'm so sorry."

But Alec kept talking, in a quiet, controlled tone as he reminisced. "It was a beautiful service. So many former students either came or delivered flowers or sent well wishes. It was amazing for us to see how many lives she had touched. Kids and parents and even some of her students' kids all converged. She knew so many people during more than three decades of teaching."

What a long career. Mallory thought lovingly of how fulfilling that must have been, not only to Alec's mother but to his whole family.

"You know she taught longer than I've been alive?" He forced a bit of laughter through what sounded like a sniffle.

"That's really incredible." And it was. Mallory had only

taught a fraction of that, and while the benefits of seeing her students succeed were grand and immeasurable, there were also failures and incidents she hadn't expected, like the major one which landed her in the current predicament. She was already multiplying her experience in her mind to intellectually comprehend the depth of so many years of devotion to teaching others. "You have every reason to be proud of her."

Alec nodded and swallowed hard. "I haven't actually talked about her in a while."

"I'm glad you're talking about her now." A happy story of teaching success was one Mallory needed to hear. *More than you know, Alec.* But instead of verbalizing, she could only bite her lip and smile with unspoken gratitude she hoped Alec could somehow feel across the table.

Alec tilted his head and met Mallory's eyes again. "I am too." And she couldn't be sure, but she sensed a trust established somehow in their surprise conversation.

Mallory had felt alone and scared for the last couple of weeks, as if no one was really listening to her. Yet here she was, the one listening to someone else who, in a moment of recollection, needed an ear.

Funny how sometimes what a person wanted wasn't at all what she got.

Other times, it was better.

AFTER THEY FINISHED their last bites of entrees, polished off the *sopaipillas*, and drained their tea, Alec and Mallory cleared the dining area. Mallory forced the Styrofoam containers into an already too-full garbage bag that needed to be taken out while Alec grabbed the paper towel roll from the counter—one of the only items left from Mallory's whirlwind packing—and started wiping the table.

Mallory was pleasantly surprised to learn Alec had a basis for understanding the world of teaching, though she was further surprised to learn about his own educational background. "I graduated from St. John's," he revealed with a shrug, as nonchalantly as someone might have said, "*I have a pet goldfish*" or "*I sometimes bike to work.*"

"You have a degree from St. John's?" Mallory stopped wrestling with the trash to make sure she had heard him correctly.

"Yes. A bachelor's degree in liberal arts."

That's the department in which I teach. Oh, the things she now wished she could say! But Mallory didn't want to cause further pain in talking about teaching with Alec as he reminisced about his mother, and she didn't want her own mind to go back to the dark place it had been for the end of her semester.

Instead, she kept the focus on Alec. "Color me impressed."

St. John's private school education was highly competitive and not just well-known throughout Santa Fe and Annapolis where there were on-ground campuses, but their rigorous curriculum was nationally renowned.

Intense reading loads, seminar-style discussion classes,

and philosophical approaches characterized the unique educational experience of St. John's. Mallory had been to the campus in town for a few professional development training seminars, and she had daydreamed about what it would be like to take a graduate class of her own there—or even, one day, teach at the institution. Mallory had so many questions for Alec.

"Favorite class?"

"I liked my logic ones. But the twentieth century literature was fun."

Right up my alley! "Favorite book?"

Alec laughed. "Too many to name."

Good answer. That was actually Mallory's own when people asked. "And did you take a foreign language?"

"We studied Greek and French."

Their intellectual chemistry kept building. Mallory was infatuated.

With Alec's education.

With Alec.

Her heart held a special place for everything that Alec was sharing. "I'm jealous," she admitted.

That solicited a grunt of laughter and another shine of a dimpled smile. "Jealous? Of a guy with a liberal arts degree who now moves people's stuff for a living?"

"About that." Mallory was curious. "Why is it that you are a mover?"

"Easy," Alec joked. "Because no one's putting out employment calls for philosophers."

Alec was right in theory, but liberal arts educations were

still highly prized, especially in certain industries. It was what she told her students. And she suspected Alec knew as much. She wasn't undercutting his choice of employment, but she still wanted to understand the switch into a job that—at least from her perspective—was largely driven by manual labor, not literary classics. "But what was your tipping point into Four Guys?"

"Three other great guys," Alec began before he started enumerating the more specific benefits he enjoyed. "I have my own company, and that's satisfying. Plus, I have steady work, good income, flexible hours, and lots of time off to read the books I want to read."

"Now that sounds like a dream job."

"I guess you could say it is."

Alec talked about being self-employed, including the satisfaction he received from helping people. "I know not everyone would see it like this, but I enjoy what I do. And I feel like I make a difference in people's lives."

Like with teaching.

Maybe Alec and Mallory weren't very different.

Alec was heartfelt, and he was pretty convincing.

In his choices.

In his conversation.

And their mental connection of shared interests came as a pleasant surprise. That, coupled with Alec's intelligence and ability to hold conversation, was something her doughy boyfriends of the past couldn't do. Not to mention his good looks were continuing to drive Mallory insane. The longer she was around Alec, the more she liked.

And liked.

And liked.

But Mallory had to put on the brakes. After all, why lust after someone who was going to be in her rearview mirror in a matter of days?

Chapter Six

B ELLA REMAINED LARGELY out of view during Mallory
and Alec's impromptu apartment dinner, and she had
been skittish the next day. Persian cats could be tempera-
mental.

"Is that your problem?" Mallory was crouched low and
peeking beneath the bed skirt in one of the last places Bella
could hide. With so much movement in the apartment, her
usual hiding places were off limits. But not this one.

She called to Bella, who stayed just out of her reach.
"Come on, girl." Mallory was exhausted enough from
making three trips to the storage unit today, and she was
ready to strip the bedding because Alec was due any minute
with his closed trailer. He was helping with one trip to the
unit for all the things Mallory couldn't move on her own,
like this mattress and frame, but Bella wasn't budging.
Mallory tried coaxing. "Want a treatie?"

Bella just stared back at her, not humored.

"Right. You're watching your figure." She rolled her eyes.
"Want to play?" She grabbed one of her sneakers and bobbed
the untied lace up and down within the cat's view. Bella was
still not amused.

Mallory eased back on her heels and tossed the shoe in

the corner. "No treatie. No exercise." She put her hands on her hips, thinking aloud for the next idea. "Want some water?" She could try turning on the faucet. Bella was sometimes entertained by the trickle of water when Mallory was brushing her teeth. It was worth a shot.

"I love you, Bella." Mallory used her hands to push up from the carpet as she stood and then repeated, "I do." She padded to the apartment's only bathroom. "But you can be one stubborn kitty." She switched on the light, turned the knob on the cold water, and flicked her finger beneath the stream absently, waiting to see if her pet emerged from seclusion.

"I'm not going to waste water for long." She looked to the mirror, silently counting the seconds as she did.

And there was nothing.

"Suit yourself." Mallory halted the water, flicked the moisture from her skin, and dabbed her finger on a towel. She was going to have to strip the bed whether or not Bella moved since Alec was due to arrive any second.

She planned to spend the night on the floor with just the bedding anyway. Then she'd wrap up the remnants, service them at a laundromat on her final trip to the unit, and leave for Seguin early the next morning with essentials packed in her car. And her car was going to be followed—by Alec.

That was perhaps the biggest surprise of their dinner. She needed the piano moved, and Tavis and Alec could load it if it were planned for tomorrow. Alec and Mallory had talked about the twelve-hour trip to Seguin, and it seemed best for her to do it before the holidays. She had some hesitation about crashing Paige and Nathan's special traditions and cramping the romantic holiday time between her sister and fiancé Everett. But Paige had been insistent over the phone that, since their parents were bound by snow in Angel Fire, there was no way she was going to let Mallory spend the days alone.

When she and Alec chatted about the holiday season over dinner the night before, he insisted his only plan was Christmas Day at his sister's house in town. The thought that he valued a relationship with his sibling in the way Mallory valued Paige warmed her. Holidays were for family.

And her friends had theirs, too, which was one reason why Mallory employed Alec. Doing so was so much more convenient than having to plan with friends and, by extension, their husbands and boyfriends on such short notice. Everyone was busy with their own families.

When she did tell her friends the news, she reassured them her absence from Santa Fe was temporary since she was only going to be gone for the spring.

"Spring in Seguin," she repeated, as much for personal consolation as a cue that she would be reuniting with everyone again at some point.

Her closest friend, Jovanna, knew about the incident with Jesse and supported Mallory's need to change locales, but most everyone else just thought she was taking a work sabbatical for the purposes of a special project.

It was so hard to see on the other side of a semester. She really didn't know what the months ahead would bring. What would happen after the sabbatical? Not only with her job, but with her? She had hoped to sort her feelings, rebuild her confidence, and feel safe in a place.

Yet what if I don't?

Maybe she and Bella weren't so different. They were both a little skittish lately. And with good reason.

Mallory walked with ginger steps back into her bedroom, deciding instead to simply strip the bed and let Bella do what Bella did.

"I'm sorry," she apologized as she laid the pillows on the floor, peeled back the comforter, and began disassembling the layers of bedding. "I know this isn't easy for you either." She sighed, a Cinderella of unfortunate circumstances who seemed to, for the moment at least, have but an animal with whom to have a conversation. No palace. No magic. No fairy godmother in sight.

MALLORY'S MOVER ARRIVED at five a.m. on Wednesday morning. He didn't ride a horse, nor was he fitted in shining armor for battle. But he was punctual, with eyes that shone from early morning alertness. He wasn't a storybook prince, but when he appeared at Mallory's doorstep ready to load the piano and the boxes she was taking to Paige's, he might well have been one.

"I'm so glad to see you." She opened the door with one hand as she held tight to her travel beverage mug with the other. She was in such a mental fog that she hoped the caffeine from her hot tea would kick in at some point.

Alec didn't seem to need tea or coffee for energy. He laced his fingers, stretched his arms in front of him until his knuckles cracked, and cheerily announced, "Let's get this show on the road."

"I'm all for that." Mallory stepped aside to let him in, and Alec's mere presence near her gave a pleasant jolt as much as the beverage she was sipping. He was dressed in worn jeans and a gray pullover with a half-zippered neck, a combination that was comfortable yet sexy in its simplicity. He smelled of fresh laundry and light cologne.

But as much as Mallory would have enjoyed staring at him for a few moments longer, Alec was not going to stand still. "Tavis should be here at 5:30. I can get these loaded"— he pointed to the boxes stacked right inside the door—"so they'll be a barrier in the front of the enclosed trailer before the piano." He then pointed to several rounded trash bags. "Garbage?"

Mallory shook her head and swallowed her mouthful of beverage. "Oh no. That's clothes."

Alec raised an eyebrow. "To take?"

"Yes," she confirmed. "But I can throw some of that in my car," she added, not wanting to cramp Alec's plan. She could tell he was mentally crafting a strategy of attack for all the items left in her apartment.

"Cat going with you?"

The brashness of the comment surprised her. "Well she's not going in the trailer!"

Alec raised both hands in mock arrest. "Just checking."

"Sorry. I didn't mean to bark." She took another sip of tea, wishing she had Alec's early morning strength and focus. Instead, her mind was disheveled and her nerves were on edge. Even Bella had stayed away from her last night. Was Mallory that hard to be around?

Alec lowered his voice. "Is there something wrong?"

So much.

But Mallory wasn't going to crack. She told herself no crying, no being sentimental. Today was about new beginnings. The gnawing sense, though, of unfinished business swirled inside of her, feeling like failure. There was so much she didn't know about her future. "Is this normal?"

Alec put his hands down. "Is what normal?"

"This." How could she explain? "To feel . . . to be, um . . . to not know."

Alec squared his stance in front of Mallory, confident in ways she lacked. "Look at me."

Alec's height made Mallory raise her chin to meet his gaze.

Once her focus was settled, he spoke in a simple yet direct pep talk. "Your life is changing. You're moving." His eye contact and his attention stayed on her. "You have a right to feel all kinds of things. You're entitled. Let yourself." And then to ease her burdens even further, he added, "Because I've got this." And with that, he pivoted, picked up the first box, and drove the reins of her morning move.

He was so self-assured Mallory believed him. When she was rudderless, he was her anchor. And that was exactly what she hadn't known she needed.

She exhaled, relaxed her posture, and let Alec's guidance wash over her. No one in the last month had validated her situation. Not Iker. Not her coworkers. Not even Jovanna, as well meaning as she tried to be. No one had acknowledged her with such direct speech that communicated an understanding of her life in flux. No one had told her she was entitled to her mixed emotions. No one validated the fear Mallory couldn't shake by staying in Santa Fe with Jesse's threat still fresh.

Alec was managing her move, but he was shouldering so much more. And, as she watched him load box after box, she wondered if he even knew.

THEY WERE AN unconventional trio: Mallory, Alec, and Bella. The boxes were loaded, the piano was anchored, and Bella was settled in the back seat of Mallory's car in her pet carrier. There wasn't much room left as Mallory grabbed all the oddities she hadn't packed. Loose mail, remnants from her pantry, toiletries, and other household products she was going to fold into Paige's house once she got there. While it wasn't exactly convenient to transport a container of barely-used laundry soap, excess paper towels, tins of tea bags, and boxes of crackers, at least she wasn't letting them go to waste.

She nestled Bella's food opposite of her carrier on the floorboard, though she acknowledged, "You can probably still smell it from there." If Bella was going to be noisy on the ride, this would be one long trip. She tipped her empty pet bowl sideways next to two bottles of filtered water that she hoped would make it easy to handle when they made a pit stop and Bella needed a drink.

Alec had loosely planned stops at two designated times along the way for lunch and late afternoon refueling. "But call me if you need it sooner. Cell phone's on, but I need you to give me a heads-up before you exit and whip into a gas station bay. This trailer takes a little more maneuvering than your car."

Mallory wanted to be sensitive to that, and though she was leading the drive, she didn't feel in complete control. She hoped that would change when she arrived in Seguin. "I'm just ready to get there." She had no plans to prolong this trip. "So don't think I'll be stopping unless it's an absolute emergency." The next twelve hours needed to go as smoothly as possible.

"Have you driven this long of a distance before? By yourself?"

Though Alec might not have meant to highlight Mallory's singledom, the comment was yet another acknowledgement to her of it. "Yes, I've been to Paige's several times. And to see my parents. We drove to the Grand Canyon once. Plenty of other long day trips. Don't worry." The last words were as much for Alec's benefit as they were for her own.

"Who said I was worried?" He jangled his keys in the air between them. "Ready?"

Ready or not, Mallory said she was. And as she pulled

out of her apartment's parking lot, she only glanced in the rearview mirror to make sure Alec was there. Her apartment wasn't even within her view.

Her negative fall semester was behind her as she set her eyes on the open road. With every mile she drove, she was able to widen the distance from her past and advance toward her future.

Traffic, signage, and the landscape kept her company on the road. She didn't see too many people like her moving at this time of year, though there was the expected sprinkling of holiday travelers, families on vacation, and long-haul truckers who filled the lanes. Her situation was unique for sure, but, as she often told her students, "Everybody's got a story." She had always said that to empower them to tell theirs when they wrote assignments for class. But this really wasn't the story Mallory Fredrick thought she would have.

Teacher gets threatened. Student suspended. Teacher leaves for a semester.

Fairness wasn't a theme of that story.

But she had her credentials. She had her experience. And she had her dignity.

And Alec.

She glanced in the rearview, his truck and trailer steady behind her while his sunglass-clad attention shone through the windshield toward her. Seeing that little bit of physical support meant so much to Mallory.

She hugged the wheel, turned up the tune from the speakers, and started singing along with the catchy pop song. Her life was wrapped up in teaching, and while she couldn't unthread those connections, she could weave a comfortable future. She couldn't think too far ahead, but with the open road, clear skies, and steady progress, she was making her way.

THEY CROSSED THE eastern border of New Mexico into the Texas panhandle three hours into their trip. After some noisy early morning mews, Bella finally lulled to sleep in her carrier and had been that way for about two hours. Mallory wasn't sleepy in the least. The more she drove, the more awake and invigorated she felt.

Which was strange.

Maybe after these last two weeks of being so low, putting everything behind her meant she could ride high. Whatever the case, she relished the feeling.

She was fueled, but she still had to keep an eye on her car's. The vehicle's efficient gas mileage meant Mallory didn't have to fret about running out, but she was cautious in watching her gauges for any sign of attention.

Alec's truck and trailer were burning more gasoline than her car, so when they stopped at their planned highway convenience station inside the Texas border, she topped off her tank to be safe. "All well?" she called to Alec from her side of the bay.

He used his hand as a buffer for the bright, midmorning sun. "Smooth. Making good time."

Mallory glanced at her watch. "Hungry? Need anything?"

"I'm good. You?"

Mallory shook her head as she slid her credit card through the payment reader and reached for the fuel hose. "This is all I need."

Alec mirrored her routine and started filling up his tank. He leaned against the side of his truck within view of Mallory. "Bella?"

It was the first time Alec had called her pet by name. And the word—Italian for *beautiful*—sounded good rolling off his tongue. For a moment, Mallory caught herself in a daydream about the word referencing her before she snapped back to focus on her cat. "Yes?"

"How's she doing?"

Mallory pressed her face to the back seat glass. There was no sign of her waking. "Handling it like a champ." She spun back around.

"That makes two of you." If Alec had intended the words as banter, they nonetheless hit Mallory as a compliment. He had a way of doing so in conversation that infused her with confidence and assuredness. But he wasn't done with the appraisal just yet. "You are something . . ." His words trailed as Mallory contemplated their tone and her cheeks flushed with more color than their rock-red driving terrain.

She hadn't been flattered in far too long. And coming from someone as handsome as Alec, the communication carried weight. So perhaps it was the hiatus of having heard words like that which made her volley his flirtation with some of her own. "If I didn't know better, I'd say this were some sort of pickup line."

Alec raised one eyebrow, the arc visible above the rim of his sunglasses. "And if it were?"

The gasoline handle clicked in the absence of Mallory's response. Her tank was revved, and so was her pulse. She spun to grab the hose, shielding her face which now was likely as bright as the gas station signage. She hoisted the hose, replaced it at the pump, and punched the electric indicator to generate a receipt. Though she couldn't see them, she could feel Alec's eyes on her every move.

Alec's tank was still filling, so he addressed her with the pet name "sweetheart" to get her attention.

You used that before on me. She couldn't blush any more than she already was.

Alec followed his call with, "Are you not going to answer that one?" Then he repeated, "What if it was a pickup line?"

She was thinking, and her immediate reaction was that the gasoline fumes must have gone to his head. They were going to be parting ways in a matter of hours. What good was even a little flirting going to do? Was it supposed to be a distraction? Maybe that was it; maybe she was misreading this. Alec was a professional, and perhaps this was just his way to maintain liveliness, doing his part to keep her alert and awake on the road.

That had to be it.

"If that were a pickup line"—Mallory gestured around her for emphasis to her sarcasm—"you have impeccable romantic timing." She cracked a smile and slid her fingers to her necklace, twirling the strand as she waited for Alec's reply.

He raised his hand to the edge of his sunglasses, tipped them to the brim of his nose, and spoke with a further playful challenge. "Then I'll work on that." He winked, replaced his shades, and finished the routine at the pump. Mallory collapsed into the front seat of her car in a putty of limbs made limp by one Alec O'Donnell.

Mallory's head was awash with conflicting messages while her heart was a veritable spin cycle of emotion. Several hundred more miles of highway partnership along with two more planned stops were enough to keep Mallory on edge with anticipating what Alec might try to say.

Or do.

She glanced back at Bella, snug in her carrier and sleeping as soundly as if she had been tranquilized. Clicking her seat belt into place, she lowered her sun visor, checked her mirrors, and eased the car into drive. As she turned past Alec's truck to take the lead in their two-vehicle convoy, she waved a jazzy-fingered *see-you-later*.

Though he would follow behind her, he might as well have been sitting in her passenger's seat because she didn't feel his absence. Even as she pressed harder on the gas, she couldn't create space between her and Alec. Not the physical kind, and certainly not the emotional kind. And that was a part of the trip she hadn't anticipated in the least.

Chapter Seven

THEIR ROUTE WAS east into Texas, head south of Amarillo through Lubbock, wind through Abilene, and coast into the Texas Hill Country through San Antonio until they reached Seguin. Alec knew his way around several panhandle and west-set towns in Texas. But throw a dart and let it hit the middle of Texas, and that would be about the spot of Abilene. He had never been further south or east than that invisible bull's-eye marker. But Mallory had told him little tidbits about Seguin when they talked over dinner, and he was anxious to see the scenery she described.

Based, though, on the speed of her driving, he was going to get to see it sooner than he anticipated.

"Slow down, sweetheart," he murmured as he watched the tail end of Mallory's car speed ahead. He accelerated to keep pace, even though it wasn't like she was trying to lose him.

Right?

They drove below a big Texas sky where wispy clouds swept in full display across crystalline shades of blue. Alec could have stared at that nature show for hours, and likely he would. "In between tailing you." He spoke as if Mallory could hear him. He probably should have reminded her to take it easy when he had the chance back at the gas station. Instead, he wanted to flirt.

Who could blame him?

Now Mallory was again out of his reach, and all he could do was look and follow. Today they were seeing a variety of weather patterns as well as landscapes. Though there were hints of sunshine where they traveled at the moment, looks could be deceiving when it came to December weather. He wanted to be safe, and he wanted Mallory to be especially so. Road conditions could be tricky with temperature drops, so Alec kept his eye on his digital dashboard temperature indicator. Then, if there were rain, sleet, or even too much morning moisture that hung in the air, lanes across bridges could ice, and smooth spots of asphalt could turn into potential disaster zones.

I should have reminded her. But he didn't when he had the chance, and now he didn't want to distract her driving with a phone call. So while he would have preferred Mallory drop her speed by at least five miles, he couldn't do anything about that. He sensed she was on cruise control. He also sensed she was in a hurry back at the gas station. Was it anxiety about the drive? Anticipation of the destination? Or was there some angst with their conversation? He had wanted to kid with her, just to liven up their first stop. Yet when he opened his mouth around her lately, his words straddled the line of professionalism. He heard the way he talked—not the way he would be if, say, Tavis were by his side and this was a multi-person job—and he enjoyed the shift into territory more personal.

He couldn't help it.

And he didn't do this with clients.

Ever.

Mallory Fredrick did something to him, and she wasn't the client he thought she would be. True, he wanted to handle her with gloves after their first phone call when he heard her cry. But she wasn't a basket case at all. She was poised and determined. And while there were some instances where Alec took charge, his sense was that she had wanted him to do just that. They were strangers, but they worked alongside one another like acquaintances. They joked like friends. And there were a few instances where Alec swore that she stared at him like a lover.

Or maybe it was just his wishful thinking.

Holiday nostalgia. Feeling a little sentimental this time of year. That must be it.

Because Mallory was moving.

A state away.

And that was that.

So Alec turned his attention back to the road, focusing again on the tail of Mallory's car and contemplating the irony in what amounted to a metaphorical chase with her in the lead and him trailing behind with his heavy load. He never had a problem in a previous romantic relationship walking a step behind his woman to let her shine, but both the circumstances and the distance of this current experience took that figure of speech to a whole new level.

She led. He was behind. And he'd never quite catch her.

Believe it, buddy, Alec told himself one final time. He

punched the heater a few degrees higher, blasted the defrost to expend the fog he had caused with all of his hot-head thinking and warm-air breathing, and tried to avoid personal thoughts of Mallory. *Keep it professional. Just get her to Seguin.*

But after a pit stop for a bite of fast food in Abilene, they resumed driving for about ninety minutes when Mallory slowed to a speed she hadn't traveled the entire day. Her emergency flashers came on next, and immediately Alec knew this was no joke.

He followed her lead as she pulled her car to the shoulder of Highway 83, though he eased even further off to the side to account for the wide trailer. She flung open the driver's side door and exited in a flash before accessing the back seat, grabbing the cat carrier, and yelling something to Alec he couldn't hear. He cut his engine, removed the key, and unclicked his seat belt. If this was about that cat . . .

Mallory waved her one free hand in a wide sweep as she pointed to the front of her car. Alec checked his mirrors to gauge oncoming vehicles and hoped Mallory would walk away from the shoulder, but she was coming straight for him. Winds whipped her blondish-brown hair in every direction, and she was fighting resistance of it against the pet carrier. She brought both hands to the handle, heaving it as she walked. When an eighteen-wheeler whirred by, it reverberated the thick air in gusts that pushed against Alec's door as he fought to open it.

His words were nearly carried away by the truck's wake. "What's going on? What's wrong?"

Mallory yelled, "Smoke!"

That one word kicked Alec's reaction into gear. "Where?" He sprang past her to see for himself.

"The engine," she called through the wind, as an uprising of steam seeped from the hood.

She left both her driver's door and the side door open, so he called back to her. "Stay there!" He lunged from a standing position to reach beside the steering wheel for the hood release latch. When he did, more vapor rose, whitish like the clouds above.

Not ashy. That's a good sign.

Sensing there wasn't a fire, Alec marched to the front of her car and popped the hood. A strong smell of coolant filled the air along with a steady flow of steam emanating from around a hose. He was no mechanic, but a quick assessment told him they were going to need one.

"Safe to come back?" Mallory's unsteady voice came from somewhere beyond the car.

He waved his hand in front of him to clear the air. The engine was still hot, but his brief mechanical knowledge told him there was no physical danger. "Yes."

Mallory rounded the side of her vehicle, shielding her nose from the smell. She stood at a cautious length from both the exposed engine and from Alec. "I put Bella in the cab of your truck. She's crying up a storm."

"There will be more tears if we don't fix this." He waved his hand again as the last hot wisps disappeared. "Did you have someone check the fluids here?"

Mallory raised on tiptoes to peer into the car. "Of

course."

"You sure?"

"Yes."

"Right before the trip?" Alec turned to look at her.

She pursed her lips in thought. Or maybe defiance. "Not *right* before the trip," she admitted.

Alec couldn't help from sighing. "How long ago was your engine serviced?"

"Maybe last year. Or when I got an oil change." She paused. "I don't know."

Alec didn't want to push too far, and an oral maintenance history wouldn't do them much good at the moment anyway. He tried another approach by venturing a guess with the smell. "There might be an antifreeze leak. Probably something wrong with one of the hoses."

"How bad is that?"

It's not good. "Don't know, but we've got to get you to a mechanic." Abilene was flush with businesses and stations, and if this had happened during lunch, they could have stopped in that town without much of a problem. But they were in the middle of what looked like nowhere, and this was not terrain Alec knew. "Do you remember the next town?" He had seen a mile marker, but he couldn't remember specifics.

"Eden. Five miles." Mallory answered with the certainty of a plaintiff on a witness stand.

"Do you still have water bottles in your car?"

"Yes." Mallory reached into the back seat and procured two full bottles of filtered water. "Bella didn't want to drink anything. She had been sleeping. Until I nearly blew us up."

"This wasn't going to explode." But even if it were—and Alec couldn't be sure—he wouldn't worry Mallory with such talk. "Let's try a few of these."

"Sure thing." Alec also retrieved a couple of bottles of water from his truck's passenger floorboard. Then, they watched the engine and made sure the radiator cooled enough before their teamwork approach of using the water. Mallory checked on Bella several times, and the cat seemed inconvenienced but otherwise okay.

"Fifteen minutes should be long enough." Alec hovered his hand atop the radiator cap, still hot to the touch. "Got a towel in the back seat?"

"Yes." Mallory retrieved one she stowed beneath Bella's carrier. Using the fabric like a mitt, Alec gripped the radiator cap, unscrewed it with care, and leaned back as a blast of steam rose in his wake.

"Be careful," Mallory urged.

Alec stayed steady handed as he filled the reservoir with the tepid water.

"Is that all the car needs?"

Alec wished that were the case. "I don't know. If we start the engine and this water circulates through the system, we're in luck. This might buy us five miles or so. I want to get to Eden and see if we can find a mechanic. Are you okay to drive this?" Alec wouldn't put Mallory in harm's way, and while she would be understandably nervous about taking the wheel, there was no way she would want to drive his truck and trailer. "We'll keep the emergency lights on, and I'll be behind you the whole way. I'll make sure you're safe."

He ducked inside the vehicle to start the engine and gave a thumbs-up when it purred to life.

Mallory's face washed with relief, though she remained cautious. "Are you sure it's suitable to drive?"

He got out of the vehicle so they could change places. "Go slow. Stay in the right lane but don't ride the shoulder. Let's keep it around fifty miles per hour. There's two lanes each way, so cars can get around you." But he wasn't worried about them. He was worried about her. "What do you say?"

Mallory's internal toughness shone as she gave a gritty answer. "Absolutely." That true grit under pressure was an attractive quality. Her heart was also concerned for more than herself. "Can Bella ride with you? I don't want her breathing that smell, and it's probably in the car."

Pets were their owners' responsibility during a move, yet there were so many special cases that Alec and the guys really needed to rethink their whole policy when it came to them. They didn't charge enough for the inconvenience of sounds, dander, and those sometimes accidents that, invariably, cats, dogs, and other varieties of best friends left behind. But he wasn't about to negotiate under these circumstances, and Mallory's words bent his own heart toward Bella. He nodded agreement for the short-term shuffling of their trio road trip member.

Alec shut the hood while Mallory resumed her position as driver. She eased the vehicle forward, slower than she had moved all day. The next five miles would be painful to drive, and Alec could only hope there would be a highway mechanic at the first exit in Eden.

IF THERE WERE a population sign for Eden, Alec missed it. Rolling hills were peppered by occasional farm houses and trees whose leaves had withered for the season. Rural residences that appeared a little closer together were the first indication that a community might lay ahead. Judging by the sparse buildings and lack of retail and restaurant choices, this was a map dot of a location.

"It's not Abilene," which was a sizable city in comparison. Alec's worry manifested, and he wondered if there really would be a mechanic here. Was there even a stoplight?

The community cemetery appeared to have more residents than its municipal lots. Alec drove as the highway gave way to the town's main street, its singular central pass where a sign for what might be a restaurant—*or butcher?*—caught his eye: Venison World.

That's a first.

Then he passed a few other locations that proved, at least, that the locals seemed to have a sense of humor. There was A Pane in the Glass, Armadillo Water Well Service, The Burrito Lady, and one lone chain diner with an empty parking lot, the Dairy Queen. There didn't seem to be much beyond Main Street, though a sign pointed off the highway for Hallelujah Trail Cowboy Church.

This was Texas, through and through.

A tire shop with the letters "E-Z" on a hand-painted sign was the only place Alec saw to stop. There were vehicles parked—or stalled—in front. A large automobile bay door was rolled up, and Mallory eased into the gravely driveway while Alec slowed the truck and trailer and parked on the road's shoulder. He climbed down from his cab first and approached Mallory's driver side. She opened the door but didn't get out. "Is this a good spot?"

Alec nodded. "You did well, sweetheart."

She expended a large sigh and grabbed her purse from the passenger's seat. "No more engine vapor. That's a good sign, right?"

Alec wanted to temper any optimism because he knew this car wasn't going to make longer distance without a checkup. "It was only five miles."

"But we made it." Mallory forced verbal enthusiasm through an otherwise strained expression. He read the look of worry across her forehead.

Alec clapped his hands together in go-get-em fashion. "Let's see if we can score a diagnosis."

As Mallory swung her legs to the left to exit her car, Alec reached for her free hand to help her stand. It was short contact, but with that brief touch, a wave of warmth crested up his arm. Her hand fit like a glove when it touched his. He wanted to linger with skin on skin, but their momentary connection broke when Mallory released her fingers, turned, and closed her car door.

They walked side by side with their feet crunching against the gravel to the only movement they saw of a man in blue coveralls hunched over a tire surrounded by three upturned hubcaps. He was examining them with the intensity of a brain surgeon. "Excuse me." Alec cleared his throat. "Do you think you can give us a hand?"

The mechanic looked up, wiped his palms on a shop towel hanging from his belt loop, and gave a greeting that might well have been from the mayor of the town itself—and, for all Alec knew, maybe it was. "Welcome to Eden. Our little town of blessings. What can I do for you?" The mechanic stood and extended his greasy hand in a show of hospitality, and Alec wasn't about to avoid grabbing it. This was his lifeline. "My name's Marshall."

"Alec." They exchanged a firm grip as Alec introduced Mallory.

"Your wife?" Marshall tipped his chin in her direction.

He sure liked the idea someone would think that, but he had to answer with honesty. "No, sir." Out of the corner of his eye, he caught Mallory with what he judged was a hint of a smile, so perhaps she liked that too. They didn't have a relationship to clarify, other than Alec relaying, "I'm just helping her move."

Marshall asked Mallory, "Where are you headed?"

"Seguin."

Marshall whistled a low note. "Now that's a mighty fine area."

Service was in the hands of Marshall, and Alec led him to Mallory's car while she went to check on Bella.

After a peek under the hood followed by Marshall banging around on a few major components and crouching low beneath the undercarriage to run his hands along some parts, he leveled his diagnosis. "You've got a pinhole leak in the radiator hose, so I need to replace that. Then I'll flush the radiator and add some coolant, so that should get her going again. It's not a hard fix." Marshall sounded upbeat.

Alec ran a hand through his hair, aware there would be a major setback to their schedule. "So you can do this?"

"It's not complicated." That was good to hear. "But it's going to take a while. I'm a one man show."

"How long do you think it will take?" Alec was more concerned about the time than the actual cost.

"About two to three hours. Maybe less."

Whew. That was an inconvenience for sure, but it wasn't completely unmanageable. "That would be great." Maybe a detour into Venison World or meeting The Burrito Lady could keep them occupied.

"I can start first thing in the morning."

Invisible reins tightened around Alec, bringing his plans to a screeching halt. "Did you say morning?"

Marshall explained his setup and how he needed to clear out two projects he promised by the end of the day before he could get to Mallory's. Alec couldn't fault the guy for his honesty. Or his work ethic. For a small-town shop owner, he appeared to stay as busy as any large city service center.

Alec asked about staying the night and was told the town's only motel, the Slumber Inn, was closed for the holidays.

"Closed *for* the holidays?" Alec wanted to be sure he heard correctly.

"Yes, sir. Proprietors sometimes take a vacation too."

"So is there any place to stay?"

"I've got a bunkhouse out back." He gestured to some vague location on the far end of the shop. "Cozy. Wood stove. It'll sleep two."

Three. The cat's got to stay somewhere. But Alec wasn't going to nitpick. "We'll take it."

Now, he just had to tell Mallory.

Chapter Eight

"ARE YOU SURE there's nothing he can do this evening?" Car trouble on a one-way trip was about as big of a monkey wrench as could be thrown at Mallory. "Even if Marshall fixes it late, I'll be fine to drive at night."

Alec had negotiated the work while Mallory was attending to Bella—who refused to eat or drink anything—in the cab of Alec's truck. But there was no altering the mechanic's schedule. "I tried. Marshall can't get to it until the morning."

If only this had happened earlier. "Could we go back in to Abilene? Try to find something else?" Surely there had to be twenty-four-hour service somewhere.

"We're not chancing the road. Getting here was a miracle." He explained the bunkhouse option, and Mallory's skepticism kicked in as Alec relayed the information about this seemingly lone place to stay. "What about the Slumber Inn?"

"Unavailable. Not even open for the holidays."

"You have got to be kidding." But Alec's face revealed no sign of a joke.

They talked through other scenarios, and Mallory at one point even asked about Alec completing the next four hours to Seguin without her. But even as she said the words, she hoped Alec wouldn't abandon her. At this point, he was much less a stranger than the mechanic named Marshall, who for all she knew could be a small-town serial killer. Fear crept into her nerves at the thought of being alone. This was exactly what she was trying to escape in Santa Fe.

"I'm not going to abandon a client in some hidden bunkhouse," he insisted.

These reassuring words consoled Mallory. She had never been so grateful. "Thank you."

Alec lightened the mood with sarcasm. "Besides, just imagine it's a JW Marriott."

Mallory's imagination had been running wild lately, so she could indeed stretch it to envision all kinds of things. "I'll try." She forced a smile, which Alec reciprocated.

Bunkhouse accommodations would not have been Mallory's first choice, but Alec was right. Turning back was impossible, and splitting up to go forward only did one of them any good. Plus she had Bella to consider, and the poor dear could probably use some room to stretch out along with fresh air.

"We still haven't seen the place. Marshall said we could go take a look."

Considering there wasn't a real alternative, Mallory hesitantly agreed.

"Good thing because I wasn't keen on leaving you here." Alec's eyes shadowed when he brought his hand to his brow, and Mallory couldn't read whether it was from nervousness or attentiveness.

"You know . . ." She wanted to break the tension that

had built from this mechanical setback. "This might make a perfect urban escape for people with a sense of adventure. Think about it. People are always looking for charming, rustic getaways. Something off the beaten path." She spun around in mock drama. "I bet nobody would bother vacationers here. It should be advertised as a total chance to rest and unplug."

If there was any charm in Alec's response, he had buried it beneath his deadpan tone. "That's one way to think of it."

She was trying to make the best of a bad situation. "And maybe there could even be a clever name. There's E-Z above the shop." She pointed to the letters. "So this could be the E-Z Bunkhouse, the Lay-Z Hideaway, the Catch Some Zzzzs Glamping Getaway."

"Glamping?" Alec clearly did not know the term.

She broke down the compound word into two emphasized parts of "glamour" and "camping."

"So you *do* think this is going to be glamorous?" Alec's skepticism oozed through his words, popping her make-believe bubble.

Mallory had no illusions, but she was trying to find the humor in her situation. She couldn't be frustrated because she knew this was her fault. In hindsight, she should have had a mechanic check everything before she left. Between final grade input at the college, her HR meeting, and trying to dodge Jesse and the wake of everything he caused, vehicular maintenance was the last thing on her mind. "Look, I've got everything I need packed in the car. That piano's not going anywhere. We'll lock up, and I'll bring important stuff in with us." As she created a plan, she might have been taking charge in the smallest of ways, but it was the first time since she had been around Alec that she was calling the shots. So she rolled with it.

"Should we go look at this bunkhouse?" Alec hunched his shoulders and leaned into the late afternoon wind.

"Lead the way," she prompted.

"And then maybe we can talk about dinner." She fell into step beside his paces as he reminded her of their choices. "Burrito or venison?"

"The variety here is overwhelming," she mocked as her stomach roiled. Between classroom worry, moving-related stress, and now this setback, those unappetizing options matched most of her other experiences for the month. Hopefully the bunkhouse wouldn't disappoint, though she wasn't counting on it.

THE BUNKHOUSE WAS a portable metal building similar in setup to a studio apartment. But whereas an apartment typically had delineations for some of the living space, this had none. A mini fridge was plugged into the far corner of the room and a two-burner cooktop and coffee maker were centered on a small Formica counter. A recliner was angled diagonally across from the only concealed area which held a small sink and toilet. There was a mishmash of wall art and upcycled décor, but at least it had essentials of plumbing and electricity.

"And two beds," Alec aptly pointed out the matching twin-sized mattresses on roller frames.

Mallory was glad for that. "At least there won't be any arguments."

"About us sharing one? Or pushing them together?"

Mallory's jaw dropped in surprise.

"I'm kidding," he insisted, shaking his head in fun. "It's not a Marriott, but it kind of reminds me of college living." He took a few steps into the middle of the space. "Like a dorm. But cleaner."

Thinking about the space that way made Mallory relax a bit, though she still felt guarded. Would that feeling ever subside?

"This actually looks quite comfortable to me." Alec patted the top of the unlit wood stove, their heat source for the night. "We'll get this going, and I'm sure it will warm this place in no time."

"I'll have to keep Bella away from that. Do you know how to light it?" The interior temperature of the metal building seemed to be cooler than the outside air. She pulled her sweater around her more tightly. There was no way she could sleep if the heat didn't work.

"For sure. And Marshall told me we could help ourselves to the wood pile we passed."

"We passed a wood pile?" How much had Mallory missed?

"You're tired," he insisted. "Sit. I'll go make sure Marshall doesn't want any cash for this."

"What do you mean?"

Alec clarified that this bunkhouse was a place the mechanic built for his older kids when they came to visit. "He normally doesn't rent this. It's just for them, an extra place to spread out." He insisted that she relax. "He said they're coming for the holidays but not until tomorrow night, and he's already put fresh sheets on the beds and swept it out." The linoleum floors were clean, at least, from what she could tell. "He's not charging us."

"Really?" Now Mallory wasn't sure what to think. It did seem like a scam disguised as coincidence for a mechanic to not be able to fix a car until the next day when he just so happened to have a bunkhouse. But if he wasn't renting it . . . She looked more closely at the furnishings. As she considered them, she did sense signs of this being built for family, not strangers. One framed piece of art was a jigsaw puzzle. Two fishing poles leaned against a corner wall. And there was a pair of fleece gloves and matching winter hat slung on two wall hooks.

"Really, he said he wouldn't accept a payment for it." Alec added, "Now maybe he'll roll the cost into the final bill or something, but I would say this is all really generous. And, look, there's even some books." A tower of books was piled about three feet high next to the recliner, almost like an end table. "Charm and functionality rolled into one."

Now that she took in the place all at once, it was homely. And there weren't amenities that made it look like a rental setup after all. "For one night." She needed to hear the phrase aloud as much to convince herself that this setback was temporary.

"One night," Alec echoed. "And," he added, "we should probably start the heat now so that it won't be one cold night."

Nothing about the month of December had been predictable for Mallory, so there was no reason for this day to be either. She never would have guessed she would be spending the night with an attractive man in a private room of a place called Eden, but there she was. Each day of teaching could be unpredictable, but so was her life now.

After unloading a few essentials, securing the vehicles, and settling Bella, they used teamwork to start a fire. After gathering wood from outside, Mallory handed the split pieces to Alec as he stacked them into the belly of the stove. He struck a match that momentarily lit his face in a brilliant flash of color, accentuating his ruggedly handsome features.

Either she was exhausted or she was seeing things because, as gorgeous as Alec was in the day, he was twice so against the glow of reflected firelight.

Mallory was going to have to be careful tonight.

THE AIR WARMED to a toasty temperature as Mallory and Alec finished their take-out dinner. "Not half bad." Alec balled his foil wrapper. "The Burrito Lady knows her stuff."

"Agreed." Mallory's hunger was satisfied, but she couldn't say the same for Bella's. The cat hadn't touched her food, and she wouldn't settle down for longer than a few moments at a time. "I don't know why she won't eat."

"She's probably stressed. This was a big day for her." Alec had never owned a cat, but surely a move like this couldn't be easy on one. "Has she had any water?"

"She didn't want to drink when we stopped for lunch, and I haven't seen her touch her bowl since we've been here." Mallory had set fresh food and water against one blank wall of the bunkhouse, but Bella just didn't seem interested. "I'm worried about her."

"See how she does tomorrow. Maybe she'll sleep it off tonight and perk up in the morning." Though even he had to admit he wasn't sure what constituted model cat behavior.

"I hope so." Mallory's face registered her worry. Playfully, she called to Bella with a click-clickety-click of her tongue, but Bella didn't respond. Instead, she raised one paw, licked it, and started bathing, oblivious that anyone wanted her attention. Mallory wrinkled her forehead. "Have it your way."

Alec was learning to read Mallory's emotions and her nonverbal cues. She was frustrated. "You really should relax." He had been up as long as Mallory, but he was used to hard days that stretched longer than a typical eight-hour work schedule, which he assumed must have been Mallory's daily routine at the college. Early rising, manual labor, and unexpected detours to plans had to be a new experience for her. "Try to take a load off."

"Easier said than done." Although Bella had her space, Mallory fidgeted as if she couldn't quite find hers. "I've been in that car all day and can't decide if I want to stretch, curl, or totally give up so I can try to fall asleep early tonight."

"Your choice." Alec wasn't one to cramp a woman's style.

"What are you going to do?"

He echoed her list. "Stretch." He reached his hands over his head, turning his neck side to side as he did to relieve the day's tension. Then, he dropped them down again. "Curl." He mimed slumber by closing his eyes and pressing his palms together as if creating a pillow. "Eventually fall asleep."

"You're a real comedian," she deadpanned.

"Not trying to be." Alec preferred to keep their company light, but in such close proximity, he didn't want to force too much of a good thing. "If you want me to be quiet, just say so. I'll be perfectly fine right here." He tapped the edge of the bed before lowering himself onto the mattress. He kicked one heel over an outstretched foot as he leaned back on his elbows, waiting for Mallory to make the next move.

But Bella beat her to it.

In a flash, the cat halted her beauty routine and bounded atop the bed next to Alec, coiling her body against his blue-jeaned thigh before he could respond. Mallory registered her shock with darting eyes and a mouth agape. Bella's purring reached Alec's ear before any audible sound from Mallory.

"How about that?" Bella was as calm as Alec had ever seen her, nestling close and slowly kneading her paw pads against the plush bedding. Her fur was soft as duck down, and she generated as much warmth as a cashmere throw. As

Alec tilted his head to get a better look at her face, he swore her closed eyes were smiling at him.

Mallory finally spoke through her disbelief. "She never does that with strangers."

"Is that still what I am?" Clearly, Bella didn't think he was.

"You know what I mean."

Do I? They not only shared talks and dinner but now this: an overnight experience. Granted, it wasn't planned or exactly idyllic, but its spontaneity did possess charm even Alec couldn't deny.

Mallory shifted in her seat, yet while her body moved, her eyes didn't. Like an artist studying a still life before committing to the next brush stroke, her focus was on Alec. But rather than nervousness at being on display, he was enveloped by a calm he didn't quite understand.

Alec's last relationship had ended when commitment issues drove a wedge between him and his girlfriend, as she couldn't stay settled in Santa Fe. It had been a while since he was at ease in the company of a woman. But with Mallory, he was. Not only here, but since they first met.

And even her cat likes me. He stroked Bella's pewter fur as her purring revved louder. *Unbelievable.*

The chill had dissipated, replaced by a temperateness of heat from the wood stove. Dim lighting, basic creature comforts, and small square footage added to the intimacy, yet those paled in comparison to the surprise delivered when Mallory rose from the recliner to shrink the gap between them. Tension cut through the air. Her body moved across the space as if pushing aside a curtain of hesitation.

She approached Alec, her eyes meeting his as she asked in a voice less concerned with an answer than with articulating her question. "How do you know how to make everything seem okay?"

She sat on the edge of the bed, their bodies close as their emotions grew closer. Intense life experiences like moving brought out emotion in clients, but with Mallory, the emotion was different.

Deeper.

Shared proximity became even more so as he responded by sitting up, moving his upper body to hers. He spoke softly. "You make it easy to feel okay." And she did. Alec wanted to be around her, and especially in this moment, not just as a client.

As something more.

They mutually split the distance, each leaning in but not daring to rock the silence that now forced their movements to do the talking.

Mallory was in charge as she closed the gap. Her lips were within kissing range and Alec enjoyed the sense of control she exuded. He liked seeing this surprise side of her that he couldn't escape.

And he didn't want to.

The woman who had been on his mind even when she was far out of sight was now a reality before him. She leaned with parted lips that invited Alec's mouth to join hers, and they kissed in a sweet expression of shared affection that took them to a whole new level.

Chapter Nine

MALLORY'S HEART SLID into her throat the moment her lips left Alec's. Immediate regret for her impulsivity caused her to stumble back. Physical space now extinguished any romantic flames that could have otherwise been fanned. "I shouldn't have done that."

Alec's expression was shell shock as he froze on the bed. He cleared his throat but besides that didn't make a sound. Bella, oblivious to the shift in human expression, was the only one of the three not rattled.

But Mallory sure was.

She grabbed one of her necklace strands and pinched it between her fingers, wishing she could rewind the last five minutes. *What was I thinking?* "That can't happen again."

Alec sucked his cheek inward as if he were going to chew on it as well as Mallory's words. Mallory stood as she slid her fingers over one of the rounded beads, rubbing away incoming anxiety as she waited for Alec to respond. His lack of any verbal reaction was as troublesome as his silence. "Can you say something?" Imploring further, she added, "Anything?"

Alec opened his mouth but snapped it shut again before words came. He arched an eyebrow in thought but didn't look at Mallory. His gaze fell to Bella, a curled ball of contentment that didn't seem to have any of the snake-bit recoil Mallory had in that moment.

"Alec?" she prompted.

If he wasn't going to speak, she didn't think she could stay here with him for the night. Car or no car, there was going to have to be an alternative. Her mind raced faster than her pulse.

Finally, Alec's smooth voice assessed the predicament with, "First this girl . . ." He shifted his weight to one elbow so he could raise his right arm to stroke Bella's back. "Then this girl." He looked straight into Mallory's frozen gaze, her concentration breaking long enough so that she could intake a breath.

Oxygen never tasted so good.

And neither did one man's lips. Alec's kiss was perfection.

Yet his reply gave Mallory no indication of his feelings. In the absence of him expressing anything, Mallory had no choice but to react only to her own. And those feelings, much like their trip, were telling her to pause.

Take a break.

Rest for the night.

Don't do anything you will regret. She calmed herself with a quick mental pep talk. This wasn't a planned overnight event. Bunking with Alec was nothing more than a road-block to her destination, and she couldn't let it carry any meaning. Alec was here for a service. He was being paid for what he was doing.

That was that.

Spending the night in Eden, then, was just a delay in the trip—nothing more. For tomorrow, the farewell would come. She would arrive in Seguin with her belongings, and Alec would be sent on his way. She would be in Texas. He would go back to New Mexico.

That was how this situation was supposed to work.

And Mallory needed to stay the course without letting her emotions slide toward Alec in another surprise kiss. To protect her heart, they needed to settle on some expectations for this overnight stay. "I think we need to set some ground rules."

"Rules?" Alec raised himself to a fully upright position on the bed but did so slowly as not to disturb Bella in the process. "What kind of rules?"

"For this place. For behavior." *Great, now I sound just like a teacher.* She added a phrase to lighten any misunderstanding of her words. "Just so we can be comfortable, you know?"

"Right." Alec nodded. "Because this"—he gestured with an upturned hand in a semicircle across the bed and Bella—"is clearly not comfortable?"

Mallory had no trouble reading his sarcasm. "That's not what I mean."

He lowered his hand, conceding to her. "Tell me, then, exactly what you mean."

Mallory was torn. On the one hand, she wanted to keep their impromptu evening together cordial. Two beds meant two separate sleeping spaces. That would be one ground rule. And how hard was that? She needed to respect Alec's privacy and didn't want to blow past another boundary.

On the other hand, Mallory loved surprises with Alec. His looks, his conversation, his outreach and that kiss . . .

That, especially, was such a good surprise.

But she couldn't have it both ways.

Ground rules were safe. And Mallory needed something safe. Since Jesse, safety was all she craved. So she was protecting herself by guarding her emotions and her future. What else could she do?

Mallory gave her sister a courtesy call when she went to her car to retrieve clothes and toiletries for the night. Upon hearing about her mechanical issue, Paige offered to send Everett the two hundred miles or so from Seguin to come and get her. "He could stay in Eden instead of you and wait for the car in the morning. He's willing to, really."

"That's such an inconvenience." Everett was so good to Paige, and while a favor like this was completely within his nature, Mallory didn't want to create trouble. She already worried about how much of an annoyance her presence would be in their relationship, and she was committing herself to doing all she could to minimize any negative impact. "But please tell him that I appreciate the offer. I'll be fine. Really."

"I worry about you."

Their tables were reversed from when Mallory was the one doing the worrying. Helping Paige through her divorce and Nathan's hospitalization were trying times for her little sis, and Mallory was glad she could shoulder some of the burden for her. But, as the older sister, she reminded Paige,

"I'm supposed to be the one who worries."

Paige's kindness shone through her words. "Nobody needs to worry alone."

Mallory was glad to have Paige in her corner. She hugged her phone closer as if doing so were an action her sister could actually feel. "Thank you." She assured her they would arrive midday and she would call with updates.

"You better. I already had to break it to Nathan that you weren't coming tonight. I said his favorite aunt would be arriving tomorrow instead."

She smiled at Paige's choice of words. "I'm his *only* aunt."

"All the more reason you're his favorite."

Mallory was glad to be headed toward family.

She clicked off the call, got what she needed from the car, and went back to the bunkhouse. In the privacy of the small bathroom, she changed into a pair of shorts and a spare T-shirt to get ready for bed. Alec asked if it was okay if he took off his shirt for sleeping since they hadn't set any ground rules about clothing. The moment he asked, Mallory ached on the inside. She wished she could have kissed those ground rules goodbye.

Shirtless? Yes, please. She surprised herself with how much she was attracted to Alec. If he wanted to peel off any other layers, she privately admitted that would be fine too.

Yet she bit her lip in saying so because they were not going to flirt. She and Alec agreed to no confronting, no coaxing, and no contact.

And there would be no more kissing.

Yet Alec's kiss was so delicious it was all Mallory could taste as she crawled between the sheets of her bed, a mere matter of feet from the man who could give her more if only she might not have set those rules . . .

But just like managing her classroom, rules were necessary. When her students knew her policies on being tardy and submitting late work, when they realized how many points could be earned through completing different assignments, when they understood the importance of taking notes in class, this made the environment better for them as well as her. Everyone knew the rules, and everyone agreed to play by them.

She just hoped Alec would play by them too. And that he wouldn't think she was irrational in her actions or words. He wasn't some student she was trying to mold into shape.

Please don't think ill of me. There was more she wished she could have told him, more she wanted to in that moment. He didn't know about her teaching, her sabbatical, or Jesse. How could he even comprehend the depth of her fears if she tried to explain? Her confidence had been shot to pieces, and she privately questioned her teaching credibility. She wrestled with a sense of failure every night when she lay down just like this, and she hoped that somehow a temporary move would alleviate that. But she felt it in Santa Fe, and she was feeling it here in Eden. Was she wrong to think she wouldn't feel it in Seguin too?

Mallory lay quietly as the lit hearth of the wood stove bathed the bunkhouse in a gentle glow. Errant crackles of its mesquite wood punctuated the silence. Bella's purring would rev and pause and rev again in direct correlation, it seemed, to whether Alec was petting her or whether his hand fell to his side. Bella didn't normally sleep with Mallory, so she was shocked by her routine reversal in staying glued to Alec's bed. Her students could surprise her, and so could her cat.

I don't seem to have a handle on much these days. She pulled the bed sheets tighter as she curled onto her side, wanting nothing more than to sleep away her doubt and her tension. *Morning will break. And Seguin will be my switch plate.* Lights out for the past, lights on for the future.

THE SUN ROSE before Mallory and Alec did, peeking through the curtained window to announce the new day to them. Bella stretched and arched before jumping off the bed, plodding with all fours onto the floor. "Did she sleep there all night?"

Alec reached his hand around the comforter to the warm spot that the cat abandoned. He could still feel the heat. "I guess she did." He had been more tired than he thought. Last night, Bella was curled atop the bed against his thigh when he crawled beneath the sheets, but he remembered nothing after his head hit the pillow. He didn't recall waking once. Save for the slight *whoosh* of the heat from the wood stove, there had been no other sound. "Sleep well?"

Mallory rubbed her eyes and rolled to face Alec. "I did. Surprisingly." She burrowed her head into the pillow, a coy look flashing across her face. Streaks of sunshine freshened her facial features. Her smooth skin looked as radiant as the new day, and soft tendrils of hair fell in loose cascades.

"Me too." Alec wasn't previously aware of how much his body craved a rest after a hard day's work. "These two little beds are deceptively comfortable."

"I'll say." Mallory squeezed her pillow, its fluff pushing against her cheek as she continued to rest her head.

Alec couldn't stop staring. She had scrubbed the makeup she wore before she climbed into bed. But seeing her so fresh-faced and bare, he wondered why she even wore any. He could gaze at her beautiful face for hours.

She broke his concentration only when she asked, "So we'll tell Marshall these bunkhouse accommodations get a five-star rating?"

Alec eased to a sitting position, the comforter and top sheet falling to reveal his bare chest. He raised one arm to the side and tugged at his elbow before repeating the process on the other side to give his upper body a proper morning stretch. "I now understand why his kids would like staying here. This is a little slice of relaxation."

Mallory made a noise he couldn't distinguish before burrowing her head again into her pillow.

"What was that?"

She kept her face hidden and muffled an answer. "Agreed."

He took the hint. "I'm going to put on a shirt." He threw back the covers and swung his legs off the side of the bed. "Do you want me to check on the car and see if Marshall was able to get an early start on it?"

Mallory still didn't raise her head. "Yes."

"Okay." He rose from the bed, retrieved his gray pullover from the day before, and slid into it. The cotton fabric was warm from the fire and held the scent of mesquite wood. Feeling its texture and temperature sent a morning rush across his skin that energized him as much as a first bite of breakfast—or a first look at a gorgeous woman within touching proximity. Yet he was following her rules and resolved to be the perfect gentleman. "Can I get you anything?"

"No thanks. I'll get up when you go out."

He was curious to see more of her, but he also wanted to respect her morning privacy. "Sounds good." As soon as he fastened his work boots, he could excuse himself from the space. But as he grabbed the top of the boots from near the door, Bella lunged at one of the dangling laces. "Hey!" The Persian swiped the air with her paw as he raised them just out of her reach.

Mallory twisted toward the commotion just as Bella took another swing. "Looks like someone doesn't want you to go."

He wasn't used to having his routine interrupted by a cat. Bella crouched low, eyeing the footwear as if it were prey. "And what would you do if you caught these?" he taunted. He separated the boots to one in each hand, and she looked back and forth and back again as if trying to decide which boot deserved a pounce.

"She gets a little excited in the morning. It's her playtime."

Alec could see that. "Then who am I to disrupt her routine?" He swung each boot like a piñata in front of her, letting the laces taunt her into a back and forth game. Her paws were at the ready, and her tail twitched excitedly.

"She will swipe at those." As if Bella understood Mallory's warning, she took an aggressive swing as her claws activated and barely missed contact with the lace.

"Oh, I know she will." Alec wasn't an expert at reading feline behavior, but he knew enough of this look that Bella was declaring it hunting time, and his boots were the prize. "Wish I had an actual ball of string for you."

"I'm sure she likes this challenge better." Mallory's commentary was making this a spectator sport. "Now what will you do if she catches that boot?"

"Make her wear it," he teased, which made Mallory chuckle. By now, she had sat up, yet she kept her body hidden behind a bedsheet pulled protectively against her chest. Her morning laugh was cute, and so was this scene.

"She's a different cat from yesterday."

"I'll say," Alec agreed. She was lethargic and largely unresponsive then, but now she was kittenish and lively. Her body radiated energy and her eyes shone with a mission. Her cat pupils grew round as marbles, zeroing in on her task. "For sure, she's gotten her personality back."

"I'm glad you were able to do that."

"Me?" Alec doubted he had anything to do with it.

"Yes, you." Mallory reminded him Bella didn't detach herself from his side for the last ten hours or so. "That cat is crazy about you."

Alec brushed off the compliment. "She just likes my boots."

Alec and Mallory watched Bella continue to play. Finally, Alec put the boots on the floor, stepped into them, and hid the laces beneath the bottom hem of his blue jeans as he readied to step outside. "Game's over," he announced. "You've worked up an appetite for breakfast." He side-stepped to her food bowl, shook the morsels to get her attention, and almost instantaneously her focus was now where Alec wanted it to be.

"That's incredible," Mallory marveled. "Finally, she's eating something."

Alec didn't know a thing about cats' diets, but coaxing her to eat her food and drink some water solicited more praise from Mallory. "Does she know I'm not staying with her in Texas?"

Mallory's response was barely above a whisper. "You may have to explain that to us when you leave."

Chapter Ten

MARSHALL PERFORMED AN early round of magic on Mallory's car, and her wheels were ready to go by midmorning. He had a roll of radiator hose in stock from a previous job, which was a stroke of luck given their location in Eden. Marshall didn't seem to charge much for mechanic's labor either.

Mallory handed him a credit card, grateful she was getting to float the expense for a few weeks. Her final paycheck would kick in at the end of the month, so this mechanical expense could at least be covered. But she wanted to be fair with him. "Are you sure we can't pay you for the bunkhouse?" With their use of the place, it only seemed right to charge them something. The Slumber Inn surely would have done so.

Marshall waved a grease rag before looping it over his belt. "Not a thing. That place I fixed up isn't much—"

"But it is," Mallory countered. She and Alec slept like tranquilized bears. "It's so comfortable." Even though the quarters were modest, it had the essentials. The fire stayed toasty, and Bella even enjoyed the accommodations. "You have a little taste of paradise right here."

"That's kind of you to say, ma'am." Marshall returned

her card and handed Mallory a receipt. "I hope you get where you're going, and maybe you'll come back through Eden soon."

"I will." She smiled, already thinking ahead to when she would be moving back to Santa Fe. She hoped the sabbatical would pass quickly and by the start of the fall she could be back in a classroom with renewed confidence and resolve to do what she felt called to do.

After a check-in text message to Paige, Mallory and Bella readied again for the road. Alec tidied up the bunkhouse, emptied Bella's food and water, and loaded the cat carrier into the back of the car. He waved to Bella inside, who meowed her own version of a farewell. Next, he turned his attention to Mallory. "Ready?" He opened her driver-side door as she slid into the seat, put the key in the ignition, and brought the car to life again. "Sounds as steady as a cat's purr," he judged.

The rhythm of the engine was much less labored than the day before. "That's a world of difference. Much better." She even turned on the heat, and the car continued to sound the same.

Alec leaned his forearm against the edge of the door, looking over the gauges as if an alert light might signal at any moment. But nothing pinged from the dash. "So you're all set?"

Mallory couldn't think of anything she was missing.

Alec shut her door to ready himself inside his own truck and resume pulling the enclosed trailer load. Mallory was going to lead their convoy of two, and she eased steadily onto the highway, slow enough so Alec could be close behind. She watched him through her rearview mirror, and a faint trepidation tugged inside of her. She accelerated slightly, still keeping her eye on Alec in her rearview. As she picked up speed and made sure Alec did the same, the realization hit. This was the farthest apart they had been in hours.

The void between them and the impersonal distance stayed with Mallory as she wound her way through the Texas Hill Country. Cresting between waves of gently rolling farmland, pastures of winter crops, and fences that held thriving livestock, she split her focus between what was in front of her—and who was behind her.

They had one metropolis to pass through, and that was the wide sprawl of San Antonio. An uptick in traffic slowed their pace, but as they emerged from the heart of downtown onto the eastside of IH-10, she drew strength from knowing Alec was there.

A small interstate pass over the folkloric Woman Hollering Creek indicated their destination was near. Legend held that when a motorist passed over the creek and screamed, a woman's wails down below could simultaneously be heard.

Mallory screamed with a voice of abandon to test the legend.

She hadn't counted on scaring the cat to pieces in the process.

Poor Bella. At the surprise, she meowed in a siren of wails to try and match Mallory's volume. Had Alec been in the passenger's seat, he would have collapsed in a heart attack from the racket.

Whether she heard any other voice, she couldn't be certain. But the scream was like a cleanse, and as she led the way off the interstate into the Guadalupe County seat, she hoped the acceptance of Paige's offer would not yield disappointment. She wasn't quite ready to scream like that again.

ALEC HAD TRIED to behave like a perfect gentleman in light of the Eden detour and once he arrived at Mallory's destination in Seguin. He hadn't ever seen this part of Texas, but he immediately understood the charm when he did. The small town was close enough to San Antonio to be convenient, yet far enough to retain its own personality. Exiting the highway, Alec saw more beauty with each mile. Pecan trees with wide limbs filled well-kept lots and shaded commercial storefronts. Parks and greenspace dotted in abundance while the emerald waters of the Guadalupe River snaked through the area. Like a fancy necklace elevated an outfit, so too did the river to the town. Acreage and residences along with municipal buildings all shared the same incredible canopy of a sky so blue he didn't know whether to squint or stare.

Mallory led Alec through a picturesque yet uncomplicated route to a small residential area where she pulled to the curb and gestured for him to back into the available driveway. While he did, she hopped out of the car to guide the trailer until he saw her ball her fingers into a fist to signal a stop.

They had arrived.

While Alec unclicked his seat belt and stowed his keys inside the sun visor, he caught a glimpse through his side mirror of a little boy bounding out of the front door and into Mallory's arms. She scooped the toddler into a tight embrace, twirling around and around as her hair fanned about her and his legs dangled as if he were enjoying a merry-go-round spin. She rained kisses across his forehead as she slowed their turns. When Alec reached to open the door of his pickup cab, he could hear the boy laughing and laughing.

Mallory talked about Nathan during their first dinner and had even shown Alec a couple of photos on her phone. In person, though, the boy was even more lively than in smiling still shots. He clung to his aunt with an intense grip that was pure love.

Nathan's mother wasn't far behind to the happy scene. A woman about Mallory's height with the same shade of blondish-brown locks joined for a three-way hug. Alec took his time walking toward the trio, not wanting to destroy the reunion.

"I am so thankful you finally made it." The woman's voice was near to Mallory's, and when she responded, Alec could hear the family resemblance. There wasn't so much a Texas twang as there was a slight Southern accent that grew stronger with every word they exchanged. They spoke in rapid-fire dialogue that even Nathan tried to match. Alec's heart was glad Mallory was in the comfort of family.

Alec got to work in readying the trailer for unloading.

"Come inside for a minute, Alec," Mallory called to him. But he didn't want to intrude on the hugs, well wishes, and welcome home greetings. He had a job to do.

That was why he was hired.

"Go ahead," he assured. "I've got to get the dolly unhooked and loosen some tie straps so we can get this stuff out of here." It didn't take him long to shift into work mode. "Tell me where you want most of this. Garage okay?"

The door to the two car area was already rolled up, with only one side occupied. The other was clean, neat, and empty. *Perfect.*

"Yes, that would be great," Mallory called.

He already judged the unloading of the boxes should go quickly. But before he could get to that, there was the antique piano. "Want that in or out?"

"In! For sure." Mallory set Nathan down on the sidewalk, and she reminded Alec of the promised help courtesy of her sister's fiancé, Everett. "He should be coming by any minute. Paige called him from inside, so he's on his way."

The second pair of hands were exactly what he needed for the piano, and he was certainly grateful. "And Bella? Do you want me to bring her inside?"

Mallory clasped her hand to her mouth before darting to the car. "I almost forgot," her admission rang through the morning air.

Surely you wouldn't. Alec shook his head, knowing how much Mallory adored her pet. Strangely, after the magnetism the night before from Bella, even he was becoming fond of the cat, which was a first for him.

But fondness for Bella and Mallory both would have to be cooled. Their time together was ending. He hoisted himself into the back of the trailer and reached for the slack end of the first tie strap, focusing on his job.

The process of unloading during a move was much more efficient than loading. And because he was putting most items in the garage, this would be even faster than he originally anticipated.

When Everett arrived, Alec directed him for help in steadying the piano. There was already a spot cleared in the living room for the instrument, not terribly spacious but easy enough to navigate. "On three." He counted down as they used teamwork to maneuver the antique. When they released the straps and the piano stood in place, Nathan clapped his enthusiastic approval.

Alec cracked a smile for the appreciative audience of one, dipping his upper body into a playful bow for the boy. "No guarantee of tone," he admitted as he straightened. "You may want to get a professional to tune that." Though he always explained the risk of moving a large piece like this to his clients, he also reminded them of it upon delivery.

"That's a project for another time." Mallory ran her hand across the top of the piano. "Besides, I'm sure it will be fine."

"Can I play?" Nathan's voice bubbled with excitement.

"Let me get the bench for you, buddy." Alec threw the tie straps across one shoulder as he headed back outside.

"I'll help." Mallory locked step behind him.

As they arrived back at the trailer, they were alone for the first time since leaving the bunkhouse. Alec's heart rate was already high from the physical work, though he still jolted when Mallory followed him into the belly of the enclosed moving trailer and was within such close proximity. Yet he needed to keep feelings in check. He was leaving this girl in another hour, less than if Everett continued to help with free labor.

"Do you want to stay for a bit? Grab something to drink or have an early lunch?" Mallory lingered near a column of stacked boxes, awaiting his reply.

If this were other circumstances, he might stay. But he couldn't delay the inevitable. "I don't think so." Originally, the plan had been for Alec to spend the night at a hotel in Seguin before heading back to Santa Fe. But that was before the detour in Eden. With the change, he had practically the whole day in front of him, and he could make good time back to Santa Fe with an emptied trailer. He would be able to burn daylight, save the cost of a room, and make it back home around midnight.

Mallory pulled her sweater close. "Are you sure?" Her voice shook, though Alec suspected the unsteadiness was more a result of the cool temperatures than anything else. "Maybe just come inside to warm up a bit?"

The work was keeping Alec warm enough, and he had the still-lingering heat from their sweet kiss. He held to the fond remembrance of chemistry that manifested in their one night together. "I'm fine. You should really go inside. Let me take care of this. I'll handle it."

Mallory didn't respond but instead grabbed a box, hugged it to her chest, and stepped down from the trailer.

Alec had helped plenty of people through the years settle into a new life by performing a move, and there was always the reward of accomplishment when the job was done. But, with Mallory, the parting was bittersweet. His duties were done, but it would be a lonely drive back to Santa Fe. Shaking the memory of this girl wouldn't be easy.

SECURITY FLOODED MALLORY with her arrival at Paige's. With the piano in one piece and her boxes mostly unloaded, major worries were now behind her. Alec and Everett were folding tie-downs and replacing the dolly, readying the trailer for the trip back to Santa Fe. She would have to face Alec to say goodbye in a matter of minutes.

But before she did that, her sister made her stand before her for a proper, focused welcome. "You're here!" Paige embraced her with a hug all to herself as Nathan busied himself at Bella's carrier, curious at the four-legged visitor.

"Don't touch her, sweetie," Mallory called over Paige's shoulder. Bella's world had already been turned upside down, and the fingers of a child prodding into her personal space were the last thing she needed. Mallory released from Paige's embrace and reminded Nathan, "She's just a little scared."

"Why?" The one-word question ignited a plethora of possibilities.

"Well . . ." Mallory could answer in any number of ways.

"For starters, she's a long, long way from her house." She crouched down to Nathan, becoming more his size.

"Why?" The question echoed again.

Mallory tried a slightly different approach. "Because we're going to stay here. For a while."

Nathan didn't miss a beat. "Why?"

Mallory called to her sister. "Didn't you tell him anything?"

She simply shrugged. "Such is the memory of a four-year-old."

Her sister was a patient woman.

Nathan knew how this game worked, and he wasn't going to let Mallory off the hook. He tugged at her sleeve, imploring her for a reply. Maybe of all the people to whom she would have to explain her move, her nephew would be her toughest critic. She chose her words carefully, not in an effort to lie to Nathan but to convey complicated reasons as simply as she could. "We're going to stay here because I wanted to come to Texas. And you and your mom have a house. Your mom said it would be okay to stay here with you." She wasn't going to set herself up for another *why* question, so she added, "What do you think about that?"

Nathan stopped pulling on Mallory's sweater and instead rested his hand against her shoulder in thought. "I like that." He dipped his head into her arm for a sideways hug. "But now can I play with the kitty?"

This dynamic was going to take some adjustment. She patted Nathan's back before reaching her hand around to the top of the carrier. "We're going to let kitty take a nap." She hoisted the carrier as she stood. "Maybe after a nap, kitty will feel like playing."

That explanation seemed to make complete sense to Nathan. He waved goodbye to Bella. "Have a good nap."

Mallory led the carrier through the living room. "Is it okay if I put her in the spare bedroom?"

"That's your bedroom now," Paige reminded her. "And as far as I'm concerned, that can be Bella's too. We'll have a talk about her litter box later." That was a matter of care Mallory hadn't anticipated. She loved her pet, but there were some aspects of Bella's life she didn't need to see. Paige couldn't expect her to keep a litter box in the bedroom. "Seriously?"

"Ground rules, Sis." She spoke with the authority of a parent.

"And to think I'm the older sibling," she murmured as she continued down the hallway.

"I heard that." Then Paige added, "We'll talk about a compromise later."

But, for now, having Bella in a confined space was best. Actually, as Mallory opened the door to the small room that would be hers, shutting out the rest of the world and staying sequestered from public view didn't sound like such a bad idea.

Yet she needed to leave Bella so she could go back outside to say goodbye to Alec.

His sendoff wouldn't be easy.

Alec and Everett were just finishing up when Mallory came around the corner of the trailer they were closing. Alec held an outstretched hand to Everett. "I appreciate all of your help."

Everett exchanged the handshake. "No problem at all. Glad we could make it work." He released and then pointed over his shoulder with a thumb toward the front door. "Are you sure you don't need anything?"

Alec dug his hands into his pockets. "I'm fine. The sooner I get on the road, the better off I'll be. I want to clear San Antonio during the lunch hour and be well on the other side by the time any traffic hits."

Mallory mentally rewound their drive from the previous day, knowing exactly the landmarks Alec would pass on the way. Everett turned toward Mallory. "I'll leave you to it. See you inside soon?" Mallory nodded, and Everett excused himself.

Alec kept his hands in his pockets, and Mallory wrapped hers around herself as a cool winter breeze blew across her. "Cold?" Alec inquired.

"Not nearly like Santa Fe." Her light sweater was an adequate layer, yet she shivered in spite of it. But maybe it wasn't the weather that caused her to do that.

Maybe it was Alec.

Or the absence of him that was coming.

But words to address their parting weren't on her tongue. Alec O'Donnell had been Mallory's rock when she needed it, and now it was going to be hard to say goodbye.

To keep herself from any emotional cracking, she kept their conversation on business. "So do you have a bill to give me for the work?" Money owed to Four Guys should be her last major expense now that her paychecks were drying up for the new semester.

"I'll put something together and let you know." He didn't seem concerned by a commitment. Maybe that was characteristic of the attitude of Four Guys. But she would certainly settle the bill. Paying it was a worry, but it was one she had expected.

Not knowing if she would see Alec again was a worry she hadn't.

He made the move to depart first, removing one hand from his pocket and taking a single step forward. "So I guess I'll be seeing you."

Mallory matched his step to lessen the gap between them and stretched out her arms. A friendly hug seemed appropriate, though even as they embraced, Mallory flashed back to their kiss the night before when she had been vulnerable and let her guard down. If circumstances were different, there could be more between them.

But timing just didn't align.

They held a close embrace that Mallory wanted to siphon emotionally, and Alec stood calmly as if to let her. Then, ever so slowly, he slackened his grip and made a motion to get back on the road, turning away from Mallory as their connection dissipated.

Alec climbed into the cab of his pickup, closed the door behind him, and disappeared from Mallory's view. Moments later with the truck and trailer out of sight, there wasn't a single sign that Alec O'Donnell had even been there with her. All she had were remembrances of conversations and bunkhouse memories, but with her head no less cloudy from the stress of the last few weeks, she wasn't even sure how much she could trust those.

Chapter Eleven

"YOU DIDN'T MENTION your moving man was hot." Paige crossed her legs beneath her as she settled on the couch with a look that begged Mallory to dish.

But she wasn't in the mood. "He's not my man." Mallory closed the front door behind her.

Paige wasn't going to let her off the hook. "You spent the night together."

Mallory didn't want to delve into details, especially since there weren't any salacious ones to share. *One kiss? Uninterrupted sleep on opposing twin beds?* "Not exactly a night of indulgence."

Paige continued teasing. "I don't know. Eden sounds pretty dreamy to me."

Dreamy? That was a stretch. "I did tell you the place was an E-Z Tire Shop, didn't I?" She didn't want to give Paige any reason to dramatize this, especially not when Mallory was still processing her feelings.

"I'm just curious, that's all." Paige sank into the couch cushions.

Mallory was curious too. She was curious what Alec was thinking at this very moment. She wondered what he felt during their final hug and what would occupy his mind as he passed again through Eden, then Abilene, the Texas border, and along the highway into Santa Fe. And she could only imagine what his life would be like once he arrived back there.

He will probably resume right where he left off. She would be delusional to think otherwise.

Paige speculated with a conversation all to herself. "I just think there are certain things you should have mentioned. Sister to sister, you know? It's strange that you conveniently didn't tell me your moving guy was your age. And not even hitched! Totally available."

"How do you know he's not married? I didn't tell you that."

"No ring." She held up her own hand, her engagement diamond cutting through the interior light in dazzling sparkles.

Even Mallory knew that fact. She had glanced at Alec's hand when they first met.

But now, in retrospect, why was that even a consideration? "I've moved," Mallory reminded her sister. "And, in case you need me to jog your memory, long-distance romances are hard." Paige and Everett had their own version of one early in their relationship, when he was making more frequent back-and-forth trips to Amarillo in the Texas panhandle. Of course, everything worked out, but Paige did have some concerns because spending time away from one another wasn't always easy.

"Yet we made it work." Paige adjusted her ring at arm's length, pivoting it admiringly atop her finger.

Mallory was ready to shut this conversation down. "My mind is really not on romance." That was the truth. "Or Alec," Mallory added.

That was a lie.

But Paige didn't need to know that.

"Whatever you say." Paige conceded the final word.

Mallory took the opportunity to change the subject. "I'm going to go check on Bella. Get her accustomed to this place. Let her settle in." But she really just wanted some time to be alone. Alec's physical absence was raw, and wounds from her professional life turning into a disaster were still not healed.

She hadn't expected her arrival in Seguin to be a magical elixir, but she certainly thought she'd feel better than she did.

For the rest of the day, Mallory cut a rut between the garage, her car, and her bedroom. Even with boxes moved, there was still unloading to do. She had clothes to share with Paige as well as her own to hang in what would be her new closet. She had her jewelry, which she didn't dare place in the self-storage unit. There were electronics and books along with file folders of paperwork and copies of important documents, some personal and some college-related. Even though she wasn't teaching, there were certain records she wanted to have in case questions arose through email.

Then Mallory had all of her personal items and toiletries, but she didn't have her own bathroom. She would be sharing the hall bath with Nathan. And she wasn't exactly comfortable with a preschooler having access to hairspray and tampons. *I should probably keep these stashed.* She had extra makeup bags and storage baskets in a box in the garage, so out she went and back she came. By the afternoon, she had most of her necessities where she needed them, and she could always rearrange later.

She'd also have to do something about Bella. In her apartment, she didn't notice the space that Bella's litter box, toys, and bed occupied. But here, when she lined them up, she barely had room to walk alongside the edge of her bed. Paige knocked on the door just as Mallory was judging the width. "Come in."

Paige eased the door open—which made the room feel even smaller as it swung inward—and stood in the frame. "How are things going in here?"

Mallory plopped onto the bed. "I'm exhausted."

Paige dropped her shoulders and tilted her head as her words validated Mallory's current state. "You should be."

But the feeling wasn't just physical. "My body. My head. Everything around me." She was like a protagonist in one of William Shakespeare's tragedies she taught in literature class. "It's like I'm alone on a stage. Curtain call. The end. I don't have anything left."

"Oh, Mal." Paige joined her on the bed, bumping her shoulder before wrapping her arms around her for a hug. "I know you're tired."

"And even my car got tired."

Paige chuckled. "Yeah, but it's running fine now, right?"

"It got me to Seguin." Actually, her car seemed as reliable as ever, with no hint of sputter or sign of smoke. At least mechanic Marshall hadn't been tired.

"It's back to normal," Paige reminded her, "and you will

be too."

That was much easier said than done.

But Paige didn't see any roadblock. "All you need is a little tune-up. And I'm here for that." She squeezed Mallory and let her upper body fall against hers as she reacted to her sister's pep talk. Her sister was trying, and Mallory was so grateful for everything Paige was doing for her.

But Mallory wasn't a car.

And there wasn't a quick fix.

Mechanics like Marshall could fix an automotive problem. But there wasn't a mechanic, a moving man, or even a sister who could magically speed Mallory's recovery from emotional scars.

ALEC WASN'T AS exhausted as he should have been when he rolled into Santa Fe after finishing the Mallory Fredrick job. He had been seated behind a steering wheel for longer than his feet had touched the ground in two days. His body should have been sore, and his muscles should have been tight. If they were, he didn't notice. Instead, he focused on a feeling aside from fatigue, more of an emotion that had been with him prior to meeting Mallory, had dissipated during his interaction with her, and had returned with a vengeance upon her absence.

Loneliness.

Alec O'Donnell was used to being by himself, but something about this round of loneliness was different. The Christmas holidays arrived, and empty emotion came in a strong dose, like a bad cold that refused to be cured. He had his sister, who was in characteristic holiday form. She insisted on a full celebration, an all-day affair with food and presents passed round and round with speeds faster than Santa's reindeer. Holiday films streamed from the television, her fireplace crackled with cheery warmth, and there was absolutely no escaping the magic of the season.

But there was still a feeling of absence.

"Dating anyone?" Christine prompted her younger brother in between passing him a holiday cookie tray and cutting sideways glances to see if his actions revealed something his words would not.

"Nope," he said simply, shifting the conversation to questions about the types of cookies.

Christine wasn't buying it. "I see what you are doing."

He zeroed in on the cookie tray instead of his sister. "Deciding between a chocolate crinkle and a pecan sandie?" He pointed to an Oreo truffle. "Just trying to make an informed decision about my caloric intake."

She rolled her eyes. "Oh, right. Spare me. As if you've ever been one to care about calorie counts in cookies." Christine did know him well.

"I can always start." He broke a sandie in two and nibbled the edge as if considering every teeny bite.

"Back to the question," she insisted.

"Oh, that was a question?" His tone was laced with cynicism. "I thought it was called being nosy."

"That's what big sisters are supposed to do."

Christine had always stuck her nose in Alec's personal life. Some of it was curiosity, he would give her that. But he didn't want her on his dating case, not now. After all, what did he have to report? A crush on a girl who just moved a state away? How juvenile that would sound. He mimed zipping his mouth shut, which just egged Christine on.

"So there is someone!" She held up her index finger as if she had just used it to identify a clue.

"There's nothing to say." Though, even as Alec tried to admit that, his mind swam in the direction of Mallory.

Privately, his attention was all on her.

Just her.

Mallory.

That was how it had begun. And when he thought of her now, it wasn't like she monopolized every hour of the day, yet even when she wasn't there, her mental presence waded in and among his other thoughts.

During his time with her, Alec sensed a brokenness inside of Mallory. It was a sadness he couldn't quite touch, yet he understood it not as a demarcation of her personality. When he met Mallory—when he interacted with her—she was not a sad person. She was intelligent and vibrant. Her effervescent personality was reined in only by her responsibilities of the day. He saw her tenacity during the move, in everything from the speed at which she boxed to the carefulness with which she made sure everything was left in tip-top shape for the apartment manager. He admired the care with which she handled Bella and the joy with which she greeted her sister and nephew. She talked excitedly about the smallest of matters, yet he never tired of listening to her. On the contrary, he wanted more.

Much more.

He sent a quick text to her with happy holiday wishes. To his delight, she pinged back with a picture of a holiday tree and reciprocal merriment.

It was good to hear from Mallory, even in this truncated way. Still, this was a woman now living a state away, and he had completed the job he had been hired to do.

THE HOLIDAYS PASSED with requisite speed. Mallory joined the family of three's celebration, and she even dragged herself to a farmhouse outside of Seguin where Everett's family celebrated Christmas a day late. "The fresh air will be good," Paige insisted.

Yet since coming down from the mountain elevation of New Mexico, her head was no less cloudy than it had been when she was there.

Nathan, though, was enjoying Mallory's presence. He wanted her to sit in the back seat with him on every car ride, and he insisted she be the one to buckle him into his booster seat. "You'll have to help me out on this, buddy." Untangling the straps and making sense of the contraption wasn't in Mallory's repertoire of skills.

But she was learning.

"Does Nathan just think of me as a big kid?" she asked of Paige when they returned from Everett's parents.

"Likely." Paige shut her driver's door as Nathan was already rushing past her to get inside. "He's having a lot of fun with you."

"I don't understand why." Mallory paused next to the vehicle to continue the conversation with Paige.

"He's an only child. And he's only ever been one. So having someone else in the house permanently is like one big sleepover that doesn't end."

"This will end," Mallory reminded Paige, the words dry but resolute. "This isn't permanent." She didn't want Paige to think there was any chance this arrangement would last longer than a semester.

"I know. Temporary," she stressed.

"That's right."

"Now you'll have to be the one to explain that to Nathan." She gestured ahead of her as she made her way into the house.

Mallory followed. "You don't think he gets it?" She had already talked to him about this more than once.

"His understanding of time is about as good as his grasp on quantum physics." Paige opened the door, ushered Mallory in, and they removed their coats. Nathan had already disappeared into his room. "I worry about him being an only child."

"I was an only child," Mallory reminded her playfully, "until you came along."

She pointed to her stomach then shook her finger. "No

way. Not happening."

"You and Everett don't want more kids?" Mallory took the opportunity to shift the conversation away from herself and focus on Paige.

"Not now."

"But you've talked about it?"

"Of course we've talked about it. We're going to get married." She separated and wiggled her fingers, flashing her engagement ring again. "But Nathan's only-child status won't be changing anytime soon."

"What about Barry?"

Paige glanced down the hall toward Nathan's room, keeping her voice low. "What about my ex-husband?"

Mallory didn't want to be insensitive, but she was curious, especially as the future related to Nathan. "Do you think he'll ever have more kids?"

Paige waved her hand dismissively through the air. "Who knows about Barry? He's not exactly the warm-and-fuzzy type. And you know how long it took him to come around to Nathan."

Mallory nodded her sympathy. The idea of having a child was one thing. But for people like Barry, the reality of raising one was something different. "How are things going now between the two of you?"

"Better."

"Improvement little by little?"

"We're cordial." She shrugged. "Nathan likes spending time with him when they do something fun, but overnights are still really tough on him. Tough on Barry too." Her sister and her ex-brother-in-law had a custody arrangement, but it was a bit fluid. Paige glanced again down the hallway, not wanting Nathan to hear. "But I get a break when he's with Barry. That's nice. Is it wrong of me to say that?"

Mallory shook her head. "Absolutely not." And she understood. Although she didn't have a child of her own, she could relate to routines and stresses and a daily grind in other ways. "We all need a break sometime."

Paige smiled and then poked her index finger lightly into Mallory's chest. "Especially you, Professor."

Mallory rolled her eyes. "I can't be a professor if I'm not teaching."

"That's actually what I wanted to talk to you about."

"Do I need to sit down for this?"

Paige pulled back her hand. "Suit yourself."

My sister. Mallory pivoted into the living room. *She has a way . . .*

"Want some coffee?" Paige called after her.

"Tea." How could they share DNA when their choice in caffeine was night and day different? She cut her path to the living room to swerve into the kitchen so she could watch Paige, who grabbed a small pot from her hanging rack and ran water from the tap as she filled it. "I'm going to have to find my kettle for you."

"For *you*," she corrected as she placed the pot atop the stove and ignited the burner. "I'm not going to be your kitchen maid."

"But I am getting you to make tea for me this afternoon, right?" She couldn't resist a sassy verbal jab at her sister whenever she got the chance.

"Don't get used to it." She winked across the counter. "Black tea okay?"

Good caffeine percentage. And Mallory could use some pep. "Perfect."

"Now, while your tea boils and takes minutes to make, behold the speed of my wonder machine that makes a beverage in half that time." Paige made an exaggerated show of using her automatic coffee pod appliance, gesturing across it as if she were demonstrating a prize possibility on a game show. She selected a pod from her shiny chrome carousel holder, punched a button, and turned to tap her watch. "Ninety seconds, tops."

Mallory wasn't impressed. "I'm not interested in the speed of drink preparation."

"You'd make a terrible barista."

"I'll remember that in case I change careers." And even though Paige was joking, the exchange was a painful reminder of her employment status. Mallory needed to steel herself against words which caused a flashback. She inhaled and refocused the conversation. "Didn't you say you wanted to talk to me about something?"

"Yes." Paige rolled out a drawer to retrieve two spoons. "Exactly."

"Well?" Mallory prompted.

Paige pushed the drawer back into place with her hip. "You know Nathan can go back to daycare on Monday. And I've got work to resume."

Mallory nodded. This holiday week wasn't a normal

schedule for anyone.

Paige continued. "And you know that you can have free range of the house."

Mallory bit back a laugh. "You think I'll throw a party or something?"

"Better not." Paige waved a spoon in a no-no gesture before shifting into a more serious tone. "Have you thought about what you'll do?"

It was all Mallory had thought about. If this were a normal holiday break from the college, she would be catching up on reading, preparing her syllabi for spring classes, maybe organizing bookshelves in her office . . . but this wasn't a normal holiday break. She didn't have the college to which she could return any time soon. "I've got plenty of books. A few emails to write. Stuff to organize." Though as she rattled off her list, she realized how mundane it sounded. In a desperate attempt to add something significant, she blurted, "Maybe I'll even get a jump start on organizing my tax receipts."

Paige just nodded politely. "Do what you need to do."

But Mallory could read between the lines. "Do you have a better suggestion?" She did want to help her sister, and she was prepared to make every attempt to keep herself as invisible around the house as possible. "I'm not going to freeload. So if you need errands run or want me to pick up Nathan from daycare, just say the word."

There was no segue. "Have you thought about a temporary job?"

The kitchen grew so quiet the sisters could have heard a

pin drop.

Mallory's heart sank inside her chest. Did Paige really feel she needed to be thinking about some local job—now? Did she truly understand Mallory's professional turmoil, or was she just pretending to do so? Because anyone who actually did would realize that being forced from college teaching due to events beyond her control didn't exactly create an optimal environment for kicking a professional life back into gear.

Paige scrambled to fill the silence as she backpedaled with "I didn't mean to imply—"

"Don't apologize." Mallory held up her hand. She understood her sister's tough love. "You want me to have something to do. I get it." And Mallory wanted something to do too.

"I'm your biggest supporter, Mal. I don't like seeing you down for the count, so I just thought, um, that maybe . . ."

But Mallory wanted her old job. She did, but she wanted it before Jesse. She wanted calm classes and productive students and safe spaces. But those weren't guarantees, and that wasn't an environment she could have. At least not now. "I can't just snap my fingers and find a four-month temporary job."

"I know that." Paige lowered her head, turned down the heat of the burner, and dunked a tea bag into the boiling water.

But Mallory sensed Paige had a reason for asking. "Spill it."

Paige toyed with the string of the tea bag, refusing eye

contact as she asked, "What about substitute teaching?"

Mallory suddenly wasn't in the mood for tea. Or continuing this conversation. While she respected all levels of education, she had fought hard to teach at the college level. That was where she belonged. Her answer was a firm "No."

"Is there anything in your contract that prohibits it?"

"I'm not going to entertain the idea." Paige didn't even seem shamed by asking, and that ate at Mallory's confidence—at least what was left of it.

"So that's that? You won't even think about it?"

Mallory didn't need to justify her decisions to Paige. And since she wasn't in her shoes, she didn't understand anyway. "No," she said simply. If she were going to expend energy on teaching, it would be at the college level. That was where she belonged.

Even though that wasn't at all where she was.

And every day in Seguin was a reminder of that.

Chapter Twelve

PAIGE INSISTED ON dialing all the clocks forward by four hours so Nathan could experience New Year's Eve. She moved with CIA-like secrecy through the house to adjust them during his nap time. "He won't know the difference." She punched a sequence of buttons on the microwave to alter the digital display. "There. Now the only one left is the living room wall clock."

Mallory watched, incredulous that she would go through such effort for a white lie. "You don't think this is just a little too ridiculous? He's four years old."

"Which is exactly why he will think eight o'clock is midnight," she insisted. "It will be dark, and he'll be none the wiser." She pursed her lips and ran two fingers across them as if she were zipping a secret only the two of them knew.

It wasn't like Mallory intended to break it to the kid. "And why exactly is this so important?"

"Because I want him to experience the fun of it." Paige had already laid out cardboard hats, goofy plastic glasses, and noise makers. "I told him we were going to have a house party, so we'll eat early, pretend to ring in the New Year—"

"Lie to a child—"

"For your benefit, after all," Paige underscored. "He'll be

so tired he'll crash early, and then you can have a peaceful night to yourself."

"Oh, goody." As if Mallory needed the occasion of New Year's Eve as a reminder of her single status.

Paige unfolded a step stool and positioned it beneath the wall clock. "You offered."

"That I did."

"But you can still back out. Say the word."

"No way." Mallory wasn't going to let Paige trap her into that. "I told you that I would watch Nathan so you and Everett could enjoy New Year's Eve as a couple, and I'm not going back on my word."

"This is very sweet of you," Paige insisted as she stepped atop a stool to reach for the clock. She flipped it around and wound the gear to move the hour hand forward. "Don't think we are unappreciative."

Martyrdom was flattering. "It's the least I can do." And it was, after all. Mallory wanted to repay favors since Paige was letting her crash for the semester. She was saving her a bundle in rent and utilities, and though Mallory offered to compensate Paige financially, she wouldn't accept a dime. Repaying her with a few offers of babysitting now and again would be her way of contributing instead.

"I told you that you shouldn't feel obligated to do anything." Paige righted the clock and hung it back in place. "It's not like it's a big event. Liz just threw this together and invited some people from the office, a few of her neighbors, probably a couple of her husband's friends from his adult soccer league."

If she were baiting Mallory with temptation of single men, it wasn't going to work. "Not interested."

"I didn't say you were."

Though if Mallory had expressed the slightest hint of interest, she was sure Paige would have dished about single guys she knew through association. But when Mallory thought of single guys, her memories slid to Alec.

She had only exchanged a few text messages with him. One was once he got back to Santa Fe. Another was late on Christmas Day where they both shared cheerful wishes. And Mallory contemplated sending another to him tonight, though she wouldn't do that with Paige standing over her. "What's the theme again?"

"It's a white-out party."

"Which involves what exactly?"

"All manners of the color white." Paige stepped off the stool and bent to collapse its sides. "Everybody is supposed to wear something white. Liz is decorating with twinkling white lights and candles. All the snack foods are white. Cheeses and white chocolate and popcorn. Chicken alfredo, French bread, and white wine are being served too."

Mallory masked her interest with words of dismissal. "Sounds bland."

"I think it's a clever idea. And it's going to be fun." Then, as if to spare Mallory's personal pity, she added, "And I'm sure not everyone who comes will be a couple. Danica will be there."

"Oh, sure," Mallory chastised. "Name your one single friend in an attempt to camouflage the coupledom."

"I'm not hiding anything. All I'm saying is that New Year's Eve—"

Mallory finished the sentence for her sister. "New Year's Eve is for couples and champagne toasts and midnight kisses." She swiped a cardboard hat from the set, stretched the elastic band, and feigned enthusiasm. "Or white wine or white whatever you're going to have there. So, cheers."

Paige walked past Mallory and bopped the top of her pointy hat. "Well I'm just glad I get to spend part of New Year's Eve with my sweet sister." Her sassy tone conveyed more than her words. "And with both my boys. First, I'll ring it in with Nathan—"

"For a fake stroke of midnight," Mallory reminded her.

Paige ignored her sister. "And then Everett for a kiss to start the new year off right."

Joy. The only kissing Mallory would be doing was with the previous year. She would stay up just so she could kiss it goodbye. Because based on how the year had ended, she would be glad to see it go. "So what time are you and Everett slipping out to your real party?"

Paige stowed the stool back in the pantry. "How about eight thirty?"

"That's a quick party for Nathan."

"We'll celebrate beforehand. Then by half past eight, he'll be ready for lights out."

That actually didn't sound like such a bad idea to Mallory either. There wasn't any reason for her to stay up late, other than to watch the ball drop in New York on one of the television networks. And with the festivities there being on east coast time, she could actually save an hour by being in the central time zone. Plus, if she really wanted to stretch it, she could pretend Paige's adjusted clocks held the true time. That meant she could stay up until the ripe fake hour of three a.m. That didn't sound so pathetic after all.

NATHAN CRASHED JUST as Paige told Mallory he would. Her New Year's toast with a glass of warm milk as his beverage of choice did the trick. He fell asleep faster than if Mallory had removed his battery pack. Because most days, it seemed like the kid had one.

"Out like a light." She breathed as she shut his bedroom door.

Paige and Everett had followed through with the mock timing, and then they slipped out to Liz's party while Mallory read Nathan a bedtime story. His eyelids grew heavy and lowered before Mallory had even reached the final page of the book. She kept reading, though, in a voice that grew softer and softer until they both lay in the silence. Mallory tucked his covers around him, placed a kiss against his forehead, and tiptoed out of his room.

Before Paige left, she insisted she needed more white for her requisite outfit. She had a winter-white sweater dress that she paired with white tights, which should have washed her out completely. But the combination of her loose, long hair and the accent of that sparkler of an engagement ring broke the otherwise monochromatic look. "But I still need something else," she had insisted. "Don't you have a long necklace or some dangly earrings I can borrow?"

And so it began.

Perhaps even better than free babysitting was the personalized style service she would be affording Paige with access to her jewelry collection. She really didn't want to make this a habit, but she had to admit it was fun to hold up different pieces and find the perfect glitzy accent. "It's not too much?" Paige questioned when Mallory layered a pearl and rhinestone pattern set in silver with a long, thin loopy three-tiered strand.

Mallory insisted the two be paired. "You look like you walked straight out of a *Sundance* catalog."

"Am I supposed to know what that is?" Paige's skepticism at the compliment sucked the wind out of Mallory's style sails.

"I'm going to have to get you on their mailing list." That also reminded her she needed to check in with the apparel and accessory company to make sure she didn't miss a catalog of her own. Not that she had excess funds to spend at the moment. Or a job to which she could wear a new piece.

"You could do that." Paige looped her finger through a tier of her borrowed necklace. "Or I could continue shopping the Mallory Fredrick collection."

"Don't push your luck." Mallory would loan. But even she had limits when it came to her prized possessions.

"I should take you to some of the local shops here. Or even along the Riverwalk in downtown San Antonio. There are local craftsmen everywhere. Any type of beads or styles you could imagine."

But Mallory didn't need to daydream about what types of jewelry she could find in Texas. She had everything she wanted back in New Mexico. Santa Fe was the epicenter of artisan delight, and she found herself turning over memories of pieces she had bought in her mind.

Even small talk about jewelry brought her thoughts full circle to Santa Fe. She remained in a mental tug-of-war with wanting to distance herself and yearning to return. She needed the physical space—that was a given—and the time away from the college classroom to regroup. But she also missed the energy and the vibrancy of little things, like seeing jewelry makers at the plaza or discovering something unexpected at a local craft fair. There was also the energy of students during the start of a new semester. She absolutely loved kicking off the first week of classes. There was something special about closing the door to her classroom and being entrusted with sharing the gift of education.

Mallory's trip down memory lane was nothing but roses, yet she reminded herself there were thorns. Bad students, for instance.

A memorable one, in particular . . .

She shook away the negative recollection. After all, it was New Year's Eve, a time of new beginnings. Mallory wanted to kick off the coming year with positivity. The negative energy that had weighed her down had every reason to slide away. As the hands of the clock announced the next day, she would resolve to live in the present and look toward the future, not hold on to her past. The last few weeks in December were especially ones she wanted to put behind her.

But maybe not completely.

Those trying times also coincided with when she met Alec. And as much as she should be excited about spring in Seguin, he was one person who unexpectedly floated in and out of her thoughts on a daily basis. Yet her encounters with him were part of what she was supposed to be seeing behind her, not in front of her.

So why did he keep appearing to Mallory, especially in pleasing mental portraits that her mind wouldn't let her shake? The hazelnut hair. Those dimples. His Hollywood smile.

She texted Alec later than night, and he replied straight away. They pinged back and forth for a few fun messages. Mallory snapped a photo of a cardboard New Year's hat, and Alec replied with a question of whether he could see it on her.

A selfie?

Before Mallory could make up her mind, Alec sent a photo of his own, a close-up that made her melt when she saw his familiar face. She didn't realize how much she missed him until she laid eyes on him.

Maybe it was a good thing that Mallory Fredrick was so far away from Alec O'Donnell. With no way to bridge their distance, at least she could protect her heart.

MALLORY NEEDED A routine.

Fast.

Her entire adult life had always consisted of one. Paige had work. Nathan had daycare. Even Bella had her version of activities to punctuate the day: bathing, sleeping, sitting on various pieces of furniture.

Mallory did those things, too, but they weren't quite as interesting to her as they seemed to be for a cat.

But she did try one new thing. Every morning, weather permitting, she went for a walk through Paige's neighborhood. Her sister kept a bike in the garage and offered that Mallory could use it, but she preferred staying on foot through the quiet streets. Even in winter, yards were manicured and evergreen plants dotted the front of houses with color. Pansies and snapdragons provided abundant shades of purples, yellow, and oranges in flowerbeds and decorative pots. A few houses proudly displayed flags or interesting yard ornaments, like copper chimes or glass garden balls on stakes. There were a few Christmas decorations yet standing as well as some trees discarded at the end of driveways for removal, a sign of transition.

She didn't run into too many fellow walkers. Occasionally she would see a homeowner collecting yard waste, rolling out the garbage, or walking a dog. She waved, but never stopped to make small talk.

She did take along earbuds on a few occasions and listened to a podcast about teaching. In the privacy of her own head as she was alone, she could try to refocus on what she loved. If she approached teaching again from the professional angle—and not a personal one—perhaps she would feel more comfortable than she did about returning.

Yet a practical reentry was different than a mental imagining.

Mallory did look into offerings at the public library for workshops and activities. She scanned for possible local book clubs she could join. And she even collected all the schedules for civic organizations just to see what was offered. But, ultimately, the fear of facing new people for a temporary amount of time kept her from taking the plunge into group interaction.

So she walked. She read. She played with Nathan in the evenings. She heard all about Paige's day and shared a drink with her after he went to bed. She babysat again on occasion so Everett could have time with Paige as well.

But she wasn't really doing anything. At least not her definition of doing.

Yet Mallory Fredrick felt safe. And that feeling alone had to count for something.

Progress, one day at a time.

After her walk, she returned back to Paige's empty house, and not even Bella greeted her at the door. "Where are you, cat?" She removed her coat and scarf, hooked them on the rack by the door, and called again.

Silence.

She was probably sleeping. Again. Since arrival in Seguin, Bella's routine had slanted much more toward the lazy side of things. She slept with greater abandon than Mallory had ever seen her do before.

She gave the door to her bedroom a gentle push inward, and she clicked her tongue. "Here, girl." Then she made a sing-song of her name as she called further, "Bella, Bella, Bella-boo. Where are you?"

She crouched down and peeked under the bed. She looked behind the nightstand. Then she opened the closet door. She reached for the light as a flash of fur in the corner caught her attention. "There you are, Bella." The cat stretched awkwardly across Mallory's pairs of shoes lined against the back wall, and as the feline angled her head, Mallory could see she was panting.

Feverishly.

"What is going on, girl?" She knelt in front of the cat and held out her hand. Bella's breathing continued to appear labored, her stomach pulling in and out with ferocity like an elastic band that shouldn't be stretched as much as it was. "Poor kitty. What's the matter?" Yet as Mallory pressed with questions, Bella's only answers were pants of what appeared to be desperation.

Mallory scooped the cat into her arms as Bella gave a pained mew of discontent. She carried her to her pet bed, gently placed her inside, and started researching her symptoms on her phone.

It was a shot in the dark, but the more Mallory looked,

the more she grew sick at what she found. This didn't look good for Bella. She was going to need a veterinarian. And fast.

Chapter Thirteen

SEGUIN WAS RIPE with veterinarians. That was probably due to all of the livestock on farms and ranches in the area. But Mallory didn't need someone who specialized in large animal care. She needed someone with delicate, careful precision to diagnose what was wrong with her sweet Bella.

After a quick call to Paige and her suggestion of Seguin Animal Hospital, Mallory loaded Bella into her pet carrier and was on her way. She pulled into the facility from Kingsbury Street off Highway 90 not far from downtown. Paige offered to meet her there and insisted she could steal away from work for a half hour.

"Thanks but no thanks." Mallory just wanted to get Bella in and out as quickly as possible, and she certainly didn't want to inconvenience Paige in the process. With no appointment, it was a gamble of a visit anyway.

The front receptionist was courteous and worked Bella in to see one of the vets on duty. As Mallory waited with Bella by her side, she immediately missed her usual veterinarian back in Santa Fe. Funny how routine everything could feel in just five years. She allowed her mind to dip in and out of memories again, peeking into Bella's carrier every few minutes to check for any change in demeanor or any surprise fluid discharge.

Hurry, hurry, hurry. She recited the words mentally as she breathed in a near pant to match her cat. Some people said pets and their owners resembled one another. If anyone had considered Mallory and Bella in this exact moment, no doubt they would see the similarities.

Abnormal.

Unnerved.

Desperate.

With each passing minute, Mallory's worry spiraled further. Her heart plunged with hypotheses that grew more and more negative the longer she waited to be seen. Finally, a technician called them into an examination room.

"What seems to be the problem?" A young technician in purple scrubs invited Mallory to place the carrier atop the exam table as she started unlatching it and cooing at Bella. Mallory explained the panting. "She seemed hot, but I know she couldn't have been." The temperature in Paige's house was no different than in Mallory's Santa Fe apartment. "She had this look about her that was wild, like she couldn't quite settle. That's not like her."

The technician raised Bella from the carrier, and Bella bent awkwardly against her arms with another painful mew. "Sorry about that, darling." She checked inside of the feline's ears, felt around her jaw, then reached for a thermometer. "We'll get you fixed up."

Mallory could only hope that would be the case.

The technician stroked against Bella's back to try and settle her as she asked Mallory more questions. But as

Mallory answered, she needed settling of her own.

"Has she had any changes in diet?"

"Same food as she's had. Just eating less of it."

"Dry or moist?"

"Dry." That was so much cheaper anyway, and although she wanted to treat Bella like a queen, she did have to consider the bottom line. That, of course, was going to be blown with a single vet visit, but Mallory didn't have a financial choice.

"So her intake has been less than her usual amount?" Mallory nodded. "And what about her water?"

"She's got access to that."

"Have you noticed whether she's been drinking throughout the day?"

Though the question was simple, Mallory didn't have an answer. "I guess she has." Yet Mallory couldn't be sure. During the days of the move, she couldn't get her to digest much of anything. She flashed back to the Eden bunkhouse and the bowl of water she barely touched. Her lack of thirst must have been temporary—right? Surely Bella's habits had changed. "I mean, she's got a full bowl next to her bed, and she stays inside the house. I don't let her outside."

The technician tried another angle. "Tell me about her behavior."

That was tricky.

Bella had been a completely different cat with Alec that night in the bunkhouse. She was needy and, now that Mallory thought about it, pretty lethargic for the whole trip. Even at Paige's, Bella played less and lacked some of her normal spunk. "She's been through a lot of changes lately," Mallory explained, reflecting on the drive, the new surroundings, and Bella's attempts to escape from Nathan's bull's-eye attention when she wanted nothing to do with it. "Maybe she's had a lot of stress?" *Because I can relate to that.*

The technician asked another series of quick questions before reading the temperature. "It's elevated." She tilted the instrument and recorded the numbers while Mallory braced Bella on the table. "I'll call the vet in, and he'll make the final diagnosis."

"Thank you." Mallory's heart plunged, preparing for the worst.

BELLA'S INSIDES SEEMED to be as knotted as Mallory's. Yet while Mallory's were nerve related, Bella's were more serious. "Your cat has a UTI," the vet announced with as much fanfare as one might proclaim head lice or hook worms.

"A urinary tract infection?" Mallory questioned. "How does that even happen?"

"Female cats can be especially susceptible," the veterinarian explained. "Especially when their routine changes or they are under stress. They go for periods without water. Then they forget to drink enough of it." Mallory nodded her understanding, following the vet's logical explanation and wondering how much she was to blame. "Then if they're eating nothing but dry food, they aren't supplementing with the hydration they would get from moist food."

Her heart bottomed out of her chest.

She was supposed to take care of Bella, not be the cause of misery to her.

The vet might as well have been reprimanding Mallory right there, for she felt like the worst kitty mother in the history of pet ownership. She sensed her lower lip start to quiver, but she found a strength of voice to ask, "Is she going to be okay?"

The veterinarian scribbled something on his clipboard chart. "We'll get her fixed up." His tone changed into an upbeat tempo as he explained the next steps. A steroid shot, a series of antibiotics to give via the mouth at home, and an in-house specialty food that would work to soothe her insides and get her bladder back on track.

"No surgery?"

"This should take care of it," the vet assured Mallory, and she blew a breath of relief. "But I want you to keep a close eye on her. And make sure she has access to clean water at all times. Try keeping more than one bowl in the house. And freshen it several times a day to keep her enticed. Some cats even like ice cubes, so you can give that a shot."

"I'll try anything." Mallory was already thinking of scenarios to coax and encourage, including introducing Bella to the faucet in the bathroom she shared with Nathan to see if she would pick up her water habit that she had back in the apartment.

"She's a beautiful cat." The vet gave a final stroke across Bella's back. "I'm glad you brought her in. The receptionist will help you get squared away. Anything else I can answer?"

How much is this going to cost? Though Mallory bit back verbalizing the question. Maybe the less she knew, the better. Still, as much as Mallory worried about money, she didn't want to sacrifice Bella's health any more than she already had guilt at somehow doing. "Do you need to see her again for a follow-up appointment?"

"Not unless there are complications." That was a relief. "Keep an eye on her habits, make sure she takes her medicine. You should see pretty immediate change in behavior within twenty-four hours." He explained the antibiotic timeline again, then handed Mallory his card. "You can call anytime or use this emergency number if there's a problem outside of office hours."

Mallory accepted the card as a lifeline. "Thank you."

The veterinarian shook her hand then waved to Bella. Mallory hoisted the cat inside her carrier and headed back into the reception area. The technician followed with the paperwork and offered to help Mallory to her car once she paid for the specialty food Bella needed.

As Mallory waited patiently for the receptionist to input the veterinarian's notes and tally the expenses, all she saw before her were dollar signs. And at this new location, there would be no long-term customer discount, friendly wave of an examination charge, or even freebie treat bag as a way to lighten the sting of payment. Mallory clutched her credit card as she waited to hear the final total.

When the triple-digit cost was leveled, all Mallory could do was force a smile and a stiff verbal exchange as she signed the receipt and incurred another surprise expense that would cut further into her savings. With no incoming paycheck, every financial hit hurt.

"NOW, WHEN YOU see Bella"—Mallory crouched low next to Nathan as he held tight to a stuffed animal toy—"be gentle. She's a little sick."

Nathan's eyebrows creased in worry. "What happened to kitty?"

"She's got a tummy ache." That wasn't far from the reality of the veterinarian's diagnosis.

Nathan nodded. "My tummy hurts sometimes."

"Then you understand. Be very gentle with Bella."

"Maybe this?" He pushed his blue snuggly stuffed giraffe to arm's length, twisting the toy like adults sometimes do for kids to entice their attention. Here, though, Nathan seemed genuinely interested in making Bella feel better.

"That's sweet." Mallory reached up to stroke the head of the plush toy. "But Bella doesn't feel like playing. She wants to rest."

Nathan retracted the animal, hugging it close. "Nap time?"

"Yes." Mallory repeated. "Nap time." Living in the same house as Nathan, it didn't take her long to develop his kid-speak. She was used to explaining things to college students, so the explanations to someone a generation younger were an adjustment, but not a completely foreign one.

"Kitty's nap time." Nathan brought his finger to his lips and started to tiptoe out of Mallory's bedroom. If she could get Nathan to keep this up, Bella could probably have some peace for the next few days, which might help speed her recovery. Mallory flicked the light switch on their way out and closed the door carefully. She mimed a goodbye wave once the door was shut, and Nathan did the same before bounding down the hall back to his own bedroom.

Mallory's worry was on Bella, but concerns circled back to her bank account and her future. She had offered to help Paige with the cost of groceries—which was only fair—and she also wanted to ease her footprint in her home by taking care of other expenses where she could. But spending money could only last for so long. As much as she hoped her mental and emotional health would improve during the sabbatical, she hadn't given serious thought to her financial health until confronted with all of these expenses.

Vulnerability swept in again. She needed to clear her mind.

"Paige"—she circled into the kitchen and poked her head around the refrigerator at her sister—"I'm going to go for a walk."

Paige stood at the counter slicing an apple, its sweet aroma wafting through the air. "Around the neighborhood?"

"Yes." At least that was an activity that would cost zero dollars.

Mallory stacked the wedges against the side of the cutting board before scooping the seeds and core into her hand.

"Can you bring the mail in on your way?"

"No problem."

"Have fun. Take a sweater." She turned to dispose of the apple remnants, looking every bit the picture of domestic bliss. Somehow, in moments like this, she made holding a full-time job, caring for a child, and preparing food all as a single mother look incredibly easy.

And I have trouble managing myself these days. Mallory forced a smile and took Paige's maternal advice. Lately, she held the maturity and togetherness of an older sister that Mallory seemed to lack. The role reversal wasn't expected, but it wasn't entirely unappreciated. Mallory was grateful, and she needed to remember to find small ways in which to thank Paige.

Mallory grabbed a sweater she had stashed in the hall closet. She finger-combed her hair into a low, temporary ponytail before swinging the tresses outside of the collar, shaking back her head to let her hair free. She opened the door as a cool blast of Texas winter wind comingled with the sun above, creating a bright and breezy dynamic for her walk.

Stepping outside, Mallory's vulnerability swelled into something more intense. She had made personal strides since being in Seguin, yet she couldn't seem to control these emotional setbacks where, in moments alone, she would sometimes feel the sting of fear.

And she couldn't quite put her finger on why.

The way forward, though, was for Mallory to push through the feeling, not cower to it. She followed the length of the driveway to the home's curb and reached around to the front of the mailbox. Inside was only one letter atop a fashion magazine and what looked like a glossy-paged freebie circular full of ads. Mallory grasped the stack, the top letter catching her attention because it was addressed to her. There was no name as sender, though there was a return address.

Santa Fe.

Mallory's gulped a nervous lump. The envelope was no thicker than a strip of phyllo dough. The letter's stamp held a New Mexico postal frank with a date blurred by over-inking. She turned the letter over to reveal no further clues from the sender. It certainly wasn't on stationary from the college.

The handwritten address looked sloppy and unfamiliar, and her mind ran through the penmanship styles of her students. Far too many to memorize, but some stood out, especially those students with whom she had special encounters, like office visits, rough draft paper submissions, class notes she saw displayed when she walked past students at their desks . . . or when they were particularly memorable students with whom she had another type of encounter.

For better.

For worse.

Mallory's mind flashed to the end of the fall semester, images of Jesse and his violent social media post that she couldn't erase from her mind no matter how hard she tried. Online messages were not one-and-done like verbal ones; even though they might be deleted from one account, their presence could linger elsewhere.

As could his words.

His "get her" promise echoed through her mind as her limbs petrified.

This was the concern she had expressed to Iker. The post had done immediate damage, but it was lingering uncertainty of future safety that haunted her. Instead of understanding that, he only responded with some line about Mallory needing to trust the college's police department and their system for handling the matter. That she had done, yet here she was. A state away and feeling no less secure.

False trust had made her vulnerable.

Mallory scissored the thin envelope between two fingers, her hands pulsing in worry. She was suddenly uninterested in a walk. She wasn't even sure her legs could carry her at this point. She just needed to see inside that envelope.

Chapter Fourteen

"THAT WAS A short walk." Mallory swung open the front door that she hadn't locked behind her—and neither had Paige. Was this typical? She hadn't even asked her sister about her methods of home protection and privacy; she had simply assumed she would have done the secure thing and safeguarded the entrance once Mallory left.

Wrong.

Mallory tucked the slim stack of mail under her arm as she spun to force the dead bolt closed with a loud click.

"Mallory?" Paige called from the kitchen, a high-pitched edge in her tone.

"It's me." She confirmed in a forced breath, knowing there was no reason to alarm her sister.

"Decided not to walk?"

Not exactly a decision. Mallory faced the interior of the house.

"Too cold out there?"

Hardly. The temperatures did not rival New Mexico, especially in the mountains. "Just brought in the mail."

"Oh, good." Paige peered from around the kitchen counter with her hands outstretched. "Anything worthwhile?"

Mallory ignored Paige's question and fired one of her

own. "Do you always keep the front door unlocked when someone else leaves?"

Paige's hand fell atop the counter. "No."

Yet that wasn't the case here, as Mallory had seen. "You've got to be careful."

"I usually don't have people coming and going. Me. Nathan. Everett on occasion. That's it. Not exactly a crowd."

Mallory wasn't sure if there was an intended bite to the comment, but it cut her just the same. "Am I a crowd now?"

"What?" Paige stepped around the side of the counter and met her, Mallory still as a statue inside the small foyer. "What is going on with you?"

Leave it to a sister to sense. "There's a letter for me." The words were coming out of her mouth, but they sounded hollow and foreign.

"Okay." Paige shrugged. "You got a letter."

"Unmarked."

"Let me see." Paige offered her hand.

Like a game of Hot Potato, Mallory was glad to shove the contents into the possession of someone else.

Mallory flipped over the letter just as Paige had done outside. "It's not exactly unmarked. It's from Santa Fe." She pointed to the return address.

"Not an address I know. That's a PO box." Mallory had a sick feeling about the whole thing. "And I don't even know if that's a real PO box."

Paige appeared to study the numbers. "Could it be sent if it wasn't?"

That was what Mallory didn't know, among so many

other things. Her mind couldn't get a handle on even the simplest of tasks, nor could she focus her attention enough to tear into something so unexpected. "Open it for me."

Paige didn't harbor the same hesitation as Mallory. She stepped back into the kitchen, unsheathed a knife from the set in the butcher block on the counter, and slid it under the flap. In one quick motion, Paige did what Mallory had feared to do, and she felt hopeless and silly and grateful and confused all at the same time.

Sisterhood.

Mallory brought a hand to her chest, the thumping of her uncertain heartbeat so loud she wondered if Paige could hear it.

Her sister laid down the knife and retrieved a crisp, tri-fold page. Mallory eyed the back of the document as Paige unfolded it to read the contents. She lifted what appeared to be a singular yellow Post-it note placed in the top right. "What does it say?"

Paige paused, her eyes darting from the document to the Post-it and back again before meeting Mallory's. "You really want to know?" There was no discerning an emotional response from her deadpanned question.

Mallory inhaled as she suspended her response, trying to flood enough oxygen into her body so she could speak clearly. "Yes."

Paige flipped the envelope on the counter to check the return address a final time. She looked again at the letter, and a sly smile played across her lips.

"What is it?" Mallory's voice was meeker than a newborn

kitten's.

Paige's lips spread into a wide grin, and she raised an eyebrow across the short distance to Mallory. "You really didn't expect this?"

Now was not the time for games. "Expect what?" Mallory braced for the worst, knowing Jesse's name was going to be released from Paige's tongue at any moment.

"This news?"

"What news?"

Paige laid the note on the counter, and Mallory's pulse couldn't race any faster as she leaned over to see it. "Looks like your moving man is cutting you a break."

Alec?

"That's an invoice all right." She pointed to the total owed, which was much less than Mallory had been anticipating. "Pennies for his time, if you ask me."

Mallory couldn't believe it. This wasn't some nefarious letter from Jesse. He hadn't tracked her down. How could he?

This was Alec.

And Alec and Jesse were as night and day as individuals could be.

Mallory slowed her breathing, coming down from the anxiety of being worked up on the basis of fear. Relief crested over her as she regained her composure, embarrassment now replacing her previous worry. Why had she overacted?

"An invoice," she repeated. That was such a normal thing to expect.

"What did you think it was?"

Mallory didn't have the words. Instead, she was just glad it was from Alec. This one piece of mail was uncomplicated. She didn't need to make it so.

Paige shrugged, pointing to the total due. "Were you expecting this?"

Mallory looked at the bottom line. The amount was far less than Alec had quoted.

Far, far less.

"No." All she could manage through the shock was a single response.

But Paige wasn't done with her questioning. She plucked the Post-it from the top of the invoice and spun it so Mallory could read the words. "Did you expect *this*?"

Mallory read the unfamiliar handwriting addressed to her. It was a simple, two sentence request. *Call me sometime. I'd love to chat and see how you are doing.* The message closed with his signature.

Paige broke the silence when Mallory didn't speak. "I told you your moving man was hot."

Mallory's emotions had been on overdrive, and she didn't know what to think. Surprise deep discounts and handwritten notes couldn't be how Four Guys operated, could it? That wasn't formal business practice, and Alec certainly seemed more successful than that. Goodness, Mallory had just spent more at the vet's office than this invoice was requesting. And that note?

Paige offered her own interpretation. "I think he's interested in you as a girlfriend."

ALEC KEPT BUSY with a few telephone inquiries into Four Guys's service while the rest of the guys continued their time off. It was a slow time of year for actual moving jobs, Mallory's road trip adventure to Texas aside.

Greg and Rory had arrived back from Taos but were waiting until their kids resumed school to commit to any big jobs. And all three of them had received word from Tavis that on December twenty-eighth, baby Alondra Anne made her debut. Alec visited the first week of the new year, popping by their house with a bouquet of cut flowers for the new mother and a case of favorite beer for Tavis.

With Tavis enjoying his time at home, Alec completed some end-of-year accounting, made out Mallory's invoice, and cut her a great deal of financial slack because, truly, the job was much easier than he anticipated. He also felt terrible about her having to delay the trip by a day, even though it was through no fault of his—or hers. Still, she seemed like the kind of woman who would appreciate a break.

So even though he had completed the job and was due a certain amount for labor, he was going to give her a major discount. The other guys weren't involved in the job—except for Tavis's small contribution of muscle with the piano—so they wouldn't care.

Alec dropped the invoice in the mail, but not before adding a special note, his way of fishing to gauge Mallory's interest in a way that was more forward than reciprocal text messages. He couldn't ignore the mental hold she had on him any more than he could forget their chemistry and their kiss.

That one unexpected, deliciously sweet kiss.

And what do I have to lose? That was the question that spurred him into a move that was safe. She could respond or not. But at least Alec would be acting on the courage to reach out to see if she was interested in him.

He found himself, though, checking his phone messages with frequency. Even his daily trips to the post office were with a bit more eagerness, a mental *will-she-or-won't-she* question weighing each day as he inserted the key to the PO box, peeked inside, and wondered whether he would see a Seguin return address waiting for him. Even if he did, a bigger question still lingered. Would Mallory be open to a relationship with him?

He had never had a long-distance anything. Romance, friendship, pen pal. He didn't even know what to think, yet he knew what he wanted. And that was someone to fill a void in his life, someone special with whom he could talk and laugh and share meals and maybe travel.

And kiss.

It was only one kiss. That was what Alec kept telling himself, yet there was no erasing its potency. He knew what a kiss was supposed to feel like, and he knew what he felt with women in the past. This was different. Special and memorable, tender and true.

And if Alec didn't at least try to make a play in Mallory's direction, he would regret it. So, by Post-it, he cast a line of interest her way.

Now he had to wait to see if she would reply with more than payment of just a moving bill.

MALLORY, PAIGE, AND Nathan triangulated around the dining table for an early meal. Paige had prepared a spectacular Crock Pot roast with baby red potatoes, pearl onions, and carrots from the local farmer's market. Mallory breathed in the well-seasoned aroma that filled the kitchen as Paige ladled tender helpings into three shallow bowls. "Incredible."

"You never make a roast? It's Mom's recipe." She passed a bowl to Mallory.

"Not really." She shrugged, not remembering the last time she made anything but a halved recipe of soup in a small Crock Pot. "No one but me to eat it."

"That's what I used to think after, well, you know." She tilted her head in the direction of Nathan, presumably so that she didn't have to say the word *divorce*.

"Got it." Mallory nodded her understanding. "I should probably try to cook more than I do. I have all of Mom's recipes and a couple of good full-color cookbooks." Mallory remembered the problem. "But they're in storage."

"You can leaf through mine whenever you want. Maybe even make something this week if you like?"

That was a not-so-subtle hint. Mallory did need to eat, but so did Paige and Nathan. And she did want to help.

"How about I hit the H-E-B in the morning, and I take care of dinner tomorrow?"

Paige agreed so fast Mallory thought maybe she heard more than an offer of one meal.

After retrieving utensils and taking their seats, they fell into a comfortable rhythm of conversation and light laughter. Nathan was a slow eater, but that made meals linger, which Mallory had to admit she enjoyed. During a lull in the conversation, Paige led with a drawn-out "So . . ." followed by a sentence she couldn't cloak as small talk even though she tried. "Public school is back in session."

But Mallory didn't want to think about that. Knowing kids were in primary school now meant the college's spring semester start was right around the corner as well. Her students would be there, revved and ready to go for a whole new slate of classes—but she wouldn't.

Paige didn't meet Mallory's eyes and instead busied herself with cutting the meat on Nathan's plate as she continued her agenda-driven outreach. "And I'm sure SISD could use some qualified substitutes."

"I know what you're doing." Mallory took a bite.

"What's that?" Paige played coy.

"Bad act." Mallory waved her fork at her sister between bites. "Not buying it."

"Who said anything about acting?" Yet the way Paige's voice rose with the question was a dead giveaway. "I just meant that there are a lot of teachers involved in spring sports, UIL events, and field trips. The district could probably use an extra pair of eyes for substituting at the high school. That's all."

"Oh, is that all?"

"That's really all."

Mallory wondered if that was truly what Paige thought, that teaching was nothing more than being "*an extra pair of eyes*" to students. She was ready to call her on the carpet for this one, but she stopped short, Nathan's presence forcing her to keep her tone in check as she settled on a straightforward reply. "That's not teaching."

"Who said anything about teaching?" Paige rubbed the side of her knife with her fork and returned her utensil to her plate while Nathan enjoyed small bites of roast. "Substituting," she underscored.

Mallory's eyes would roll out of her head if she didn't respond to that. "Even substitutes have duties to perform." But short of delivering a thesis on education to her sister, she kept her response short. "Besides, there's a difference between high school teaching and college teaching."

"Maybe." Paige shrugged. "But you should look into the pay."

Mallory didn't need to do that. "There's no way the compensation is even close."

"Maybe you shouldn't be choosy—"

"And why not? Why shouldn't I have some pride in what value I bring to a place?" Mallory worked hard for her credentials and for her spot in higher education, and she continued to work long hours to meet the needs of her responsibilities at the college. Up until this spring, it was go-go-go every week of the year. She occasionally taught summer school in addition to long semesters, and even holidays gave little reprieve because she was busy preparing syllabi, lectures, research, and exams for the next semester. "Besides, I have a job, remember?"

Paige didn't back down. "But there's no contractual obligation against substituting, right?"

Mallory had to concede that.

"So why not try it? You know, keep your feet in the game. See how it feels." She cleared her throat and lowered her voice as she pressed a step further. "See if you can go back, you know?"

Could she? Mallory's negative memories of the classroom were still so raw, and while she hoped she could get over them by avoiding a campus environment entirely, her logical wheels turned in such a way that prompted her to consider Paige's plan in a meaningful way. Still, she admitted with a hint of exasperation, "I don't know." Because she really didn't.

"It's money." Mallory needed that. "And it's a chance to test the waters in a completely new environment. Totally safe." Paige added what Mallory needed to hear.

Still, Mallory wasn't certain.

After a few moments of silence, Paige verbalized what Mallory was thinking. "How do you know what you're capable of until you give it a shot?"

Well played, Sis. Mallory didn't know. And when would she? How would she? The fall semester was so far away that if she just completely shut down her professional life, she might lose much more than she already had.

Additionally, there were Bella's expenses. And upkeep for her car. Not to mention day-to-day living expenses. Yes, she could use the money. "Maybe," she voiced before stuffing a bite of food into her mouth to avoid committing to anything further. That was her answer.

For now.

Chapter Fifteen

COOKING WAS A way for Mallory to take her mind off things, and she was eager to contribute to the household and show Paige and Nathan a bit of love through food.

"Anything off limits?" she asked, flipping through one of Paige's countertop cookbooks.

"Absolutely not. I have no demands when the meal is being cooked for me," she said with a smile.

Mallory instantly rewound in her mind to Alec, though there was no internal warning for it happening. She wanted to respond to his Post-it note and call him, but she needed to decide on when. Not during the day since he might have a new client. Maybe one evening. She'd shoot for Thursday night.

That simple decision felt good. And right.

Because something about Alec felt good. And right.

Light remembrances and pleasant flashbacks of their conversation over the hot meal he delivered were still fresh in her mind. She turned them over like photographs, savoring the memory. Her hand stilled on the page of the cookbook, and she realized her daydream only when Paige's voice broke through the silence. "So what are you making?"

Mallory decided on a teriyaki chicken dish served with

basmati rice and steamed asparagus. "Will Nathan eat those?"

"I don't ask. I just put the food on his plate, and when he questions me if he's tried it before, I always say yes." Paige sealed her kid cuisine tip with a tight-lipped smile.

The things mothers do. Mallory was already learning a lot from being around her little sister for such an extended time. She closed the cookbook and replaced it in the stack on the counter. "Fair enough."

"And when you go to the store, can you pick up some coffee creamer? French vanilla in the refrigerated section." She grabbed her travel mug from beneath her coffee maker and called to Nathan. "Time to go."

Nathan came bounding down the hall with only one shoe. "Can't find it, Mommy." He pointed to his shoeless side. His sock was only halfway on, its heel against his toes. The loose fabric flapped like a swimming fin as he walked.

"Want me to help you?" Mallory offered, stepping from the kitchen into the hallway.

He spat, "yes, yes, yes," then turned like a scuba diver descending back into the depths.

"Hurry," Paige called after them. "I've got to be at work by eight. Three back-to-back closings this morning." Clearly, business was brisk at the land and title office.

Mallory had no intention of dawdling. Seeing them out the door on weekday mornings was a trip, and some days Mallory wasn't sure if she should help, watch, or stay out of the way.

But this morning she helped, even as her mind was half-focused. Did Alec have any little ones in his life like Nathan? Nephews, nieces, or cousins? She didn't know specifics about him, yet she wondered. A relationship with him wasn't unreasonable, but it would be complicated living a state away. And as much as Mallory's heart tugged in his direction, she also didn't need to create personal difficulties through starting something that would have to be done at a distance for several months' time.

She was trying to make things less difficult, not add layers of uncertainty to her life.

Either way, she didn't know how to put thoughts of Alec on permanent pause. Nor did she want to fully do so. Thoughts of him warmed her. They made her feel less alone. *Daydreaming was safe*—and normal—*right?* So holding on to these little mental images brought comfort.

But Nathan reminded her of reality. "My shoe?"

"Right," she said. "Let's look."

This morning, Nathan's mysteriously missing shoe was found on the foot of one of his teddy bears. "How did it get there?" Nathan's voice was as cute as the scene, all of which made Mallory smile. She righted his sock, Velcroed the shoe, and embraced Nathan with a quick hug before sending him on his way after his mom.

Even Nathan had a routine. Even he went to school.

So if Mallory had the chance—even through substituting—maybe she should take it.

Maybe.

She was still holding on to that answer.

Mallory was also turning over the idea of resurrecting a

project she first thought about earlier in the fall semester. She had plans for new section development of a sophomore-level literature course she wanted to share with Dean Vanguard. With the sabbatical time stretching in front of her, she could focus on that and rebuild a sense of purpose toward the future. There was a lot to do to make such a big departmental change occur, but she had the luxury of time.

Originally, she thought the new literature course could be on ground. But her self-assurance was still raw, a hollow place carved where confidence once grew. Maybe she should pitch the class as an online section.

Or was that just delaying the facing of fears head-on?

If she could quiet her mind enough to concentrate, maybe her resolve would return. Still, she was trying not to be too hard on herself. Little by little, she was getting there.

After Paige and Nathan left, the house was silent, just like Mallory's own apartment on mornings when she awoke. It was her and Bella, though admittedly the cat made very little noise most mornings. Here in Seguin, she pretty much avoided all early commotion. No doubt the cat was still healing after her visit to the vet, though Bella was handling her medicine well and resuming most of her normal feeding and grooming activities.

Mallory also had day-to-day activities of her own. Presently, it was a trip to H-E-B, the Texas market chain that was the physical definition of a company that had simply built a better grocery store than any competition. She really missed access to those stores in New Mexico. She also wanted to stop by the local chamber of commerce to get a map of businesses she could keep in her car instead of relying on her phone since she needed to curtail her data usage. And she wanted to scout for a decent salon where she could get a trim sometime in the next few weeks. She wasn't thrilled about facing an upcoming Texas spring season with a head full of split ends.

Or a heart full of regret.

Should she be letting the events of the fall drive her future? Should she be letting thoughts of Alec do so?

Or were her priorities all wrong?

BUTTER SIZZLED AND slid to coat the bottom of the pan as Mallory turned down the temperature. She added three chicken breasts, little wisps of heat and spurts of sound rising in their wake. Nathan played with the asparagus stalks by the edge of the counter, posing and balancing them as if they were green army soldiers.

"Clever," Paige acknowledged. "That's one way to get him to eat his vegetables."

"I learn from the best." Mallory winked at her sister.

"Well, you didn't learn this from me." She leaned over the stove's edge to peer into the pan. "That smells delicious."

Aroma of fresh lemon, garlic, and teriyaki lingered over the steam, all ingredients of the sauce just waiting to join in culinary harmony.

"Lift the lid on the rice over there." She directed Paige,

not wanting the pot to boil over.

The three of them together in the kitchen created a busy and joyous buzz of activity. She ruminated on their many years of sisterhood. Yes, they were happy sisters—but sisters with habits.

And, sometimes, not all habits were happy ones. "Stop that." Mallory waved a spatula in Paige's direction when she caught her dipping her finger into the teriyaki sauce.

Paige jumped back as she popped the tip of her index finger into her mouth. "Yum."

"Okay. That's all for you. Out, out, out!" Mallory shooed her away. "Give me fifteen minutes in here."

"My stomach is going to eat itself." Paige comically clutched her belly. Nathan followed suit, though his over-the-top shenanigans outdid Paige's.

"Watch that one," Mallory warned, getting caught up in the hysterics. "He's got a little thread of drama."

"If only you knew." Paige scooped up Nathan, twirling him around as he laughed and laughed.

Mallory finished preparing dinner, and the food was an all-around hit. Nathan ate every scrap on his plate, a feat Mallory took as personal accomplishment.

Cleanup went quickly as evening descended. After dinner and Nathan's bedtime, the house grew quiet. Paige disappeared to take a shower, and as Mallory readied for hers, she was startled when her phone signaled. A name flashed on the screen, which sent instantaneous shivers through Mallory from her fingertips all the way to her toes.

Alec.

Mallory took his Post-it invitation to heart, yet even though she hadn't yet called, she was thrilled he did. She took a deep breath and answered with all the confidence she had.

"Well, hello to you, too." His Hollywood-suave voice returned.

More tingles.

"What's new in Texas? Taken the bulls by the horns there yet?" Alec's conversation put Mallory at ease, even as tiny shocks of intensity at hearing from him continued.

"Wouldn't you like to know." She played coy in her response. "No bulls, no rodeo."

"Isn't there a season for that?"

"Rodeo? Oh, yes. You better believe it." Every major city and nearly every small town in the Lone Star State had its own version of roping, riding, and wrangling.

"Do you go?"

"Me?" Mallory certainly had opportunities when she lived in Texas years ago, but, today, rodeo arenas weren't high on her priorities for recreation. "Not really."

"You don't like that scene?"

That wasn't it. There was plenty about rodeos to like. "I like being outside. And I like animals. And competition." *And hot men.* But she kept that thought private. "But I prefer other outings."

"I suspected."

"Oh, you did?"

"Yes."

Who is leading this conversation?

Clearly Alec, who continued, "I think I've got you figured out pretty well."

"Oh, do you now?" Mallory was intrigued, and her lips curled as Alec spoke. "Tell me more."

"About you?"

"If that's what is on your mind." Mallory gulped at her own forwardness.

Alec spoke clearly. "You are."

I've been on your mind? Mallory gulped again, nervousness and excitement teeming.

Alec sustained her attention with a simple question that was both tender and thoughtful. "How are you?" Coming from anyone else—in any other circumstance—the words would have been mundane. But from Alec, they were anything but. And there were so many ways Mallory could answer that question.

Yet when none of those answers formed on her lips, she resorted to the pedestrian response she was apt to give anyone. She answered simply with just one word. "Good."

Alec called her out. "That's a lie."

Mallory's chest tightened as she was taken aback. "What?"

"Mallory." Her name still melted from his lips. She loved the way her syllables sounded, even from hundreds of miles away. "You just moved. To a different state. With rodeos for miles and miles. You've got to have more to say than *good*."

She liked the way Alec didn't let her off the hook with an easy answer. He heard her. And he wanted to hear from her.

And she wanted to be heard.

Before she even knew how the time had passed, it did. She was telling Alec about Bella's trip to the vet, Nathan's antics, her cooking success. But she also told him about work. No details, just that she missed the college. "The energy, you know? Students and ideas and the comradery."

"I know exactly what you mean." Alec cut in only at appropriate times to add his thoughts. "St. John's had that. Just by stepping on a campus, you feel sort of—"

"Energized."

"Exactly." Alec agreed. "So, is there none of that in Seguin?"

"It's early." And it was. Not quite a month. Had she given it much of a chance?

Yet Alec asked, "So why not come back?"

"Where . . . um . . . what?" Her tongue tripped on the questions.

"To Santa Fe."

Mallory didn't know what to say with the turn of the conversation.

"Mallory," his voice lowered, his tone imploring her to listen. "I'd like to see you." His silence heightened his next request. "And I was calling to find out if you would be interested in seeing me too."

Here was a man who did not mince words. "You want to see me?"

"I have an event. In February. Here, in Santa Fe. I thought you might like to consider coming." He added, "I *want* you to consider coming. With me."

Mallory certainly liked hearing those last two words.

"What kind of event?"

"The last weekend in February, my family is renting a community hall and getting together. It's something we do every couple of years."

"Like a family reunion?"

"A family reunion." There was no fanfare at the words, but their quiet simplicity spoke to Alec's sincerity. "It's a day of food. There's a potluck meal with more tables of casseroles than you can count. My aunts host this crazy cookie decorating competition. We get some live music, something simple, but guitars fire up during the last few hours. There's probably some other surprises that I don't even know about."

"So this is an . . . um, *event*?" Mallory really wanted to ask if it was a date, but the word didn't exactly come. Still, Alec must have understood as much. Did he know her this well already? "It's an event, yes. But it's an event I'd like to be at with you."

So maybe it was a date.

An offer of one.

TWO CUPS OF tea weren't enough to calm Mallory's jitters after that phone call. And she had even brewed a caffeinated variety. Maybe that wasn't the smartest thing to do as nighttime loomed. She wouldn't be able to sleep a wink.

Because of the tea.

Because of talking with Alec.

Paige returned from her shower in a bathrobe and grilled her after the phone call, wanting to know exactly what Alec's intentions were.

"If I knew, I'd tell you." Mallory was as confused as her sister.

"But you have to have a sense," she implored, not satisfied by her dismissal.

"I sense this guy wants company at his family reunion."

"Mal." Paige spoke as if she were reprimanding a puppy. "No guy just asks a random girl to a family reunion."

"I've been called a lot of things." Mallory's mind flashed to semesters full of student evaluations where classes rated her like education were some sort of fast food service. The open-ended questions on the anonymous evaluations sometimes made her smile and sometimes made her cringe. She couldn't ever remember being labeled "*random*" by a student. "But I've never been called that."

"I think there's more going on with Alec than you're telling me." Paige tucked her legs beneath her on the couch, settling in as if getting comfortable would make Mallory reveal something. She pulled the edges of her terrycloth robe tight against her chest and waited for her sister's reply.

Mallory was in no hurry to respond. Absently, she finger-combed her hair to one side, sweeping it across her shoulder and wringing her hands around the center of what she gathered. "If there's more going on with Alec, then I don't know about it."

Paige shook her head. "For someone so smart, you sure can be naïve."

Mallory's hands stilled. "Now you're just being catty."

Paige lifted her hand into the air and bent her fingers to mime a cat's paw with sharp claws. Mallory rolled her eyes.

"Look, do you like this guy? Do you not like this guy?"

"It's not that simple." *Nothing in my life is.*

"It should be that simple."

"Easy for you to say."

Paige had her Prince Charming. And she didn't have to go looking for him. Everett found her, and their lives were folding into each other. But Mallory didn't want to look for anyone, and she certainly didn't need the complication of a romantic relationship when she was supposed to be using this time to get her professional confidence back on track. She tried to articulate that to Paige—again. And though her sister was listening, Mallory wasn't sure how much Paige was hearing.

Outsiders thought the world of education was textbook perfect. That it was a series of days filled with academic enrichment always polished and pristine. No one talked about the emotional pitfalls when students stopped attending class or dropped out of college altogether. No one talked about the rollercoaster of professional betrayal when it came to cases of cheating and plagiarism. And absolutely no one—no one—talked about what to do when students who were supposed to respect their professors bullied and belittled them through digital posts and social media messages that spiraled into viral cruelty.

Mallory wrung her palms against her hair again, not wanting to swerve into a *woe-is-me* rehash of the past month.

She was already doing plenty of that in her mind.

Paige tried a new angle. "You have to decide what you want."

"But that's the problem." Mallory looped a strand of hair around her finger and wound the end as she spoke. "I know exactly what I want."

"You do?" Paige leaned forward.

"Completely." Mallory wound tighter, the hair slipping once she reached the end only to be pinched by her thumb so she could slide and start again.

"Then what is it?" Paige's voice quieted. "Mallory, what do you want?"

Her fingers kept twirling her hair. She could have curls for days if only her fingers held a little bit of gel. Instead, the tresses slipped, falling through her fingers and eluding her grasp. Not unlike her professional job, for the time being, and her confidence.

Holding on to nothing but the air, she answered Paige's fair question with an answer equally so. "My life. I just want my life back."

Chapter Sixteen

A WOMAN ON sabbatical in central Texas with a master's degree in liberal arts wasn't exactly a hot commodity. Mallory knew this.

But Paige kept forgetting this.

"Just try, Mal. You're in such perdition with Santa Fe College," Paige insisted.

"Wrong," Mallory corrected. "Perdition would mean I don't have a job. I have one."

"You have a job promised. No paycheck."

Do you have to rub that in?

Paige didn't drop the subject. "Why don't you just check out colleges around here? See what they have. Weigh your employment options."

"First substituting and now college visits?" Mallory wondered when her sister would give it a rest.

Apparently, the answer was no time soon. Paige continued at a mile-a-minute pace. "And you can start right here. In Seguin."

"TLU?" The private college campus of Texas Lutheran University was the town's only higher education institute, and the student body was small. "It's nothing like Santa Fe."

"Who said it was? Besides, that's just one college. You

can always look further. There are several in San Antonio."

"Look further for what, exactly?" If Paige was angling for something, she needed to cut to it.

"Just see about jobs. Get out there. Explore places and faculty opportunities. Keep an open mind. Maybe there will be an option that's more perfect for you than going back where you intended."

Mallory didn't know if Paige was offering advice or dictating fortune cookie lines.

True, there was no harm in scratching an itch of curiosity to see what instructor positions existed at nearby colleges. Maybe doing so would even give her a fresh perspective on her situation in Santa Fe. Comparing salaries and understanding the competitiveness of full-time positions might even reignite her professionally more than her sophomore-level literature course proposal.

Mallory, though, didn't want Paige to think she was going to jump ship. Sure, she could safely visit colleges and even access online employment opportunities, but it wasn't going to be more than a scavenger hunt.

"I'm on sabbatical," she reminded Paige again. "I'm not unemployed." She was, in effect, on a break for one semester.

So why did that one semester feel more and more like a death sentence?

And why could no one—not even her sister—fully understand her crisis of confidence?

Even though she was physically removed from the space that had shaken her, Mallory's professional uncertainty remained. Everything she did seemed so distant. She privately questioned whether she would have the strength to go back to face-to-face teaching and whether she'd even be productive in the classroom if she did. There might be more students like Jesse, and there might be other tests of her willpower and strength. She had no idea how much she could take and still stand tall as a teacher.

These thoughts required her to wrestle. In still moments when she was alone in her bedroom, these were what lay next to her. She was constantly wondering, constantly worrying.

There was no absolution.

So when Paige planted her idea, it lay alongside everything else already in Mallory's mind. Then, after importunities from Paige resurfaced over several days' time, Mallory finally caved and told her she would go.

"TLU has some part-time positions posted online," Paige called after her on the way out the door.

"I'll keep my full-time one," Mallory replied, biting back her frustration. Paige's line of thinking was from her eight-to-five job, not an academic one. Paige sold and prepared home and land deeds, which wasn't anything like Mallory's career in education.

Paige's life was measured in weeks. Mallory's was measured in semesters.

Paige worked for paychecks. Mallory worked for yearly contracts.

Her sister could give two weeks' notice at her title company and choose a job anywhere in another sector. Land offices, appraisal districts, municipal services sets, county seats. These jobs were ripe for the picking any time of year.

Vacancies came and went. A position was open, applicants filed, and it was filled. Unemployment one week was not a static sentence through the next.

Paige was trying to be helpful—this Mallory knew—but her sister also couldn't fully see inside of Mallory. Mallory had to be in charge of her own introspection.

And to get herself on track, she needed to believe in herself, believe in her abilities, and believe she could make a difference in education. That started with small steps.

Mallory's collegiate email account, for instance, was still wildly active with regular updates. Her dean kept her apprised of departmental happenings, while various offices—of the registrar, of student services, of financial aid—sent instructional reminders for her to pass along to her students.

Except it seemed like no one outside of human resources at Santa Fe College got the memo: she didn't have any students.

But she did need to remember she would have them again in the future. And a trip to a college campus, even though it wasn't hers, could remind her of that. So she was off to visit TLU during a weekday afternoon. Paige seeded the idea, but Mallory made the exact reasons for visiting her own.

Seguin's population didn't rival Santa Fe's. Santa Fe was the capital for the entire state of New Mexico and a hot-spot tourist attraction. That meant more buildings downtown, more restaurants, more hotels, and more pockets of places to explore. Mallory never tired of the scene.

She especially liked Santa Fe's Railyard, a historic district turned commercial with everything from shopping to strolling to live outdoor performances to even a farmer's market. Seguin didn't have such a spot, though its farmer's market and special events made great use of the town square, Central Park, and the city's Starcke Park near the Guadalupe River. Each place had its charms.

The smaller size, though, of Seguin didn't lend itself to more than one college, but what it did have was impressive. There were other Texas towns about Seguin's size that managed to sustain four-year colleges, but something about Seguin was different. The campus wasn't relegated to the edge of town, nor was it part of an expansive system that tried to make it a little pocket of a larger institute in a different place. It was its own place and had its own identity.

Just like Mallory wanted.

Even though Mallory had spent her high school years in Seguin, she really hadn't paid much attention to the campus. But, now, she wanted to do just that.

She parked in a visitor spot on campus with the intention to stroll, sampling the area and tasting its general flavor. She kept her eyes aimed high to hold her head so, and she followed meandering sidewalks in leisure. Her footfalls reverberated in low-toned thuds against the concrete, creating a metronome of pacing. Leaves rustled from live oaks dotting the manicured site. Little pops of color from red-tipped shrubs and knock-out rose bushes surprised her eyes as she walked. The private college's buildings weren't large or showy, but they were stately and inviting. The TLU campus was, indeed, a pearl nestled inside of Seguin.

Her eyes glossed across greenery, walkways, and building entrances. Students congregated to talk, shoulders heavy with their backpacks and their semester's responsibilities. Some assembled beneath trees. Some paired at outdoor tables. Others walked alone with purpose before disappearing through doorways that no doubt lead to classrooms and instructors' offices. She knew this pace of an academic environment. Everything surrounding her was familiar . . .

Yet foreign.

These were not her students.

This was not her college.

Paige insisted Mallory visit to get a feel again for the space. "To test the waters," she had said. As if visiting one college could wipe away negative memories of another.

But, so far, no slate was being wiped clean for Mallory. Each step was a challenge in personal fortitude. Could she be resilient enough to spend a few hours on campus? Would her body and mind allow her to blend back into an environment that had been home to her for five years, or had her last semester been a career deal-breaker? This was what she wanted to find out.

As Mallory roamed the campus, she fought feelings of nostalgia as well as fear. Looking around, this scene was idyllic. Students engaged with one another, their faces eager at the possibilities to learn. But she also knew the reality.

Some of these students were probably failing. Rather than having conversations about classroom activities, some were likely complaining about grades. Some who sat would glance to check their phones when their screens lit. And what was happening on those devices? Banter? Gossip? Complaints?

Mallory tugged at her purse strap, righting it higher on her shoulder as she tried to shake away the chip of bitterness at thinking the worst. Perhaps these students were checking their email, seeing if grades were posted. Or maybe they were arranging their work schedules, coordinating with bosses, coworkers, and babysitters. There were plenty of students who were honest and hard-working. They weren't all like him.

Like Jesse.

She needed to stop her paranoia. Jesse was one student. His actions were not indicative of an entire group of individuals.

Don't paint a group with a single brush. Mallory quickened her pace and steadied her feet. She couldn't stop thoughts of Jesse from resurfacing, but she could work to manage them. Like a wave, she would allow it to come toward her, but she would mentally let it crest and move on rather than hold onto it. Once it did, she was free of the thought.

This had been part of her coping, and it worked. Still, she wished the waves would stop coming altogether. Perhaps, with more time, they would.

But today, she needed to deal. And she was here to, in part, do that. On this campus, she wanted to try out the environment, see and feel what it was like to again be on college grounds. So part of that was reacting, and part of that was being active. For the latter, she decided on entering the campus library. If any place could help her feel like a college professor again, surely it would be that environment.

Stepping into the Blumberg Memorial Library building in the heart of campus was like being wrapped in a blanket of familiarity. As an undergraduate and graduate student, she had spent countless hours in libraries. Even as a professor, the library was where she still came when she needed to focus on research, get fresh ideas, or grade a large stack of student essays. There was always a private work area she could carve out for herself in the stillness of such a building to claim as her own for a few hours.

That was what she planned to do here.

Inside, the library spoke serenity. Whisper-quiet spaces, dim lighting, and rows upon rows of books greeted her, universal signs of what she expected. Even though she didn't know this exact library, she knew how calm this would make her feel.

And it did.

This also wasn't a place in which to get physically lost, just to mentally disappear.

Mallory made herself at home by walking with assured-ness through the interior that radiated a sense of welcome. Without even stopping at the circulation desk for a site map, she headed to the stairs, taking a guess that the most private spots would be on the top floor. She wanted to find a quiet corner, grab a couple of pedagogy books, and peruse their pages to see if there was anything that caught her eye for teaching or classroom management—or even for professional confidence rebuilding.

They weren't hard to find. As she plucked books from the shelves and lost herself in passages of the ones she found, she recaptured a sense of productivity she hadn't experienced in weeks. She was using her mind, and she was back in career mode. It felt good.

Manageable.

After several hours, she leaned back in her chair to stretch her back and arms. Scraps of paper, pages of notes, and armfuls of books spilled around her. She was back in the saddle, and she was proud of her focus.

Four pages of notes, three hours, two stretch breaks, and one trip to the bathroom later, she stacked her finds to take a picture of the spines so she could have a record of their titles and authors. Her composition book and her mind were both brimming with the excitement of learning something new, a habitual yet slightly dormant feeling she was glad to reignite.

With late afternoon descending into evening, it was time to finish savoring her productivity and head back to Paige's. Mallory threw away scraps of paper she had been using as bookmarks, carried the books she borrowed to a nearby cart for re-shelving, and replaced her phone, pen, and notebook that she had removed from her purse. She exited her private little research corner with a smile as she made her way to the center of the library, descended the stairs, and reached the front entrance. Her heels clicked again in tiny beats against the floor underfoot, and the slight noise carried her past the circulation desk until she swung her purse in front of her to ease through the security exit. But loud beeping stopped her dead in her tracks, a paralyzing series of sounds crashing through the silence as all patron eyes fixated on her.

"Miss," a voice called to her. "Stop right there."

MALLORY AND PAIGE had once conspired to shoplift mood rings from a craft fair. It was a juvenile choice, and they had, in fact, been juveniles. When their mother discovered their thievery was the root of their giggles on the car ride home, she U-turned the vehicle so fast they practically got whiplash. Their mother marched them back to the booth where they had swiped the goods and made them return the merchandise and apologize until they were on the verge of tears.

At home, punishment was sealed through a month of being grounded. But the feeling of internal shame was far worse than four weeks of house arrest.

That sense of shame came cascading back as Mallory shifted her unsteady feet, legs weighted with jitters. The beeping of the security siren continued as loud as the pounding of her heart. She brought the palm of her hand to her chest, her necklace and purse strap tangling in the way.

"Miss," the voice called again. "Step over here." Mallory turned to meet the steely, bifocaled eyes of a librarian whose cutting gaze was more chilling than any craft booth proprietor's.

Mallory stepped backward from the exit, but years of training to be quiet in a library made her hold her tongue. Thankfully, the siren stopped when she moved away, though she was sure all eyes from everyone else in the library were still on her.

This had to be some mistake. Mallory didn't have a faculty or student ID badge, but surely that didn't mean she was unwelcome in the library. The circulation desk attendant was followed by another staff member. *Now they're going to prevent me from leaving? Great. Just my luck.*

One woman cut to the chase. "We need to check your bag."

"What?" Mallory found her voice, but she was befuddled.

"Your bag, miss," the other echoed. "We track the books that come and go." The sass in the comment was not lost on Mallory.

Oh, that's what this place does? Track books? She wanted to lambast back. She removed her hand from her chest and shimmied her waist so her purse could fall to the front of her body. "I don't have a campus ID, and I was just looking at some books—"

"Do you have any in there?" The attendant pointed at Mallory's bag but barely waited for a response as she peered close to her.

Mallory pushed the sides apart to show the deep recesses of the interior, stuffed full with her wallet, phone, water bottle, lipstick, pens, a half-eaten bag of trail mix . . . and something that took up space the bag barely had. "My notebook," Mallory admitted, but even as she did, she sensed something wasn't right.

The notebook shouldn't be that big.

She extracted it by its spine, and in doing so, sheepishly realized it wasn't only her notebook. Closed inside of it was a paperback pedagogy book she had taken from the shelf. It was the smallest of the bunch, though she had sworn she put it back with the others.

Except she hadn't.

The accusatory eyes, embarrassing security siren, and public humiliation were all evidence to the contrary. "Is that our book?" one of the women asked, already knowing the answer by its protective cover, barcode, and Dewey Decimal number.

Mallory's voice was no more intrusive than that of a mouse. "Yes." She stammered out a pathetic, "I'm sorry," then a phrase about misunderstanding that didn't make sense. She held the book between her and the two library staff members, willing one of them to take it before it slipped from her palms, sweaty from embarrassment. "I don't even know how it got in here," she admitted, though she did.

She had been careless. She wasn't thinking. She must have just closed her notebook and not even counted the books that she returned.

"Thank you." The circulation attendant accepted the book, though the gesture was more cold than courteous.

"This was an accident. I didn't mean, I, um . . . I was just reading and got—carried away." Yes, that was plausible. Happened in the library all the time, right?

"We try our best to keep materials available for everyone." The attendant passed the book to the woman as her lips sealed before turning into a tight-lipped frown.

"I understand—and I appreciate that. I so do." Mallory tripped over words in a flurry of continued apology. "Really, truly, I don't steal books."

"No?" The attendant raised an eyebrow.

How did she even get into this mess? She was an educator, and attempted library thievery was a cardinal sin as far as she was concerned. "I just wasn't paying attention."

The librarian who now held the book ended the impromptu interrogation. "We thank you for the return of the book." Then she gestured for Mallory to try the exit again.

Mallory hung her head and scraped together what was left of her dignity as she turned on her heel. She pushed her palm against the top of her purse to hold the bag closed and steady her hand from shaking. Some people had this type of physical reaction to being pulled over by a police officer or having a cavity filled by a dentist.

She had the jitters from shame by librarians.

And the feeling was little different than she felt in December with Iker as she sat in the human resources office. Was there something about Mallory that invited attention? Did she sometimes get so rushed or careless she brought about these situations? She couldn't control Jesse, yet just as she had hastily packed the book by mistake in her purse, maybe there was something she had done without knowing . . .

Her confidence crashed in that instant, and even stepping outside into fresh air only brought temporary tranquility. She blew out the breath she was holding, but there was no expulsion of the indignity she held.

That was more permanent.

The saving grace of the whole humiliating encounter? At least they didn't ask her name. Yet the damage to her confidence was still done.

Chapter Seventeen

"YOU REALIZE YOU'RE turning into a gypsy." Paige lifted the lid on a glass-jarred candle that she placed next to the stove. Stale air from dinner hung throughout the kitchen though it was no match for soy-based wax with triple wicks wrapped with a vanilla frosting label.

Mallory temporarily avoided her sister's verbal jab. "That smells incredible."

"Made in Fredericksburg. They're the only kind I buy." Paige struck a match and lit each wick in quick succession.

"I can see why." Mallory savored the sweet scent as the heat carried down into the wax.

"Everett orders some now and again for me too. Good gifts." She waved the match to extinguish it.

"He's a keeper, you know."

"That's the plan." Paige ran the match tip beneath the faucet before tossing it into the kitchen garbage. "But back to you. And your new gypsy lifestyle."

"I'm taking one trip back to New Mexico," Mallory corrected her. "I hardly think that qualifies me as a gypsy."

"You're bunking with someone."

"Jovanna." Mallory reminded Paige of her friend, who had offered her a place to crash while she was in town again for Alec's family reunion.

"Alec didn't offer you his place?"

Mallory knew her cheeks were reddening at the thought of spending another night with Alec, especially in a space so intimate. "No."

Paige shrugged. "He should have."

"And what makes you say that?"

Paige squared her shoulders to face Mallory more directly, counting on her fingers. "Number one, hot guy invited you to a family event." She extended a second finger. "Number two, hot guy should offer you a room."

Mallory mimicked Paige's finger movement to underscore the reality of Alec's situation. "He lives in a one bedroom apartment—"

"Perfectly cozy!" Paige threw her hands in the air. Her dramatic reaction to Mallory's love life—make that anti-love life—never ceased. "Look, this guy likes you."

"So?" Mallory still didn't know exactly what to make of Alec's weekend invitation and whether there would be more than a reunion for them. But when she called Jovanna, her longest-time friend in Santa Fe, she immediately offered her couch for the weekend. She would be a good buffer, and her friend could even serve as an excuse if Mallory needed her for any reason.

"So, what are you going to do? Lead him on or start a relationship?"

Mallory angled her head. "That's forward."

"Look, gypsy—"

"Watch it." Mallory held up a finger.

It was a playful warning Paige promptly ignored. "Blow back to Santa Fe. Test the waters there. See if the O'Donnell family is sane, crazy, or somewhere in between."

"The family isn't my reason for going."

Paige crossed her arms. "Then what is?"

It was more than a one-word answer.

"Spill it," Paige demanded.

Mallory flashed back to one of their prior conversations. "You had asked me what I wanted."

"I remember." Paige was matter-of-fact.

"Do you recall what I said?"

"Yes." Paige challenged her sister. "Do you?"

Mallory skimmed her hand across her hair. "Yes, I mean, I remember what I said. But maybe I didn't see far enough."

Paige uncrossed her arms. "You're not sounding too confident."

Mallory tossed her hair over her shoulder. "But now I do." She hoped Paige would hear her mounting confidence in the way she spoke. "I don't want my past. I want a future."

Paige knitted her eyebrows in puzzlement. "That doesn't make sense. You have a future. Everyone does."

"Living with my younger sister, bunking with Jovanna, not earning a paycheck. That is not a future. It's certainly not much of a life."

"It's a gypsy life!" Paige proclaimed in triumph, her words coming full circle.

Mallory rolled her eyes. "Exactly my point."

"Look, you don't have to explain everything. You don't

even have to know everything. You're free not to know, okay?"

Mallory had always been the think-it-through type. The organized one. The planner. She was sensible. And smart. But so much about the last few months were outside of her realm of planning.

That included Alec.

The man who swooped into her life, slid in where she needed it, anchored her during a difficult time, but then was physically absent. These were the circumstances.

For the present, at least.

But for the future? That was what she didn't know.

What she did know was that she thought about Alec. And talked to him. A few times since she had been in Seguin were over the phone.

And a few times had simply been in her mind.

That was a whole new experience. Pretend conversations were not normal for her.

"But I do know one thing," Mallory offered, ready to admit something to Paige.

Paige's interest was piqued. "And what's that?"

"Alec hasn't left my mind. Some guys do." She looked away from Paige as she thought about him. "But Alec hasn't." The handful of memories she held of him were small in number but rich in substance.

"Then go." Paige swept the air with her hands. "Fly away, gypsy." She gave Mallory a sideways wink. "Alec might just like that kind of girl."

ALEC HAD JUST kicked off his shoes when his cell phone buzzed. If that were his most recent needy client, he might have to let it go to voicemail. His latest job was a real challenge. When the wife in a divorce case told Alec during his estimate of her home that she was allergic to cardboard, he realized he really had heard it all in the moving business.

Allergic to cardboard? Was that even possible? Alec and Tavis both suspected it was probably a ploy to try and get more money or sympathy—or both—from her ex-husband. Either way, they both quickly gave an option of plastic crates that they completely overpriced, thinking the figure might scare her off to another moving company.

Wrong.

It was as if the challenge proved she could get what she wanted.

Alec flipped his phone expecting to see her name, but instead it was a woman who sent his nerves in the opposite direction. He suddenly rushed to answer the call. "Hi, Mallory. Your timing is perfect."

Her voice rang with cheer through the other end. "Well, hello to you, too."

"Did you know I needed a distraction?" Alec let his toes sink into the plush carpeting of his living room as he plunged onto his couch.

"I like to think my perception has been keenly developed through years of practice."

"I'll say. You're saving me from a call with Orchid." Saying his client's pet name aloud, the one she insisted Alec use, nearly left *him* allergic.

"Come again?"

"Orchid," Alec repeated. He glanced at his arm, concerned hives would break out any minute. "She's my latest Santa Fe client problem."

"With a name like that?" Mallory joked. "She sounds like a real prize."

"I guess I should feel like a winner then." Alec shared the woman's antics and outlandish requests, including Orchid's explicit instructions to Bubble Wrap each individual piece of silverware. "But when I asked about these two sculptures on her mantel, she could have cared less."

Mallory tried to stifle her laugh, but she wasn't successful. "Maybe the sculptures are from her ex?"

"Likely." Alec asked few questions of the woman. With clients like her, it was best just to take orders. That was the fastest way to collect a paycheck. And she didn't appear to be a woman exactly hurting for money. "The house has all kinds of paintings, too. Like she's got some Georgia O'Keeffe complex or something."

Mallory put the brakes on her giggles. "She doesn't actually have originals of those, does she? I love O'Keeffe's watercolor flowers. Larger-than-life and so incredible."

"Doubtful." Alec was sorry to burst her bubble and told her so. "Maybe reprints. Or maybe knockoffs. They're mostly orchids anyway. Go figure."

"Did O'Keeffe even paint orchids?"

Alec flashed in his mind to what he remembered when he visited the Georgia O'Keeffe museum in downtown Santa Fe. She was the city's most beloved artist, and her modest museum tucked on a side street from the plaza drew visitors from year to year. "I don't remember."

"Maybe you should ask Orchid," Mallory nudged.

"The less of a conversation I have to have with her, the better," he insisted. "Not that I mind talking about such things with other people, though."

"So you like talking about art?"

"Not as much as I like looking at it."

"Good answer." Mallory then shared her own memories of seeing O'Keeffe's paintings for the first time, and Alec was glad to hear her enthusiasm as well as have the distraction from Orchid herself. After Mallory expressed a desire to visit the museum again, Alec offered, "We could do that."

"This upcoming weekend? During the family reunion?"

"Well, maybe not this weekend," Alec clarified, clutching the opportunity to keep an open-ended offer on the table with Mallory. "But another one. They've got some summer special events we could look into." He really wished he could see Mallory's face to read her expression. "They even hold these drawing workshops. For amateurs, of course. But it might be fun."

"That does sound like fun," Mallory agreed.

"It would be much more enjoyable to go with someone." Alec wanted that to be clear.

He heard Mallory's soft breathing on the other end of the line, but she didn't voice an answer.

Maybe I pushed? He quickly covered with an off-handed, "No pressure."

Mallory's verbal reply was hard to interpret. "I just don't even know when I'm coming back to Santa Fe full-time." Alec sensed a slight sadness in her words, though he couldn't be sure. "Let's see how the weekend goes."

"Fair. And I promise, no Orchids will be at my family reunion. The flowers or the female."

Mallory's tone lifted a little. "So, what should I expect?"

Alec couldn't see into the future. The presence of Mallory would keep questions of who he was dating at bay. His family would probably whisper and speculate, but they were unlikely to pry too much with someone by his side. Of course, he didn't want Mallory to feel used; that wasn't his intent at all.

He liked this girl.

He liked her more with each passing month. And he had only known her for a couple.

So, while he didn't have a crystal ball, Alec did promise Mallory this. "It will be a weekend to remember."

"ARE YOU SURE about this?" Mallory balled a scarf and tucked it into the side of her suitcase.

"Go." Paige leaned over the bed to close the luggage's top. "Before I change my mind."

Mallory's shoulders sank. "See? That's exactly what I'm

worried about."

"I'm kidding." Paige clasped her nearest arm, forcing Mallory's attention. "You need to relax. Bella is going to be fine."

Mallory cast a glance in the cat's direction. She was curled in her pet bed against the side wall, but one eye was slanted open as if she was keeping watch on the sisters' conversation. "I've never left her for more than a day."

Paige loosened her grip and righted her posture. "She's a cat, not a newborn child."

"She's a baby to me." Mallory pushed her lower lip into a pout as she stared at Bella.

"You know she's not going to react to that." Paige pointed to Mallory's face.

Mallory bit back her lip as she crouched down beside Bella, barely fitting in the slim aisle of space between the bed and the wall. She scratched Bella behind her ear and spoke to her in a sing-song pitch. "Are you going to be okay all by your lonesome?"

"Oh, that's right," Paige chided from over Mallory's shoulder. "Because you are going to be all alone here. You poor, poor cat. The humans will be gone all day and never even feed you or play with you or pretend like you are even—"

Mallory drew her elbow backward in a quick swipe that just missed Paige. "She can hear you."

Paige elbowed Mallory instead, a vulnerable yet playful hit on her shoulder that reminded her of the women's wrestling moves they used to do. Mallory, being older, always got the best of her. But now they were about equal in size. And Mallory was low to the ground. "What do you think I'll do?"

Mallory arched her back and lunged forward to the nightstand to try and escape Paige's punches. The verbal as well as the literal ones. "Just be a good cat auntie while I'm gone."

"Done." Mallory rolled over to face Paige, and she extended her hand to help her up. "Because that Persian may be the only niece I ever get."

Mallory pulled back on her hand. "Not fair." The longer they were together in the same house, the more they turned back to their teenage behavior of picking and prodding.

Paige dealt one more sassy comment. "Unless you're going to tell me that cozying up to Alec will net a marriage and kids sometime in the future."

"Out, out, out." Mallory extended her arms to steamroll Paige from the room. "I'm leaving at six in the morning. Don't get up. But remember to feed Bella at seven."

"Whatever you say." She smirked as Mallory closed the bedroom door, alone with her nearly packed suitcase, Bella, and her still-looming confusion about Alec. The more she mentioned him and the more Paige asked her about him, the less she seemed to be able to answer. Not that she was responsible for answering to her sister about her relationship with him.

Or friendship

Or whatever this was.

Whatever this became.

Mallory zipped her suitcase shut. She still wasn't sure of a status with Alec. But she was sure about Santa Fe. She hoisted the suitcase onto the floor and pushed it against the wall. Bella lifted her head only halfway, as if she might be interested but thought better of it. She yawned in a wide, showy expression before lowering her head to her paw and watching Mallory through barely-opened slits.

"Keep your thoughts to yourself," Mallory directed of the cat. "I've already gotten plenty from one girl in the house, thank you very much." Though, truly, she couldn't be curt to Bella for any length of time. The Persian wouldn't allow it. And as if on cue, she started purring to prove it.

"Oh, Bella." Mallory's heart softened. "I am going to miss you." She crouched down again to nuzzle her. "Promise me you will be good. Stay out of Nathan's way. Drink your water." The litany had become her credo for the cat every time Mallory left Bella alone. "Because I cannot afford another expensive vet bill. Not with more Santa Fe expenses coming soon." Gasoline was the biggest, though associated costs of other car maintenance along with food while she was away were going to be hits to her pocketbook. Being settled was so much more cost-efficient than being unsettled.

Not to mention normal.

This trip back would be a good way to test the waters. Surely she'd be able to gauge her confidence and comfort of being back in the city once she arrived there. True, it wasn't going to be in her old apartment, and she wasn't going to be reporting for work. But navigating and mingling and putting herself into a larger group of people would be like a test run for the fall semester.

Mallory heard Santa Fe calling back to her. Pushing aside the landscape of her profession, it was the physical space that sang loudest. She missed the elevation and the desert air. The low rise of city buildings that mingled with adobe architecture. She missed the trains. Starlit nights. Being enveloped by colors that ran through nature and buildings and fashion.

Seguin was good. But Santa Fe was home.

Chapter Eighteen

JOVANNA GREETED MALLORY with a late Friday night hug that was as big as her heart. "You, Professor, have been gone too long."

"I know." Mallory gave her friend a squeeze, glad to have arrived in Santa Fe without a hitch. No car trouble, no surprise Eden stopover. "And you're the first person to call me professor in months." Jovanna and Mallory had kept in touch through messages, social media posts, and a few phone calls. "I'm glad to be back."

"Say that again." Jovanna released her and held her at arm's length. "How have you even managed to not be teaching? Ever since I've known you, your head has been stuck in a book. Or a stack of papers."

"It's been a challenge," Mallory admitted, which was an understatement.

"How's your sister?" Jovanna stepped aside to usher Mallory into the small house she rented just a few blocks off the downtown plaza. It was a great location being centrally located, though the side street was actually pretty quiet. That was the benefit of a small piece of property surrounded by neighbors who were weekenders and artists.

"She's good." Mallory followed Jovanna's lead before she

took her luggage and closed the door behind her. "She had been calling me a gypsy for bouncing around to houses like this, freeloading and—"

Jovanna cut in with laughter. "Two houses? Oh, please, girl." She rolled Mallory's bag to the edge of the living room. "Temporarily staying in two different houses hardly makes you a freeloader."

Mallory stepped to the couch and let her purse slip off her shoulder. She settled into the cushion next to where her purse landed. "I'm not used to this. Not having my own place."

"There's a rental just down the street that opened up." Jovanna hitched her thumb over her shoulder. "Such cute curb appeal. I thought about you the minute the sign posted. And it's a one-bedroom like this one. Affordable."

"It will be gone before I'm ready to come back." Mallory rested her shoulders against the back of the couch. "No use getting my hopes up."

"Never know," Jovanna shrugged. "We could be neighbors. Plaza lunches every weekend. The best jewelry finds early in the morning. No hassle walking for live music during festivals."

Those were some of the events she missed about Santa Fe. "That does sound like a dream."

"Could be a reality, Professor."

"You don't have to keep calling me that."

"If I want to make sure you come back to New Mexico and reclaim your job, I do." Jovanna softened her voice and asked with sincerity, "So how's that going?"

Mallory shrugged, wishing the weight of worry could fall from her shoulders as easily as her purse did. "Okay, I guess." Her shoulders lowered. "I'm not getting a paycheck, which is probably the biggest hit I've taken."

"Better to take it in Texas than here though." Jovanna was just trying to be nice. Mallory appreciated the attempt and verbalized as much with a hasty echo of some of her friend's words before Jovanna continued. "I'm sure the cost of living is better in small-town Texas than in Santa Fe."

"Depends." Mallory shrugged again. She and Paige had plenty of conversations about that exact subject. True, there was affordable housing and land as well as lot ownership possibilities all around Seguin, but that was for those who wanted to stay in the area. Veer north toward New Braunfels, and prices climbed. Head west toward San Antonio and the prices skyrocketed, especially in newer suburbs and planned communities.

"Thought about staying?" Jovanna edged.

I've thought about everything. Mallory wanted to unload all of her jumbled thoughts and professional pressures. Perhaps by verbalizing them to Jovanna she could be like a temporary Sherpa, carrying them for Mallory just for the weekend so she could breathe a bit easier. But Mallory was never the type to burden beyond a physical space to crash. So instead of unloading her emotional baggage, she kept that to herself as she deflected back to Jovanna's prior comment. "Tell me more about that house nearby."

And before long, the two were gabbing as fast as Realtors. Yet their exchange was effortless, more like two neighbors who routinely crossed paths. And as Jovanna waxed poetically about this jewel of a home, it could be a possibility.

ALEC WRUNG HIS hands onto themselves. Tiny beads of sweat settled between his fingers, and that was the last thing he wanted Mallory to feel.

She had texted him late the night before to let him know she arrived in Santa Fe. He was relieved to hear from her and didn't let on that he was so wrought with worry that he kept his phone on the highest volume all evening just so he wouldn't miss a message from her. He was happy when he didn't—happier still to know she wasn't stuck again in Eden. Not that he expected car trouble to strike a second time, but he worried just the same. All day, his thoughts bent toward her, with his greatest reminiscing occurring when he re-wound stored memories of their coed time overnight. That single evening spent in Eden was their closest contact, and every night when he lay down in the darkened interior of his own bedroom, he could recount so many details from that surprise time shared in close quarters.

Alec had spent romantic nights with women in the past, and he had been in far more intimate settings than an E-Z Tire Shop bunkhouse. But there was something about the spontaneity and the circumstances that made that one night different. It was both unexpected yet quietly memorable, not in traditional ways but in unassuming ones. There was an ease at which Mallory placed him, which was the antithesis of how his pulse climbed during most moving jobs. With her, the rate of increase was for a completely different reason.

It wasn't the job that ignited his core being. It was Mallory.

Their conversation, their banter, their humor. Alec hadn't known her long—he didn't even know her well—yet every exchange was as if he had. So when Christine reminded him of their upcoming family reunion, he didn't want to go alone. Better still, he wanted to ask Mallory. She was on his mind, being the person she was.

But there was also physical attraction at play.

Her petite body was full of spunk. She joked and laughed and moved in memorable ways. He couldn't forget her blondish-brown locks, which were so silken he wanted to thread them through his fingers until they got lost.

He conjured memories of her lips, the way they curled in subtle lines he learned to read so keenly in just their handful of encounters. And because he knew them, he swore those lips begged for a kiss beyond the special one they shared.

He envisioned Mallory's coy looks that lit her face in ways she didn't even know. But Alec did. Because he couldn't stop stealing glances at her every chance he got, whether they were boxing her things or sharing a snack or fawning over Bella.

He knew Mallory because he could recall everything about her.

Alec double-checked the digits on the mailbox, making

sure he had the right address. The numbers matched, but so did the car parked on the opposite street. He knew her car since he trailed it all the way to Texas. Now, it was back in Santa Fe.

Mallory was back in Santa Fe.

And Alec couldn't stand another moment of not seeing her.

He parted his hands and wiped them on the surface of his blue jeans. He grabbed the key out of his truck's ignition, placed a hand on the door, and took his first step toward Mallory after nearly two months of physical absence.

One foot in front of the other. He was so shaky with anticipation he might as well be going to the White House instead of a simple stucco on this downtown side street. Mallory Fredrick sent him off-balance in a way other women didn't do.

There was no doorbell on the modest porch, but there was an antique brass knocker squared in the center of the wood door. He lifted and lowered the handle three times, his nerves jolting with each point of contact.

"Coming, coming," he heard a voice call from inside.

Mallory. He smiled to himself. He recognized the melody of her words even without seeing the composition of her face.

The door swung open, and his breath caught in his throat as if an unexpected breeze had just blown. Instead, it was her.

This time he said her name aloud, the syllables escaping his lips in a whisper. "Mallory." She curled into the embrace he made for her, a warm and comfortable exchange months in the making. "Welcome back." His lips skimmed the top of her head as she cupped her own arms around his torso and squeezed her version of a hello.

He would stay in that position as long as Mallory wanted. Every nerve ending of shared contact brought a satisfaction he only experienced when he was with her. And this he knew—because he had searched for that same feeling in her absence.

And Alec couldn't find it.

Here, Mallory's mere presence was a rediscovery in familiarity laced with a little bit of fire. As Mallory pulled back, her eyes ignited her face in a great expression of joy. Her grin from ear to ear was as wide as the emotional hole Alec experienced when he drove away from her in Texas, leaving her in his rearview mirror. But now, holding her, all of that dissipated.

It was the two of them.

Together.

And he had just one weekend to make Mallory realize that Santa Fe—not Seguin—was where she belonged.

MALLORY INHALED THE scent of Alec as she settled against his chest. The soft cotton of his tee mingled with his cologne beneath, a heady mixture of masculinity and coziness. His body felt incredible.

And that made Mallory feel incredible.

"Welcome back." His words made her melt faster than chocolate on a sunny day.

"It's good to be back." The words had been traveling with Mallory all the way to Santa Fe, and they found a home with Alec.

"Good trip?" Alec sheltered Mallory tightly in his embrace.

Mallory inhaled and didn't mince her words. "Better arrival." She had no predetermined plan of how she would act once she saw him, and any plan would have been thrown out the window anyway. Her emotions were in charge. That was par for the course so far this year.

Yet the emotions with Alec were a complete turnaround from the tumultuous swirl of the end of her semester. And for that, her heart was freed.

Alec lowered his gaze. "Anything in particular about your arrival worth sharing?"

He was baiting her, and Mallory knew it.

Yet she bit.

And what reason was there not to? Here she was in a hug more intimate than friendly with Alec, completely unlike the one she extended to Jovanna the prior night. Their actions spoke more loudly than even their words, though she wanted to bring those up to pace. Her answer followed as fluidly as their movements. "I didn't expect this." She slackened her hands and arms so that she could meet his eyes, yet she didn't release the embrace. "I expected a mover." That was why she hired him. Yet Alec O'Donnell moved more than her stuff. He moved—her. "I just didn't expect to feel this."

Even though she couldn't quite articulate more than that, Alec seemed to understand. His dimples exploded like parallel fireworks across his face, the happy sight causing Mallory to mirror happiness of her own. But ever Alec, he tempered the seriousness with an edge of humor. "Just don't forget that feeling this afternoon at the reunion. You know, right about that time when my family members are parading past and asking ridiculous questions that I swear are questionable parts of my gene pool."

The family reunion reminder brought Mallory squarely back to the present and her reason for returning mid-semester to Santa Fe. "About that . . ."

"Here we go." Alec finally released Mallory and took a small step backward. "Question time. Let me have it." His arms dropped to his side, vulnerability on full display.

Mallory immediately missed being in his comforting hold. But she certainly had questions stored she had wanted to ask but that seemed impersonal over the phone. Face-to-face, she now had nowhere to hide her fear of asking them. "Well," she cleared her throat. "Since you are offering—"

"I knew it." He pointed a playful finger. "I knew you had questions."

"You invited me across state lines to meet your entire family. And I haven't yet met so much as one member. You didn't think there would be questions?"

Alec stood inches from Mallory, so close it was hard to concentrate on just his words. "I figured you'd ask them if you had them."

"And I do."

"Good." He grinned.

Mallory's knees softened. *Compose yourself. Say a full sentence.* "I'm flattered that you invited me to this. And I'm really glad to be back here." She cleared her throat again. "But why me? Why this event?"

Alec's grin dissipated, and he nodded shared understanding for the fairness of her questions. "Can we sit?" He motioned to the porch steps.

"Sure." Mallory took his hand for balance and lowered herself onto the middle step as Alec poised on the top one, stretching his long legs below.

"My family has these reunions every two years. Clockwork, these get-togethers. Always in spring. Always in Santa Fe."

Mallory offered him silence to continue.

"I told you about the antics of it all. You'll see as much today, mark my words for that." He brought his hand to his brow and tugged at his skin. "But my family also is very close, and they ask questions. They want to know about relationships and marriages and family. Futures are important to them."

Mallory nodded, reflecting on her own parents' desire for stable and happy futures for both her and Paige. She certainly understood that aspect of family.

"I had a serious girlfriend during college. And I introduced her to the family. She got close to my sister Christine and my mom. The whole bit. But after St. John's, she just couldn't see a future in New Mexico. She started looking out of state for jobs, and she wanted me to do the same."

Mallory swallowed, knowing the weight of such a decision. "And did you?"

Alec shook his head. "My life was here. And Santa Fe is where I wanted to start my business. Traveling is one thing, but coming home has to feel right. This city feels that way."

Mallory didn't ask the woman's name. Some details were better not to know. But she was curious about the location. "To where did she move?"

"Portland."

Mallory had only ever seen Oregon in photographs. "That's a far cry from this place."

"You can say that again." He looked around Jovanna's yard. "Oregon's beautiful, no doubt."

Mallory imagined what Alec might have seen as she verbalized, "Towering trees. Forests bursting with foliage. Air so fresh it probably tastes sweet just by walking outside."

Alec nodded, but he didn't look convinced. "Maybe." He looked around Jovanna's yard some more. Her small lot was dense with characteristic Santa Fe xeriscaping of succulents and yuccas and scrubby ground cover. From far away, all the colors looked like shades of green and brown. But up close, especially from this perspective on the steps of the porch, burst of colors in lavender sprays, dots of mahogany, and tiny yellow buds could be appreciated. Only those who took the time to look up close could uncover these plants' secrets. Much of New Mexico's outdoors was like this—underappreciated—but Mallory knew how to look for the natural surprises. Alec did too, and he practically read

Mallory's mind by saying, "But I like this too. Right here."

Mallory aimed to fully understand, and she chose her words carefully. "So you chose place over a person?"

"I chose a future of my own making," Alec answered instead. "Does that sound selfish to you?"

Who was she to judge? Besides, charting one's own path was sensible. It was advice she tried to impart to her students. "Not at all."

Alec's next admission landed suddenly. "She wasn't the one."

"Not what I was wondering." Though Mallory had some vague curiosity about the ex-girlfriend in that regard.

Alec plucked a leaf from a nearby shrub that had been pruned into a rounded shape. Its new spring buds were just awakening. Alec pressed the leaf between his fingers and rubbed it like a worry stone. "I'm too old to play games. I know what I want. And I know what makes two people compatible." He stilled his fingers and looked straight into Mallory's eyes. "Best case scenario? You enjoy me and my family so much today that you decide to make a relationship of this when you're ready. Maybe when you come back permanently to Santa Fe."

Mallory gulped. There was the answer to their status of which she was wondering. "And worst case scenario?"

Alec pondered that in silence before he settled on an answer. "Worst case scenario is that today's family reunion sends you running back to Texas."

Mallory shook back hair that had fallen into her face as she dismissed, "I don't see that happening."

"What do you see?" Alec's eyes stayed on Mallory.

With her hair tucked like a curtain behind her, she leveled her gaze and locked eyes with Alec. "A future in Santa Fe."

Whether that was with Alec O'Donnell as a permanent romantic partner was yet to be determined. But making one decision at a time was fulfilling. She was here—in Santa Fe—and something about this sense of place, even though she had no address to call her own, simply felt right.

Chapter Nineteen

MALLORY WALKED SIDE by side with Alec into the community hall his family rented for the event. He dipped his head close to her and kept his voice low. "Are you nervous about today?"

Mallory didn't know what to feel about anyone in Alec's family, so she deflected the question back to him. "Are you?"

"Not nervous, no. But whenever I get together with my family, I'm curious about what news I've been missing."

That was fair. Mallory looked around at the hundred or so people who dotted the interior of the hall. "This is a lot of family." She thought about her tight clan of mom, dad, and sister. Sure, she had extended family—but nothing like this parade of folks.

"This amount of people in one place only happens every two years." They stopped at a table near the entrance and Alec grabbed a permanent marker. He slid two adhesive name tags off a stack. "That's why we wear these."

"Really?" Name tags at a family event seemed more like a conference setting than a family one. "What should I write?"

"Your name is a good start," Alec quipped.

"Funny," Mallory deadpanned. "I mean first name? Last name?"

"Whatever you want." He uncapped the marker and scripted *Alec O'Donnell* across the tag. "Or you can make up a name."

"Oh, that would go over well." She accepted the marker as he passed it to her.

"Who would know?" He stripped the backing of the name tag and placed it on the left side of his shirt, pressing firmly against his chest to make sure it stuck.

"You would know."

"I'll call you whatever you want, sweetheart." He leaned with one hand on the table, as if daring her to write that pet name on the tag.

I'm tempted. Mallory's stomach fluttered with a quick rush of flattery at hearing the label. She was getting more and more used to it every time she heard it. Stuffing the intensity of emotion down again, she leaned over the table. Then she said a bit under her breath, "I'm used to just signing Professor Fredrick."

"Professor?" Alec's inflection raised. "You're a professor?"

"Surprise." Mallory scribbled her first and last name instead, sans her title. She recapped the pen and placed it on the tabletop. "Liberal Arts at Santa Fe College."

"How did that never come up in conversation? I thought you worked at the college in an office."

"Oh, I have an office," she corrected, trying not to sound pompous but probably doing so just the same. "And I do plenty of office-related work."

"So is that what I call you now?"

"No," Mallory pivoted as she pressed her own name tag

into place. "You can still call me sweetheart."

"Deal." They sealed the flirtation with an exchanged wink. The ice was broken between them as a couple, and Mallory suddenly experienced a rush of confidence in her ability to chat, mingle, and even have fun for the day. "Any other surprises I need to know about?" Mallory could hear the interest pique in Alec's question.

"If you did"—Mallory stepped forward, full confidence trailing in her wake—"they wouldn't be surprises."

"You know how to keep my focus, Professor Sweetheart."

Mallory threw her head back in laughter, the weight of her chandelier earrings pushing the drape of her hair. "Now that's a name I've never heard." *But I like it.*

Alec layered on a final line of charm. "Then I'll be sure to use it again." He placed his hand gently on the small of her back as they stepped further into the din of activity.

This was going to be a good day.

Aromas from casseroles, warm entrees, fresh salads, sides, and desserts of all manner and variety teased their noses. Laughter sprang from children who ran in circles playing impromptu games of indoor tag. And groups of smiling O'Donnell family members of all ages congregated in standing groups and around tables. People looked around from time to time, but no one stared or pointed. She wasn't sure what she had expected—*more attention, maybe?*—but this extended group of people seemed like any other gathering.

Buzzing with conversation.

Happy with activity.

But normal. Quite normal.

"Anyone you want to talk to first?" Mallory wanted to make sure she didn't hold Alec back from visiting or mingling.

He stretched his gaze to a far corner and nodded in the direction with his chin. "I do want to show you that." Mallory followed his motion and spied several tables set in a horseshoe shape, each with a tented tag next to a stylish display.

Of cookies.

"Is that the cookie decorating contest?"

"Looks like the entries have arrived," Alec confirmed.

Mallory's stomach churned in sweet appreciation. Shortbreads, sugar cutouts, fruit bars, and chocolate delicacies jockeyed for attention as they walked closer. "Incredible." Not only was there food for days at this reunion, but there were enough sugary confections to feed a small army. "And these are judged?"

"Competitively," Alec stressed.

"On taste or appearance?"

"Both." They paused at the helm of the displays. "And more. They have a rubric."

Mallory practically spat her surprise. She used rubrics for grading papers at the college level, but that was for writing. This was such a different world. "You mean for judging cookies?"

"Oh, Professor," Alec consoled with an edge of spirited mockery. "These amateur bakers can get so feisty. Consider yourself warned."

"Nothing looks amateur to me." Up close, Mallory admired the clean edges of the sweets as well as artistic use of colorful icing, confetti sprinkles, and edible glitters. "I've got to take some pictures." She reached into her purse to grab her phone. "You probably think I'm nuts."

Alec shadowed her from behind. His warm breath tickled Mallory's ear as he joked, "I reserve such judgement only for family members."

"In that case"—Mallory centered a shot before she shuttered the phone in a series of camera clicks—"these nuts have my complete culinary admiration."

"Just save room. Because after lunch and the crowning of a winner, we get to eat the entries."

Mallory's stomach somersaulted in approval. This day was already too sweet to handle.

To Mallory's credit, she jumped right in to this reunion as if it were with her own family. If she had any reservations about fitting in, they weren't showing.

She was glowing more brightly than a firefly at dusk. She smiled as they walked past families chatting in groups, nodded in acknowledgement of elderly individuals seated around tables, and even stopped to pick up a baby's blanket that fell from a stroller. "There you go." She tucked the fabric around the infant as she cooed her thanks.

There was nothing that seemed to rattle her.

"Having fun yet?" Alec pulled out a chair for her at a table's edge that no one had yet claimed.

Mallory placed her purse across the back of the chair before she sat down and pushed up her shirt sleeves, her bangle bracelets jangling in tiny clangs of metal on metal. "This is all really charming."

"Glad you feel that way." There was, indeed, a certain allure to the togetherness and common buzz of activity that celebrated family as friends. It was an easy day of relaxation, and Alec was glad to have Mallory at his side to help him feel that. Otherwise, he would be sucked into conversations, called on to settle a friendly argument, or have his back slapped as older family members asked him questions about who he was dating and whether marriage was on the horizon. Mallory's presence spoke to him having a social life, but it deflected the family from peppering him with prying questions.

Just as he had hoped.

But where Mallory kept complete intrusiveness at bay, her attendance did invite direct interest from some people.

"Long time, no see." Two hands bared down on Alec's shoulders as a voice surprised him from behind.

Alec turned to face the noise, even though he recognized the female's words. "That's not true at all."

She gave him a squeeze. "I haven't seen you in weeks."

"Two," he corrected, lifting his hand to pat hers. "Don't pretend you're some long lost relative."

"Closest kin there is." She learned in to place a peck on

his cheek before standing and tousling his hair.

"Hey," Alec called, ducking to the side but not escaping the razzing. "I've outgrown that."

"Older sister says you haven't." She ground her fingers into his scalp one final time before she pulled back.

Alec smoothed his hair with his palm. "Excuse this one." By way of introduction to Mallory, he announced, "This is my sister, Christine."

"Pleasure to meet you." She stretched out her hand as Mallory did the same across the table. "Alec has told me so much about you."

"He has?" Alec watched Mallory raise one eyebrow.

"Not a thing." She grinned before releasing her hand. "My brother shares very little. You could be a crown princess for all I know."

"Maybe I should have written that as my title?" She pointed to her name tag.

"It would have made for good gossip. Not too late." She gestured to the table near the entrance. "I'll bring you the Sharpie."

"Forgive my sister," Alec cut in. "She's a little intense for some people."

"Is that what you're calling it now?" she countered in condescension. "And all these years, I thought you were enchanted by my behavior."

"Enchanted," Alec repeated, "implies a storybook relationship. And I would say we had, oh, how shall I put it?" He poised a finger playfully against his chin, searching for words. "A sibling rivalry for decades that has been anything but enchanted."

"Typical." Christine pulled out a chair and sat next to him. "Here I am trying to compliment you to your girl, and you go and ruin it."

Alec's eyes darted to Mallory, aiming to read any visual reaction she had to Christine's implied status of her as *his girl.* But she didn't so much as blush, just offering instead a simple smile before she pulled the thread on Christine's line to start a conversation between them. "I'm prepared to hear all about Alec. Childhood, teenage years, embarrassing moments. Anything you want to share."

Christine twisted in her chair, her full attention on Mallory. "Oh, girl, have I got stories to share!" She immediately launched into gossip mode, as if his past was the most interesting thing in the world.

Maybe to Mallory. Her eyes shone like ignited orbs, and she leaned across the table as if closer proximity to Christine might help her soak up juicy details.

But what did he have to hide?

Alec and Christine were close siblings. She was gutsy but golden. Totally harmless in her fire.

Christine spoke a mile a minute, and seeing as there was no stopping this train, Alec eventually excused himself to get a drink. "Can I bring you girls anything?"

Mallory declined, and Christine simply dismissed him with a wave of her hand. The two were locked in conversation, as if long-lost friends. Admittedly, he was glad Mallory connected with Christine, even if it were over the common ground of his past.

"Have fun," he said at his expense, but they were too absorbed to even hear him at that point.

Alec shook his head as he paced toward the coolers against a side wall that held soda, beer, and bottled water. He fished a bottle of water out of the slushy bath of ice for himself, twisted the top, and tipped it back in a long, satisfying drink. He brushed the back of his hand across his lips just as two women sandwiched him on each side.

Aunt Irma and Aunt Faye.

They extended on tiptoes to frame him with a kiss on each cheek. He cringed as he had no choice but to accept the affection just like he accepted their holiday fruitcakes every December. Both the kisses and the cake were unwanted, but he knew how to play the part of the good nephew.

Still, that makes three kisses from family members. Zero from Mallory. Urgh.

"Alec!" they squealed in unison. "You get taller every time we see you."

"You've been saying that since I was five years old." He turned to give Aunt Irma her requisite hug, followed by one to Aunt Faye.

"That's because it's true," Faye insisted. "And so muscular too." She took liberty with squeezing his bicep like he was a piece of produce she were considering from a farmer's market. "Are you taking steroids?"

His face contorted in reaction to the absurdity of the question. "Steroids?"

"Because your late mother, rest her soul, she would never want that. But you know that we're supposed to keep our eyes on you so we're just checking."

"You have nothing to worry about." He turned to Irma. "Or you."

His honesty did little to curb Faye's assumption. "Because if you think for a minute that steroids are the way to—"

"I don't."

But there was no derailing her motherly lecture. "You are much too precious to be poisoning your body with that."

"Much too precious," Irma echoed. He wouldn't be surprised if they both pinched his cheeks in warning.

"We love you, Alec."

"And I love you too." *Now drop this nonsense.*

"And since your mother passed, you know—"

He finished the line they were going to speak anyway. "That you just want the best for me." They really were acting like he was five, even though his mother's death was nearing its second anniversary. He wasn't sure if Mallory had put two and two together in her head, but this was the first family reunion he was attending without his mother present. That was part of the reason he didn't want to come alone, yet he struggled to explain that to a woman whom he genuinely liked. Going into this day, there was no escaping the reality of her death. Any reminder of that created a possibility for him to plunge into a dark place for which he had worked so hard to climb from after her funeral. And he wasn't going to go back there.

Aunt Faye meant well. Aunt Irma did too. But Alec shut down their spiraling concern with a finite, "You have nothing to worry about."

They each looked at him with kind eyes, insisting, "We just want the best."

"I know." And he thanked them for it. Every time he looked at them, he was reminded of his mother. That was hard, but it was comforting, too. "Now if you'll excuse me . . ." He reached down to grab another two bottles of water from the cooler, just in case Christine and Mallory were thirsty from all their gabbing. "I have to get back to a couple of special women."

"Oh?" Irma didn't miss a beat. "Spill."

"Christine's talking to—"

"I see her over there." Aunt Faye was so excited she wouldn't let him finish. "Who's that woman? That one in the lavender top."

"That really is a great color on her. Perfect for her skin tone." The women clucked like hens in their own little world, only vaguely remembering Alec as the source of their banter when he cleared his throat to remind them he was still standing there. "Who is she?"

"Her name is Mallory." Now what, exactly to call her . . . "She's a friend of mine."

Aunt Faye wasn't buying it. "Friend? That's what you called your Little League teammates—"

"Or your poker buddies," Irma chimed in. "But not a woman."

"She's my friend," Alec insisted, not wanting to offer anything more. At least not yet. He excused himself by raising the water bottles and bowing out of their conversation. "Now before they send out the search party, I should be on my way." Like his aunts, Christine was no doubt leading the charge back with Mallory. Female conversationalists were part of the O'Donnell family DNA sequence. "I want to take these drinks to the ladies."

"Tell them we said hello." Faye and Irma waved as Alec retraced the path toward Christine and Mallory, though as he approached the women closer, he expected to return to two happy faces. Instead, Mallory's brow was furrowed in concern, her eyes lowered as she leaned forward and rested a hand atop Christine's. Even before Alec could see his sister's face, he knew something wasn't right. Placing the two water bottles he held by their necks on the edge of the table, he was only able to see Christine's countenance when he lowered closer to her. She tucked her hair behind her ear and dabbed the corner of one eye. Tears spilled from where they had pooled, staining her cheek as she choked back a sob.

"Christine," Alec's concern rose as fast as his heart rate. "Why are you crying?"

Chapter Twenty

MALLORY WAS RELIEVED when Alec returned. In five minutes' time, her conversation with Christine had turned from harmless childhood reveals about Alec to what Mallory thought was simply a casual mention of Christine's only child.

"How old is he?" When Christine indicated she had a son but didn't give his name, it seemed like a logical question for Mallory to ask.

"Nineteen. He's in college."

Now the conversation was right up Mallory's alley. "What's he studying?"

"That's the problem." Christine heaved a sigh. "He's a smart kid, but he has really struggled in college."

That was the case with so many students. "Lots of students do. Is this his first year?"

"Yes."

"That's the toughest." And that was part of the reason Mallory enjoyed teaching freshmen. She liked helping them through struggles and getting them over the hump of their inaugural year in college.

"You don't know the half of it." Christine put her hand to her forehead, the lively color from earlier draining from her face. Mallory wondered if this were territory into which she should have so willingly followed Christine. But when Christine shared a litany of heartfelt reasons for her son's rough start in college—his long hours at a job more full-time than part, unreliable transportation after getting rear-ended in a parking lot, food poisoning that kept him in bed for the better part of a week where he missed class—Mallory actually understood.

"It can be hard for young adults to manage all of their responsibilities." Mallory really did feel for students like Christine's son. "It's a good thing he's still standing. He can get his feet under him for a semester, right? Or maybe come back in a year when he's ready. College will be there when he's more sure-footed, you know?"

By Mallory's quick appraisal, Christine certainly played the part of a loving mother. She nodded, but her lip trembled even though she didn't speak.

There was more.

When moisture started pooling in the corners of her eyes, Mallory's reaction was immediate. "Christine?" she prompted, extending her hand ever so gently across the table. "Are you okay?"

Christine's lower lip quivered some more before she bit it. Then she forced her eyes to widen, trying to keep the mounting tears pushing on her lower lids at bay. Yet those tricks didn't work. Mallory placed her hand atop Christine's again in a show of emotional support.

Alec walked up just in time to see Christine tuck back her hair as she wept. The sobs were quiet and contained, yet that made Mallory feel all the more uncomfortable. What had she stepped into during this conversation with Christine? Luckily, Alec asked the question that was on the tip of Mallory's tongue. "Why are you crying?"

Christine stifled what she could of her emotion with a deep sniffle and a forced change in her posture. Her eyelids blinked in rapid succession as her whole face stiffened so as to compose herself.

As Christine readied to answer—or not—Alec's eyes shot to Mallory.

Don't look at me. Mallory had few clues.

Alec pushed a bottle of water in Christine's direction. "Want something to drink?" He seemed determined to get her to respond with one question or another. She grabbed the bottle and lifted it near her chest in a swift move to unscrew the top. That was certainly more of an answer than Mallory got to her question.

Making progress. Though she really wanted to scream, "Tag, you're it," then take off to hide in the restroom as Alec dealt with baggage that she was likely not supposed to see.

Alec slid out the chair next to Christine and spoke to her with kindness and control. "Is it about Mom?"

Mallory immediately rewound what little she knew about Alec. His mother had passed, but how long ago? And from what, exactly? Maybe Christine's focus on her son was really a mask for what she was feeling about her deceased mother, something interconnected that Mallory couldn't know. That could explain the suddenness.

But Christine spoke through another round of nose sniffling. "No, not Mom." She inhaled as if to reclaim what had already escaped. "I'm sorry." She lifted her eyes now to Mallory, a look of apology replacing her outburst. As much for Alec's clarification as to get back into a talking tract, she explained, "This is about my son."

"In college." Mallory spat the two words in haste, as if saying something could take the edge off an uncomfortable situation. Even if the words were what Alec already knew. Of course he would know his nephew was in college.

Alec's retort was as hasty as Mallory's. And it was the shortest sentence he could offer to identify her occupation—and about all he knew. "Mallory teaches."

As if a dam had instantly been created by those words, Christine's eyes dried. She pounced on that bit of knowledge. "You do?"

All of the ease from earlier in the day had dissipated. Replaced now by air much heavier in emotional weight, Mallory didn't know how she'd survive an entire reunion if this first meaningful family member conversation were any indication. It was as if she were on a skyscraper's ledge brokering Christine to step back and Alec to just stay where he was. "Um, that's right . . ."

Christine's demeanor instantly perked. "Then maybe you can help."

Mallory was happy to offer generic advice. There were certainly talking points she made with her first-year students, but rarely did she ever do so with their parents. While there were exceptions, avoiding parental conversations was one of the reasons she sought college teaching instead of high school. But, here, she didn't have a choice. "Shoot."

Alec flashed an appreciative look as Christine dove deeper into her son's challenges during his freshmen year. Alec added a couple of echoed comments—"He's a good kid" and "Really works hard"—in between Christine's barrage of unloading.

Not that she was debating those things. What did she know of him?

Christine continued. "And at Santa Fe College—"

"That's where I teach."

"Oh!" Christine lit more expressively, probably assuming previously that Mallory was a secondary school teacher when Alec announced her occupation.

Most people did. She didn't have the stereotypical cat-eye glasses, polyester suit, or penny loafers that, though entirely antiquated, most people with whom she spoke for the first time expected of a college professor.

"That's perfect. I'd love for him to hear from you about the importance of a college education. Maybe just a quick pep talk? Coming from a teacher would really make a difference."

Mallory could certainly do that. "Sure."

Christine practically sang her gratitude. "That would really mean a lot. Help him get back on track. What is it that you teach there?"

"I'm in the liberal arts department. Mostly writing classes. A little literature." Mallory had to keep herself from sliding into a daydream about teaching again and all of the classes that she didn't have at the moment. Her colleagues were in the peak of the semester. But she was in the valley of sabbatical, a far cry from routine.

So, too, was Christine's next admission a far cry from anything Mallory expected. "Jesse took an English class."

Mallory's entire body seized, a cold and unwelcome rush of frenzy hearing a name that had been the source of her current situation. Surely, it couldn't be . . . yet she had to ask. "What is your son's name?"

Christine, perhaps sensing a change in Mallory's demeanor, knitted her eyebrows as if daring Mallory to respond more forcefully. "Jesse," she repeated, though it wasn't just the first name that was the problem. When she heard the last name, she knew. "Jesse Sands is my son. He's Alec's nephew."

And now it was Mallory who wanted to cry.

ALEC WATCHED THE volley of emotion between Christine and Mallory grow more intense. It was hard enough to determine why Christine was crying and harder still to understand why Mallory's eyes reddened when his sister mentioned Jesse. Like being a spectator at a beach volleyball match, the game changed in an instant.

"Do you know him?" Alec wanted to simultaneously move toward Mallory yet move away as he watched her face heat up. Her clavicle splotched with light red patches as if she were immediately allergic to something. "Do you need some air?"

Mallory reached her hand to her neck, setting her palm against her collarbone. Perhaps she knew this tell. "I need to know . . . to know." Her words caught in her throat, not in a completely restrictive way but more in a cautious use.

Alec edged the second water bottle in her direction, a small gesture that at least was practical. Maybe a drink would help refresh her. "Mallory? Are you okay?" Clearly she wasn't the same as when they entered the reunion. Or when he left her alone with Christine. She seemed to be enjoying fun, feisty conversation with his sister, but in a few minutes' time, that had changed. He wasn't with his aunts long, but what had he missed in that absence?

Christine must have sensed as much of a change as Alec. "Did I say something wrong?" Though it wasn't much of a question to answer. "If you don't want to talk about the college, I understand."

"You're his mother? Is he here?" Mallory's eyes shot past Christine then Alec then to the sides of them.

"Yes, Jesse is here."

"Here today?" Mallory brought her hand from her chest and grabbed the edge of the table, as if readying herself for some physical surprise where she may need to leap, lower, or take cover.

Alec had never seen her like this. This wasn't the Mallory he knew.

Mallory rose from her seat. "I need to talk to you, Alec. I'm sorry, Christine, I can't, um. The college and students . . ." She wasn't making sense, and Alec wanted nothing more than to swoop in and save her from humiliation and a situation he didn't fully understand. But something had set her off.

"Christine, Aunt Irma and Aunt Faye want you to say hi." He pushed his chair back and stepped around the table to reach Mallory. "We're going to step outside for a minute and—"

Mallory's voice was frantic. "Not outside. I can't stay here."

"Okay," Alec soothed, as if needing to talk Mallory down from a cliff. He reached for her purse strap stretched across the back of the chair, looped it through his index finger, and raised it to Mallory's shoulder, stiffened even though she stood. "Follow me." She took his lead in accepting the purse, moving in rigid, mechanical ways.

Christine read Alec's cue and excused herself quickly. "It was nice to meet you, Mallory." She extended her arm across the table for a handshake but drew back in midmotion as if realizing that any touch would prolong this uncomfortable turn of events. Instead, she wiggled her fingers in an awkward half wave before she pivoted and left Alec with Mallory, who was already turning on her heel in the opposite direction.

Taking two large steps to follow her, he whispered at her back, "Are you having a panic attack?"

"Nearly." She huffed, heavy footsteps reverberating against the floor in the direction of the exit. "Have you lied to me? Is your last name really Sands?"

"What?" Alec reacted as if he had been snake bitten. He

hadn't lied to Mallory about anything. Of any woman whom he wanted to date, his interaction with Mallory Fredrick was the most genuine, most natural. That was what was so special about his feelings toward her. There were no pretenses, no pressures. He was 100 percent honest and truthful. Lying never even crossed his mind for any reason when he was with her. "No."

"Because if—"

"You know my name." Surely Mallory didn't really assume he had lied about his name. It was fortified in Sharpie beneath his "*Hello. My name is*" tag affixed to his shirt. "Sands is my brother-in-law. Jesse's father."

Mallory quickened her pace in short, determined strides, and Alec kept up with effort. This girl could move. "So Jesse really is your nephew?"

"Yes, my only nephew." Christine had complications after Jesse's birth, and while Alec could have had a conversation about that under normal circumstances, this was anything but normal.

"That's just great," she mumbled, pushing over the door from which they entered with one hand. She ripped her name tag from her shirt with her other and balled it into the trash can on the way out. "I need to go back to Jovanna's."

"What?" Alec was trying to keep pace with her steps and her words.

"I need to go," she repeated, firm as her footfalls. *"Now."*

Alec didn't want to make a scene. "Whatever you need," he assured her. And he was sincere, though likely that fell on deaf ears. He wondered if Mallory would hear anything he said. He had never seen her like this, so closed off and frantic. "But I do think we should talk about what went on back there."

Mallory did not share those plans in the least, for she stopped dead in her tracks, spun to face Alec, and spoke through tears. "Your nephew tried to destroy my career. End of conversation."

THE SILENT RIDE in Alec's truck back to Jovanna's didn't take more than ten minutes. But it felt like ten hours. Mallory would have called a cab—she would have even walked—but Alec's truck was the fastest getaway from a situation that made her as queasy as a roller coaster loopty-loo.

She leaned her head against the passenger side window, the seat belt of Alec's truck the only thing keeping her upright. She closed her eyes and tugged at her dangling earring to keep her hands busy, wishing away the last thirty minutes of her life.

Alec O'Donnell was Jesse Sands's uncle. She couldn't undo that genetic thread.

And that thread had nearly undone her employment future at Santa Fe College. Shaken to her core after the social media sabotage, she was getting her confidence back. Moving to Seguin had helped her create distance that allowed her to regroup, recharge, and reenergize. That was just what she needed, and it helped remind her she loved teaching, especially in the college environment. Arrival the previous night in Santa Fe made her feel like she was home again. So did this new relationship with Alec.

Until today.

A family connection with Jesse Sands was too close for comfort.

Ending her contact with Alec O'Donnell wasn't a decision. It was a choice already made, a line she needed to draw. But that didn't make sitting next to him in a vehicle any less difficult.

Several minutes into the ride, Alec broke the silence. "I know there's something you're not telling me. And I can't fix it if I don't know what it is."

"You don't need to fix anything." She kept her eyes closed, as much to maintain her own sanity as for fear of even looking at Alec and losing her composure all over again.

"I do," he insisted. "I need to fix this."

But there was nothing for him to do. Mallory retreated into herself, a defense mechanism to protect what she had privately rebuilt. If she was going to move forward, she needed to do so with a clean slate.

No bad memories.

No connections to Jesse Sands.

No Alec O'Donnell.

This—whatever this was with Alec—had to stop.

Finding the headspace to explain was a challenge. She didn't want to pin Alec into a compromising position.

Family was important to him, and Jesse was his family. She was probably just collateral to him compared to that. Even if she explained Jesse's actions in detail or showed the dirty posting and violent words, Alec had familial allegiance to his nephew. He would never fully feel the sting of pain with which she had to live. For all she knew, he might see her as nothing more than a sensitive college professor scorned by an angry student. What would Alec care about that?

Mallory preferred to be speechless, but Alec wanted to talk. "I'm not letting this go. I'm not letting you go. Mallory, please help me understand."

"I don't know how." Because she didn't.

"Could we start by talking? If not now, later. Call me this afternoon when you're ready? Or meet me for breakfast tomorrow? Or next week or something?" They were within blocks of Jovanna's house, and Alec's desperation for an answer rose with each offer. "I'm so in the dark about this, and when I go back to the reunion . . ."

Of course he would go back to the reunion. Mallory knew that, and how could she blame him? If anything, she was completely ashamed for having been a yo-yo visitor, strung out and then retreating. Yet a close connection to Jesse Sands was Alec's reality.

It just couldn't be Mallory's.

"You need to understand," Mallory conceded, opening her eyes, forcing herself to name what had been done. "Your nephew hurt me." Alec turned onto Jovanna's street, their time together slipping. More tears welled and her heart stiffened in her chest. "I was Jesse's teacher, and my sabbatical is a result of what he did." She paused to muster further strength. "He threatened me, and criminal action was taken by the police department for doing so."

Alec made a guttural noise. From the corner of Mallory's gaze, she saw astonishment wash over his face in a paled response. His hands clenched hard on the steering wheel.

"I'm not going to relive that by describing it all, but if you want to know specifics, ask Jesse. Talk to your sister." She swallowed her emotion as best she could so as not to shatter into a million pieces. "He's suspended from campus."

"From the college campus?" Alec voice rose as high as she had ever heard it.

"Surely you knew."

"Absolutely not." Alec stopped the truck with punctuated force, Mallory jerking forward in reaction to the abruptness. "Sorry," he apologized as he turned the ignition off.

Mallory clicked to release her seat belt and grabbed her purse. "I'm sorry too. I wasn't ready for this to end." *But it has to end.*

She twisted at her waist, leaned sideways, and placed a single parting kiss on Alec's cheek. His skin was alive with heat, and even in such a swift motion, human energy jumped from Alec back to her. She winced at the shock of it, her body telling her not to leave as her mind insisted she get out quick.

Masters level work in humanities courses helped her understand human culture. But nothing prepared her for this.

She reached for the door, opened it, and swung her legs from the cab. She left Alec alone without a parting word, hurrying down the sidewalk to retreat into Jovanna's house.

She didn't even look back.

Chapter Twenty-One

THE LIGHTS IN Jovanna's living room were cut as Mallory pushed open the unlocked front door, the dim interior matching her dark mood. Her bangle bracelets jangled an arrival announcement as her eyes squinted to readjust from the bright desert sun outside. Inside, the only small source of illumination was an ivory-colored pillar candle lit on an end table. Soft meditation music sailed through the air, a tender welcome that juxtaposed with the tune of her demoralizing day.

Jovanna posed on a yoga mat in the center of the room, her limbs triangulated in downward-facing dog. Through an upside-down view, Jovanna called between her legs to Mallory, "Back so soon?"

"Hello to you too." Mallory didn't try to hide the tartness in her voice. Not that she had any reason to take something out on Jovanna. "Please don't ask."

"You know I will." Jovanna inhaled through her nostrils, the type of cleansing breath that Mallory needed. "But first let me finish my reps."

Good. Mallory needed the space to breathe. "Don't mind me." She stepped to the couch as she slid her purse from her shoulder, tossing the weight of it onto the cushions with abandon. Jovanna didn't so much as flinch. Mallory slipped the bracelets from her wrist and stacked them next to the purse, wishing she could be half as relaxed as her friend. "Comfortable?"

"This does wonders for my back." She stepped one foot forward and shot her upper body vertically into warrior I. Now, she was at least upright with Mallory.

"We used to do this religiously." Yoga class was where she'd initially met Jovanna. Mallory embraced it during her first year in Santa Fe, a way to simultaneously meet people and get involved in a routine outside of her apartment. She did love it—and the knowledge stayed with her—but she hadn't done more than token stretches in the last few months. "I've got clothes you can borrow."

Yoga would be a complete one-hundred-eighty-degree turn from the reunion disaster. And to Jovanna's credit, she was good at not pushing. When Mallory left Santa Fe, Jovanna didn't try to talk her out of it, nor did she pry beyond what Mallory chose to share. For so much more than just the offer of yoga clothes, Mallory avowed, "You're a good friend."

"Geez, something did happen today." She stood completely upright, clicking her bare heels together with her lean limbs on perfect display.

Mallory was glad the lighting was dim. Perhaps she could conceal the defeat she wore on her face.

"You look like a train wreck."

Or not.

"You can tell me now or tell me later." Jovanna dropped

back down to the mat. "Or you can join me for a cobra pose."

Mallory certainly felt like shooting venom.

"Perfect stress relief," Jovanna teased.

"So is wine." Mallory pointed to the kitchen. "I'm going to get something to drink."

"It's a little early for alcohol."

"It's never too early for alcohol." Mallory didn't have lunch, but she had no appetite. "Have you eaten?"

"Sandwich." Jovanna stretched her body, elongated her neck and shoulders, and held as gorgeous a cobra pose as Mallory had ever seen. "I'll make us two smoothies after I'm done."

"Show off," she teased.

"My culinary skills or my yoga skills?"

"Both." Mallory padded into the kitchen, ready to embrace the first guilty pleasure she saw. Wine would do, but so would chocolates, potato chips, or even a box of mac and cheese. She needed something for comfort.

"Help yourself," Jovanna called, her voice carrying with the music.

Mallory threw open the two cupboard doors Jovanna used as her pantry. Trail mix and chia seeds were front and center. Behind that were some wheat crackers, a couple of cans of soup, cereal, and a bag of chocolate chips. She reached for the bag.

Milk chocolate. Promising.

She held the bag like a one-pound free weight. Then she read the labels on two bottles of liquor. One was brandy, and one was a nearly empty bottle of rum.

"Vodka's in the freezer," Jovanna called.

Tempting.

But Mallory needed to do something. And not yoga. Drinking would just make her feel worse. She needed to be productive.

"Can I make some cookies instead?" Warm chocolate chip cookies would be comfort enough. Plus those entries from the O'Donnell family reunion contest were still fresh in her mind. The only way to eliminate the memory of those confections was to make some of her own.

"Be my guest." Jovanna shifted into a sitting position on her mat as Mallory started grouping measuring cups, a mixing bowl, spatula, and a baking sheet. Next up was making sure she had all the ingredients. Jovanna's ear must have been attuned to the sounds of everything in her kitchen. "Teaspoons are in the pullout drawer on the far left."

Mallory slid out the drawer. *Bingo!*

"And you'll have to substitute with wheat flour."

"Of course," Mallory muttered under her breath. Health benefits in warm cookies were the least of her concern. But Jovanna's arsenal of cage-free eggs, organic sugar, and Madagascar vanilla extract might fortify her with enough of an earthy jolt to feel more human.

Because, at the moment, she was feeling pretty out of touch.

With people.

With herself.

With everything.

ALEC WAS READY to wring Jesse's neck.

Jesse had done something to Mallory. Then, he lied to his family. Those reasons were enough for Alec to confront him. But seeing the hurt in Mallory's eyes created an added layer of legitimacy to a situation that Alec needed to understand.

Now.

He shifted his truck into gear with forceful fingers. As much as he wanted to trail the sidewalk after Mallory and beg her to talk to him, she made it clear she was in no place to do that.

Mallory left in shock, but Alec was in as much of a state himself. He couldn't blame her—her face wore a look of absolute devastation from the moment he joined her and Christine back at the table to the moment she left the cab of his truck at Jovanna's—yet only Jesse could help him fully comprehend the circumstances. That was the only reason he was headed back to the community hall.

Not to make small talk with distant relatives.

Not to hear one more nostalgic comment about his deceased mother.

Not to wax poetic over his aunts' cookies entered in the decorating contest.

He needed to talk to Jesse.

Alec was going to get to the root of this. What should have been a day where his relationship with Mallory blossomed had turned into the exact opposite. And all Alec knew was that if Jesse Sands had not been mentioned, that wouldn't have happened.

Alec cut his truck into the exact parking spot he left. He crawled out from the cab and immediately started scanning the lot for Jesse. He was nearly Alec's height, but he was still growing into his frame. Teenage awkwardness was slow to dissipate. The same hazelnut-colored hair as Alec must have been genetic, but Jesse's hair always looked like it was in need of a trim. Paired with his clean-shaven face, Jesse looked more like a teenager than an adult even though he was in college.

Or was he still in college? That point of fact was muddied after what Mallory communicated.

That was one aspect he needed to clarify. And the exact role Jesse played in Mallory's move was the most important of them all.

"Jesse!" Alec barked to grab his attention when he saw him standing around the bed of a pickup with several other boys about his age. He paced toward him, a straight line of ballistic missile-type targeting.

"Hey, Uncle Alec." He waved, as if this were a normal exchange.

That boy. He had to hold back from spitting nails until he could get Jesse away from this crowd.

As Alec closed the distance between them, Jesse encouraged him nearer. "Come see this new toolbox. State-of-the-art design. I bet you've never seen a truck-bed toolbox like this."

Alec could care less about a toolbox. "I need to talk to you about some stuff." He nodded an out-of-order hello to each of the other boys, but to Jesse said, "Come on over here. It'll just take a few minutes." Alec forced his emotion to stay inside his chest, his shoulders rising and falling to control the tension.

Jesse was oblivious. "Have you been inside yet?"

Alec pointed to his name tag. "Sure have."

"Then do you know if it's time to eat?"

Typical question from a typical teenager. Alec shook his head. "Don't know. But you'll eat after this. Follow me." He nodded a quick exchange as he left the group of boys who continued to ogle over trucks and their accessories.

Jesse caught up with Alec out of earshot of the others. "What's wrong?"

"Sit with me here in my truck." Alec didn't have to point to which one because Jesse knew it. He knew so much about Alec. Now, the question was, how much did he know about Mallory?

"Are we going somewhere?" His voice held every bit the boyish tone that characterized Jesse during his teenage years when he and Alec grew closer. But they were over a decade apart and a world away when it came to maturity level. Those facts were augmented by Alec's difference in voice, one that was deep and mature. "Not until I figure some things out."

Christine had Jesse young, and especially in Jesse's later years, Alec helped raise him because his brother-in-law worked on the road for weeks at a time. High school graduation had been a major milestone, and Christine was so proud when Jesse started classes at the local college. Not because he wasn't capable with academics; just because he strayed off path as a high school student and didn't show much interest in textbook learning. But enrolling seemed to be his ticket back on track.

Alec had been a good role model with his completion of St. John's. And Alec had kept Jesse accountable by asking him about classes. Though it was surface-level discussion, Alec used every opportunity to give Jesse some encouraging word or bit of advice about time management or persistence. Jesse needed to hear those things.

But he obviously needed to hear much more.

They both climbed into Alec's cab—Alec in the driver's seat and Jesse in the passenger's—and closed the doors. Alec wanted the privacy because he didn't want to chance anyone hearing this conversation. And he didn't want to give Jesse any opportunity not to be honest with him. That was the first ground rule he set. "I'm going to ask you some things. And I need you to be truthful. No lies, no omissions. Got it?"

Jesse must have expected something completely different than the seriousness of Alec's directive. "What's going on?"

"You're going to tell me that," he leveled, his tone weighted in authority. "Was Ms. Fredrick your professor?"

Jesse cocked his head, a look of surprise with such a left-field question. As if he needed to shift from wherever he had expected this conversation to go, he answered with a slow affirmation that was still noncommittal. "She teaches at

Santa Fe College."

"I know she does." Alec was above playing games. "Tell me, was she your professor?"

Jesse looked down. "Yes."

"Did you fail her class?"

Jesse didn't look up. "Guess you could say that."

Alec wanted to make sure he didn't forget the rules of this conversation. "No lies," he reiterated. "Be straight with me."

He took a deep breath, raising his chin. But instead of meeting Alec's eye contact, Jesse stared straight ahead through the windshield of the truck. "I didn't finish her class."

"You stopped going?"

His voice trembled ever so slightly. "I was told to stop going."

Now, it was Alec's turn to hold his breath as he listened to Jesse spill details of the December end to his semester. "A stupid mistake," he offered. "A really bad decision" and "can't take it back," he explained of posting threatening words on social media about Ms. Fredrick, using her name.

What Alec heard made his blood boil. Still, he asked, "Just words?"

Jesse's look of shame told Alec that wasn't all. "A picture too."

Alec clenched his fists, his knuckles turning white in frustration as his mind raced with sickening possibilities. Yet he had to know. "Of what?"

"It wasn't her," Jesse backpedaled. "A stupid picture I

found online that wasn't even real."

He hadn't answered the question, and Alec wasn't going to let him off the hook. "Of what?"

His quiet answer was as weak as his morals and hard for Alec to hear. "This picture of a teacher being roughed up."

Alec released his fists before balling them again, enraged by his nephew's callousness. Did they share blood? "What made you think that was okay?"

"It wasn't okay. I know that—"

"You didn't know that!" Frustration coursed through Alec's veins like hot lava, his body a volcano of rage only controlled by their confined space. "Otherwise, you wouldn't have done it!"

"But I've deleted everything. I don't even have that account anymore," he insisted.

Alec opened his fists and pressed both palms against his kneecaps, digging his fingers into his legs in an effort just to keep his hands to himself. He had never been so fired up, so completely ready to burst. He had never actually wrung his nephew's neck, but this certainly qualified as the most justifiable circumstance.

"It's a misdemeanor. But that's what got me suspended."

And that was even more of a shock. "You're not in school?"

Jesse hung his head again. "Can't go back. For a year. I don't even know if I will after that."

Alec's heart had always tugged toward Jesse, but now it pumped in angry throbs. All this time, he thought Jesse was enrolled for the spring semester. He had lied to him. Had he lied to Christine? Or did she know? And had she been keeping the secret from Alec too? Whatever the answer, Jesse was a coward. And Alec told him so.

"I know I am." He berated himself further. "A stupid idiot who screwed up beyond belief. I made a whole mess of my life." His voice shook. "And I can't even take it back."

No. You can't. "That's the nature of our actions." But Jesse hadn't just affected his own life. "Did you know Ms. Fredrick isn't teaching?"

"No." Jesse looked genuinely surprised. "Why? Because of me."

"I'd venture that has a lot to do with it." Alec stopped short of saying she had moved.

He didn't know all the facts, and surely Mallory Fredrick wanted to shield her privacy under the circumstances. In hindsight, Alec's head spun with realization that maybe that was why she was in such a hurry to move out of her apartment. Again, thinking back to December, Mallory was like a wounded bird. And whether Alec had helped her fly or clipped her wings by getting involved, now he wasn't even sure.

As Jesse sat stone-frozen, he retreated into himself in complete shame. "I am trying to make up for all of this. Really, I am."

Alec burned at his core in anger for what Jesse's reckless actions had caused for Mallory. Yet even as his body heated up and his limbs fidgeted, Alec's heart lurched toward this kid who he knew all his life and loved with every fiber inside of him. "Does your mother know?"

Jesse emptied the surprise answer. "Everything."

So Christine knew this whole time and didn't tell me anything. It was just Alec who was in the dark.

"That's why I haven't gone inside." Jesse looked toward the hall. "I don't want people to ask me about college. I don't even know what to tell them."

Alec could understand that.

After a brief silence where more questions still hung in the air, Jesse asked one of his own. "How do you even know Ms. Fredrick?"

Now that wasn't easy for Alec to answer. "A client," he said first. But if he expected Jesse to be honest, he needed to do the same. So he clarified with, "But I was hoping she'd be my girlfriend."

Jesse's mouth shot an expletive.

"Watch it." Alec had no tolerance for that.

"Sorry, man. I just had no idea." Jesse looked from Alec out the window and back again. "How did that happen?"

But Alec's head was swimming with so many thoughts he couldn't pin them all down. Nor did he even want to explain, which was probably best since it seemed Jesse never even saw Mallory at the reunion.

When Alec didn't answer, Jesse offered more apology. "Blame me for all of this, really. I was mad at my grades in class and didn't think it through. I was never going to do anything to her. I've apologized to the college. Wrote a letter to Ms. Fredrick that the police chief said he wouldn't even give to her. Kicked myself for being so stupid in the first place. Been working like a dog to try and earn enough money to make Mom proud of me for something." The kid certainly seemed to have his penance in order. "And I haven't had any trouble. Not a lick. Not even a speeding ticket."

Alec remembered Jesse's warning for speeding and his ticket for running a stop sign after he got his license. The two incidents practically gave Christine a heart attack, so Alec could only imagine what this legal black mark did to her. It must have paralyzed her with embarrassment, too, enough to keep it a secret from Alec. But he had also been so busy he didn't notice if there had been a change with Christine or Jesse. Not that he kept full tabs on either one, but still. He should have sensed something.

Maybe he wasn't that good at reading people.

Christine.

Jesse.

Or Mallory.

Alec spoke in a much more subdued tone than when their exchange began. "So where do you go from here?"

Jesse explained the legal ramifications and the exact terms of his college suspension.

"You're lucky that's all you got."

"That's what Mom said." His voice was quiet, and shame was written all over his face.

Alec brought his knuckles to his chest, cracked once on his right hand and once on his left, and decided against wringing Jesse's neck. It wasn't that the kid didn't deserve punishment. He most certainly did. The college had leveled that, but so had the police. Jesse Sands needed to walk a straight line, and Alec reminded him of that. "That's the only way to make this right."

"I know." Then Jesse offered, "If I could take it all back, I would."

"Too late for that."

"So I've been told." He turned his head away from Alec, his shoulders slumped so he looked more like a shell of himself than the nephew Alec knew.

College freshmen could be so foolish. Alec certainly fell into that category at one time, though he never did anything that would have been considered criminally violent. Still, he understood the age, and he knew Jesse well enough that he understood his actions were not meant to be malicious. But that didn't minimize their effects.

He wasn't excusing what he did; he was trying to make sense of it.

Even so, the law didn't care about intent. The law was only concerned with actions. What Jesse did crossed a legal line, and for that he was punished. Plus, he hurt Mallory, more than just personally. She moved states. She cancelled the lease on her apartment. And Alec would understand if she never even wanted to be a professor again.

He certainly understood her wanting to bolt.

Jesse turned his head back to Alec. "Can I tell you something?"

At this point, Alec didn't know where to take their conversation. Now, all he could think about was Mallory. He gave a half-interested, "Shoot."

"Ms. Fredrick wasn't that bad of a teacher. She was actually pretty cool."

"I bet she was." At least they agreed on that.

Alec told Jesse to go on in to the reunion. Lunchtime was probably passing them by, though Alec had no appetite for food.

Jesse exited the cab and disappeared between vehicles as he made his way into the community hall. Alec stayed in the pickup a while longer to make peace with being alone. Because that was exactly what he was.

Chapter Twenty-Two

MALLORY STAYED THE night at Jovanna's before tackling the long road back to Seguin once again. She drove with a lead foot, eager to put distance between her and the hurt that resurfaced at being in close proximity to Jesse. What she had thought could be a step in the right direction was a misstep into a relationship with Alec that was too close for comfort.

Yet she missed the man who was all hard work and Hollywood.

Alec had helped her when she needed it, being her rock when she was unsteady. As she passed through Eden, an amalgamated mix of hurt and happiness welled inside of her for memories shared and love lost. She couldn't hold Alec accountable for the actions of his nephew, yet a relationship with him would be too conditional.

That was what she told herself.

Later that evening before bed, she took a seat on the piano bench in Paige's living room as Bella pounced next to her. "Make yourself comfortable, sweet girl." She stroked her soft fur as Bella stepped onto her lap and bent into a donut shape before settling atop Mallory. She had missed her darling fur baby. Mallory placed her fingers gingerly on the keys and started a melody she knew by heart.

"Memory" from *Cats* seemed appropriate.

"Whatcha playin'?" Nathan bounded into the room halfway through Mallory's rendition. She moved one hand to pat the wooden seat next to her. He hoisted himself onto the seat then practically glued himself next to Mallory, his lips now zipped in silence as she played. He only raised his hand to pet Bella or stroke a single key at the edge of the piano without depressing it as he listened intently.

Mallory swayed gently at the prompting of Nathan's feet, which pumped back and forth as if he were on a swing. "More," he insisted when she stopped, just like he did on the playground.

"That's all." Mallory showed her hands. "End of song."

Nathan burst into applause, which startled Bella into jumping off Mallory's lap and onto the carpet. She darted out of reach of either of them.

Typical cat. Mallory dismissed Bella's manners but reveled in Nathan's. "Thank you, thank you." She bowed at her waist from her still-seated position to offer theatrical appreciation. "Now you." She helped him spread his toddler fingers across two keys and had him alternate the notes. She added accompaniment via a couple of black keys in a duet completely of their own making.

"That's a pretty song." Paige rounded the corner into the room, doting on both. "And a pretty sight."

"I'm playing piano!" Nathan beamed, his fingers sliding off the keys as he turned to look at his mom. "See me?"

"I see you, kiddo." She walked behind him, planted a

kiss atop his head, and placed a hand on Mallory's shoulder. "Aunt Mallory will have you playing like a pro in no time."

Mallory retracted her hands, letting Nathan continue to experiment. "I'm just glad this piano is getting some use, especially after all that trouble of moving it."

"I'm glad it has a home." She gathered Mallory's hair into a low ponytail with her hands and then tucked it behind her shoulders, almost in the manner they used to do when they styled each other's hair as teenagers. "And you have one here, too."

These were dear words for her sister to say, but Mallory really didn't have a home, not her own anyway. Seguin became a now permanent retreat. Mallory licked her wounds the night before at Jovanna's, then hugged her friend good-bye as she fled back to Paige's. She talked through all the pros and cons of staying in Santa Fe after the sabbatical even if she was offered her old job. And that was a very big "if." The Santa Fe College board had not yet met about fall employment contracts, so she was in complete limbo. She would just have to wait.

Still, Mallory had little confidence in feeling comfortable in Santa Fe. She couldn't face Jesse. She couldn't even continue a relationship with Alec. Her whole emotional stability was worse than she thought. Clearly, Santa Fe would do nothing but disappoint her. She couldn't simply return because her life was not the same there.

And, just maybe, she would make a life here.

"More job searching on the agenda this afternoon?" Paige kept prompting Mallory with little reminders like this throughout the next week.

"Yes," Mallory sighed. "There's a pretty campus over in Universal City from the San Antonio community college district. I might go back there and speak with human resources."

"Have you heard anything definitive from Santa Fe?"

"My dean liked my idea about a new section development for a sophomore-level literature course." She had pitched it through email.

"That's fantastic!"

Mallory had felt so. At least she had done one thing right. "I hope. But there's no guarantee. She's not sure about enrollment numbers."

"Is the class listed on the fall schedule?"

"No." And that lack of commitment from the dean was what had Mallory most worried. "And I can't count on digital promises at this point." Messages and spreadsheets didn't carry any weight. Only a signed contract did.

And without that in hand, Mallory stayed in employment purgatory.

Paige was as supportive as she could be. "I think it's good to keep your options open at this point."

That was one way to put it. But, truly, Mallory didn't feel like hunting for a job was *optional*; at this point, it was more like desperation.

She had already sent resumes to all the nearby colleges, not only TLU but also colleges and universities in San Antonio. She went as far north as Texas State in San Marcos to try for an adjunct lecturer position, which would be prestigious but a serious reduction in pay from full-time work. Plus she extended herself to as far of a commute as she could handle, including the Victoria College center in Gonzales and the Blinn College campus in Schulenburg. She explained this to Paige. "No word."

"Give it time. You know how committees work."

That was the problem. "I know exactly how committees work. Slow. Ineffective. Nonresponsive."

"That's pessimism talking," Paige insisted.

"That's realism," Mallory corrected, which was why she was going to try the human resources route instead to see if she might have success in speaking with someone there about the hiring process. But in working through that, she had also decided to give the local high school a try.

"Have you been cleared as a substitute?"

After all of her sister's prompting, Mallory finally conceded to the idea of secondary school substituting, even though there was little fanfare in the work. "I have a gig on Wednesday."

"That's wonderful!" Paige beamed as if her sister had just announced a lottery win.

"I'm overqualified."

"Can you afford to be picky?"

Mallory knew the answer to that.

Paige added perspective. "It's guaranteed pay for a day's work."

At this point, Mallory's expectations were so low the prospect of any employment check sounded good. But her heart was still in higher education, and she reflected back on colleges in the area. "The market here is just so saturated." It was different from New Mexico.

"Something will work out," Paige offered little in the way of constructive advice. "Suck it up, buttercup."

"Nice try," she said of Paige's attempt, though it was just filler since buttercup was their father's pet name for Paige. He only used the phrase on her as the baby of the family. "Dad's pep talk doesn't apply to me."

"Then I'm out of ideas."

Which was completely lame. "I just think you're done talking about employment."

"That too. Look, you have a substituting job. Try it out. See what it's like to be in the classroom again. Just take it one day at a time." Then, Paige turned her attention to Nathan, who had bounded into the room.

"Can we play a game now?" he asked with bright-eyed enthusiasm.

Entertaining a child seemed like a constant activity.

"Maybe. How about Candy Land?"

"Yes!" He squealed. "Aunt Mallory, will you play too?"

She shrugged. "Sure thing."

For the next thirty minutes, the three of them took a journey through mythical confectionary lands of the Peppermint Forest, Gumdrop Mountains, and the Lollipop

Woods. Nathan won—*was there any skill at all in this game?*—and he beamed with delight. Mallory, on the other hand, didn't even make it close to King Candy and his colorful Candy Castle at the end of the Rainbow Trail, which seemed like the universe's cruel reminder of her current situation.

Unable to win.

"Don't be sour grapes," Paige teased as she gathered the cards and Nathan gathered the game pieces to put back in the box.

"I didn't see any of those on the board," Mallory deadpanned.

"We could play again," Nathan offered.

"No thanks." She had landed on one too many licorice spaces and was stuck for some turns, which were also ironic metaphors for her employment status. Could she not even escape her life for half an hour in a preschool board game? "I'm going to go check on a few things. But good job." She reached out her hand for a sportsmanlike shake with the four-year-old.

"Good game," he concurred. At least the kid was a gracious winner.

Mallory slid into her bedroom, plopped onto the bed, and grabbed her laptop to retreat into a digital world where she could feel more like an adult.

Maybe for a short time.

She checked some routine pages, scrolled through the news, and then logged in to her work email. There were lots of messages that cluttered her box with no applicability to her, so she started clicking radio buttons to delete, delete, delete. She paged through more emails than she realized she had, though one unread message caught her attention.

Course evaluations from the fall semester were attached.

"Do I really want to know what my students thought?" Mallory mumbled to herself, hovering her mouse over the link as she considered clicking. She anticipated a train wreck of comments.

Student evaluations were always a mixed bag. Some students—usually those who performed well—would complete favorable evaluations. But those who didn't usually crucified her, as if their failure to turn in work or attend class was entirely her fault.

But that was part of the bargain in teaching freshmen. Students in first-year classes didn't have a point of comparison for the work they were doing, and so many were just learning to navigate the ebb and flow of the college environment. Freshmen were also highly opinionated, so most filled out the evaluations to completion, including optional comments about her instruction.

Mallory took a deep breath and clicked to open the first electronic file for her 8:00 a.m. Tuesday/Thursday class. That early class was one of the last to fill, so its roster included a fair share of late registrants and students who really didn't want to be there anyway.

The file opened in a new window, and Mallory adjusted the size to see the data clearly. The first section held results of scaled questions, including how useful students found certain assignments on her syllabus as well as the textbook, library services, and other college offices. The results were pretty typical as they generally swung to the "useful" but not "very useful" end.

That was good.

Then she paged to the percentages section, which culminated in a penultimate question where students rated the overall effectiveness of the instructor. Mallory got to see her score in contrast to the departmental average of all liberal arts instructors. For the fall semester, the average from her combined colleagues' classes was 3.9 on a 5.0 scale.

Her average was 4.7.

Could that be right?

She increased her screen resolution, the number appearing more crisp as she did. This was higher than her evaluations had ever been. And for a class that she thought of as her toughest critics.

Wow. She certainly didn't expect that.

She scrolled further to the optional text comments that students could make, which were collated from each of their individual evaluations. The resulting page was a testament to what they saw in her.

This professor knows her stuff.

Ms. Fredrick walked into the class with a smile every day.

I love her enthusiasm for writing. I never liked English before this class. But now I do.

Professor Fredrick has a way of explaining things that makes class fun.

One really made her laugh. *My favorite thing about Ms. Fredrick is seeing her jewelry every day. I want to raid her closet.*

She kept reading, energized by the fun of comments that

were more glowing than she had ever seen.

She never made me feel stupid. Even when I didn't know something, she helped me. Now I know how to write a college essay.

Ms. Fredrick treated everyone with respect.

I am glad she was my first college teacher. She's really good. Give her a raise.

Mallory was ready to second that! Though she'd really just settle for full-time employment again . . .

Then a comment punched her right in the gut. *This teacher is tough, but she cares so much. That makes me try hard. I want to do well. I want her to be proud of me because she always seems proud of us.*

Mallory's heart swelled with a pride she hadn't felt in months. Her heart raced back to these students and the classroom environment as she eagerly clicked on the other evaluations. Was this one section just an anomaly?

Each of the five section files was a numeric and textual testament to her teaching in ways she had never seen.

4.9.

4.6.

Another 4.7

4.8.

Every class offered high ratings and heartfelt comments. Even the class in which Jesse was a student contained a litany of affirmative comments that spanned beyond her wardrobe. Students praised her everyday demeanor, her instruction, her humor during lectures, her fun writing activities. Yet a few even mentioned her academic standards and the way she held students accountable. *She expected a lot*, one wrote, *but that's what college is all about.* When first-year students understood that, she had done her job.

Mallory leaned back against the headboard of the bed, basking in the digital discovery that touched her more than these students would ever know. This was a time when she needed their affirmations the most.

Paige was wrong. Mallory couldn't just use her skills in substitute teaching. She needed her own classes. She needed to work with students for the long-haul in the way she knew she could, in these ways that they told her she was good at doing.

She needed to be back at Santa Fe College.

IN THE DAYS following the reunion, Alec oscillated between feelings of frustration and failure. After talking with Jesse, he understood a fraction of what Mallory must have experienced. She poured her energy and soul into teaching, a noble profession. She was obviously intelligent and capable, and Jesse insisted again she really was a good teacher. "I just don't like to write," he admitted, which didn't come as a shock to Alec. "But that's not her fault," he quickly covered. "She did do this really neat thing where she made us close our eyes and we had to imagine our favorite vacation spot. Then we got to write about it but couldn't describe it with its actual name."

"That sounds interesting." Alec's mind slid to what Mallory was like in the classroom. Professional yet spunky? Feisty but fair? He was sure she could command a room.

"That was one assignment I really liked."

"So maybe you should have just focused on that."

"Hindsight," Jesse insisted. "Like I said, I was mad and stupid when it came to research. She had us doing all kinds of library stuff."

"Because it's an English class . . ."

"I know that now." Jesse had already explained his apology to Alec, but he did it again. "And she called me out for not being prepared one day. And my grades weren't good either. So I snapped. When I got home, I went on a tirade online."

Alec verified what Jesse had said about deleting the social media account. It was not only deactivated but completely wiped from the virtual strata. Maybe there was a lingering screen shot or digital download captured somewhere on somebody's machine, but at least a general web search did not result in his post being found.

"Words hurt." Alec wanted to make sure his nephew understood that.

It was a tough lesson for any age. "I know."

His nephew wasn't the first person in need of a reminder for that. Alec saw cases all the time. Between couples he was hired to move. Angry customers in restaurants. Careless drivers on the road. Impatient patrons waiting in lines at events.

Though there was so much beauty in words too. This he uncovered at St. John's, especially with his love of humanities. He reminded Jesse of this very important fact. "Words can heal too."

He nodded solemnly. "I tried that."

"Maybe you haven't tried hard enough." And that was when Alec got an idea, an epiphany lighting above him as brightly as an incandescent bulb.

He explained his idea to Jesse, whose moral reconciliation had kicked in before Alec even asked him a question. "Count me in."

"Are you sure?" Alec had the idea, but Jesse's willingness to participate needed to be his own.

Jesse nodded. He admitted he was nervous for the outcome but insisted, "I need to do this. I need to do right by Ms. Fredrick."

It would be a long shot, but the biggest risks carried the greatest rewards. They had to give it a shot.

For Alec's sake.

For Jesse's.

And for Mallory's.

If Alec couldn't win Mallory Fredrick's heart, at least he could try to make it whole again. He just hoped it would work.

Chapter Twenty-Three

"ARTSFEST ONLY HAPPENS once a year. Are you sure you don't want to come?" Paige had implored Mallory to come yesterday, and she was trying again this morning.

It wasn't working.

"You and Everett deserve some time by yourselves." Nathan was at his biological dad's house for the weekend, so Mallory really wanted her sister and her fiancé to make the most of having time for a date. "Go. Have a great day." She did wish she could get out from underfoot with them. Now about two and a half months in to her visit, she sensed she was overstaying her welcome.

That wasn't because of anything in particular Paige said or did. It was more of a feeling. She and Bella were crowding their lives, even though Paige would never admit it. And Mallory's presence made it hard for Paige to have a full relationship with Everett. Whenever he dropped in or stayed for dinner, Mallory was like a sore thumb.

Paige looped an infinity scarf around her neck before smoothing the pleats on her cascading pastel-colored maxi dress. "Do these match?"

"Impeccably." Though she and Paige didn't share the

exact same style sense, her sister knew how to own an outfit.

"Thanks." She tilted her head to judge her silhouette in the reflection of the front window. "You can always come to ArtsFest later. Did I tell you that there would be representatives from the local chamber of commerce?"

"You mentioned it was a city event."

"They help with the ArtsFest booths." Paige explained that artisan craft vendors were set up all throughout Seguin's Central Park area next to the courthouse. The block's park plaza featured a fountain, gazebo, and cute manicured landscaping framed by stores and restaurants. "Court Street Coffee is nearby."

"Coffee is your vice, not mine," Mallory reminded Paige, not falling for the caffeine tease.

"They have tea." She grabbed her purse. "Either way, Everett and I are definitely stopping there."

"See? You two have plans already." There was no need for Mallory to be a third wheel.

"You can always drive yourself. It would be good for you to meet people. Maybe make some professional connections there."

Local job leads and prospects were not on Mallory's radar. Especially not after her anticlimactic substitute teaching gig on Wednesday. She didn't expect fireworks of student reverence or beatific teachable moments. She just expected . . . something.

Anything.

More than she experienced.

Which wasn't much. Substituting was absolutely nothing

like having a classroom of her own. And although she would keep her name available through the end of the school year, she had no delusions about making this part of her professional routine. Not in Seguin. Not in Santa Fe. Not anywhere.

She responded to Paige's offer, "Thanks, but no thanks."

"Or you could just come for fun."

"I'll pass." Everett's truck tires rocked across the asphalt as he turned into the driveway, vehicular sounds reaching the interior living room where they both stood. "Really, go. Don't think about me. Or Nathan." Mallory was ready to shoo her out the door. Although her opportunity for romance was nonexistent, at least Paige had the chance. "I know you'll have a wonderful time."

Paige turned away from Mallory and trailed a two-finger wave on her way out the door. As Mallory closed it behind her, she turned into the house, resting her back against the frame. It was her and Bella alone, just like in their old apartment. The whole day was at her disposal. The hours were hers to do as she pleased, and she had a long list of private indulgences.

First up would be an intense yoga workout. She would channel Jovanna's skills—maybe she'd even call her—until she broke a heavy sweat. And even if she did so prematurely, she told herself no less than ninety minutes.

She really needed to get back into a routine, and this focused time was her ticket.

Then, she was going to treat herself to a long soak in the tub with zero interruptions from a certain four-year-old with whom she normally shared the bathroom.

Finally, she'd decided on a home pedicure and manicure. She had the perfect pink polish that screamed springtime. With any time left, she was going to indulge in some online window shopping and then a good book that would whisk her into the late evening when Paige would arrive back home.

Divine. Absolutely divine.

Time alone was so underrated.

THE HOURS PROCEEDED in smooth and steady rhythm, a perfect Saturday of Mallory's making.

She made a simple dinner salad with grilled chicken and brewed a mug of hot chamomile tea. She sipped at leisure, rejuvenated and refreshed from the day. She pulled her laptop open on the dining table and decided to check her work email. Again, her box was filled with the digital noise of messages that she deleted without even opening. But a Friday message from her dean caught her attention. It wasn't a mass memo; it was addressed only to her.

Opening the correspondence, her eyes scanned fast as she took in words she had longed to read. The college board had approved fall contracts, and her dean was pleased to share that hers in the liberal arts department was extended for one academic year. Early enrollment numbers were shaping up better than originally anticipated. Mallory would have a full-time slate of classes in the fall.

If she wanted them.

Dean Vanguard explained in the message she had spoken with Iker in the human resources office, and Mallory's sabbatical status would be cleared at the end of the semester. So she could start again in the fall with her previous salary and all employment benefits fully restored. She'd also be given a shot at the sophomore-level literature class section she had pitched.

Mallory's excitement erupted as she squealed in utter delight. She was so grateful, and she couldn't wait to share the news with Paige.

There were details to finalize, and she wanted to frame her reply carefully. She could do that tomorrow, for tonight was about basking in the satisfaction that her sabbatical had been worth it.

After she finished her tea, Mallory grabbed a light sweater and headed outside to appreciate the stillness. Evening greeted her like an old friend as she moved from the porch to the driveway.

Storied stars scattered across a fresh night sky. Mallory stepped further down the concrete to get a better view of the emerging constellations before Paige arrived home. She and Everett were having dinner after ArtsFest, so Mallory's time to herself would soon come to an end.

She slid into the black wrap sweater and cinched its band at her waist, the long cotton sleeves making her upper body disappear into the darkness. She tilted her head until she stared deep into the part of the world she didn't observe often enough.

There was too much light pollution in Santa Fe for her to see the night sky as clearly as she saw it here in Seguin. But outside of Santa Fe, on highway shoulders and roadside parks, the mountain elevation created a glorious stage for discovery. High above the clouds were incredible treasures, and whether in Texas or New Mexico, she never took enough time to consider them.

Mallory inhaled the sweet spring air, cool breezes whisking past her and teasing her nostrils with scents of wildflowers from hills nearby. Tendrils of her hair lifted and lowered on the wind, her skin prickled by each movement. Insects sang their nightly lullabies while neighbors closed curtains and blinds as they prepared for sleep.

The serenity of the day was perfectly encapsulated by this evening, and Mallory was soaking up every moment.

Just as she readied to head inside, two headlights broke through the placidity, grabbing her attention. A vehicle slowed along the street's curb, idling into park in front of Paige's house.

Everett? Mallory squinted her eyes trying to identify the pickup truck's body style. When the passenger door opened, the occupant who exited most assuredly was not her future brother-in-law.

Not even close.

Her pulse spiked as her heart pounded with a force she had never experienced. She wanted to scream, yet her voice was paralyzed in surprise. Every fiber of her being kicked into an urge to flee though none of her limbs would move.

Mallory's legs petrified, her feet immobilized in complete fear.

"Professor Fredrick," the voice broke through the dark.

Her body seized with recognition. The silhouette. The height. The way he addressed her.

"Jesse," Mallory called back, mustering every ounce of personal strength to try and sound tougher than she felt. "What are you doing here?"

"Mallory," came a second voice, as recognizable as the first but for an entirely different reason.

She squinted again, trying to make sense of the outline of two people she least expected coming closer to her. "Alec?"

His frame advanced in slow steps, his boots, jeans, and tight tee silhouetted against dim backlight from a faraway streetlamp. "Hold on a minute," he called, placing his hand out to slow Jesse's movements. Then he stopped far enough away from Mallory that she could pivot and run into the house before either was able to get to her. "We didn't expect you to be in the driveway."

I didn't expect you at all. "What's going on?" She crossed her hands over her chest, wrapping her top tighter and enclosing herself in a hug for personal strength and protection.

"I'm sorry." Alec kept his hands out of his pockets with his fingers spread, as if he were showing Mallory that there was nothing he was hiding. "This was all a big gamble. We didn't even plan on stopping tonight."

That sounded like stalker talk, and Mallory reconsidered bolting. She hadn't locked the front door, right?

"You must think we're crazy."

Precisely.

"And maybe it was crazy to drive all the way here without letting you know. But this weekend was the only time Jesse could get off work—"

"I'm here to apologize." Her former student cut in, not unlike he did during class. Alec immediately tried to shush him, but instead Jesse was fueled with a frenzy of emotion that sprayed apologies like a lawn sprinkler. "I was a total screwup, and I know I can't go back in time. But I can make things right for you." He delivered lines of regret and remorse unlike any expression of contrition Mallory had ever heard. All of this was from over twelve feet away, in the dark, on a Saturday night, in Seguin—from a boy who lived in Santa Fe.

And Alec stood by, himself now a statue in Jesse's shadow.

"You don't have to forgive me. You don't have to even say anything." Mallory wasn't. "But I need to say that I was wrong and I was immature. I am sorry for all I have done. I won't take words for granted again."

It was certainly a strong sentiment, though Mallory's head swam in the spontaneity of it all, not sure if she was treading the water of this experience.

Or drowning.

She opened her mouth but only gulped a mouthful of night air. She sank back into the ocean of darkness, letting Jesse's words of retribution crest over her. He kept his distance, and so did Alec. Perhaps he was giving his nephew space for his monologue. Perhaps he was giving Mallory space. Either way, there was no escaping the words that were meant for her alone.

Jesse was her student, and his final lines were filled with the type of simple wish she carried for everyone in her class. She aimed to make them better by the end of the semester than they were at the beginning. Sometimes, that took the form of grades. Other times, that took the form of personal growth.

Jesse was polished in his words. "I've learned from you. I'm a better person for having you as a teacher." His apologetic eyes met hers, and she couldn't look down or away. In that moment, she saw Jesse Sands for who he really was—a young adult finding his way. He asked her to consider one final thing. "Don't let my stupid mistake keep you from continuing to do what you're really good at doing. That's being a professor."

No one spoke for several moments, Mallory caught in a triangularization she never expected but appreciated.

It was never too late to apologize, to try to make things right. This Mallory knew. What she didn't know was the role Alec played in all of this. He clearly drove Jesse here for face time, but was this prompted by him? And to what end?

Jesse sounded genuine, and he would gain nothing tangible from speaking with Mallory. It wasn't like his misdemeanor would be wiped away or his college suspension would be lifted. Those were set. But was this all a favor to Alec, an attempt at retribution for the sake of saving their budding romantic relationship? Jesse couldn't answer that, and now wasn't the time to ask Alec. This wasn't about him anyway. So Mallory mustered her voice enough to focus on Jesse. "I appreciate the apology and that you took the time to tell me." She relaxed her arms from around her torso but clung to fabric on each side, as if doing so would keep her guarded.

Rarely did Mallory have encounters with her students after the semester ended, rarer still with students who didn't complete the class. But Jesse Sands was in a whole different league. His actions—his mistakes—were not indicative of freshmen as a whole. She forced a tight smile, and he returned a look of gratitude.

But she had no intention of prolonging this. "You should probably both go now."

Each nodded in her direction. Then, Jesse Sands and Alec O'Donnell drove away as stealth-like as they came. The neighborhood was once again as it was. The night returned its former silence. And Mallory Fredrick was alone.

Something lifted from the air as the truck drove away. Mallory felt it first in her shoulders, then deeper at her core. A resiliency broke through the shadows of personal doubt that had followed her for months. She was a teacher, and while she didn't always succeed in reaching each one of her students, she realized none were hopeless. For even with painful mistakes, there was a chance for penance.

Jesse boldly owned his mistake with a face-to-face apology. Even though his actions had been immature, this move had been the opposite. Mallory's past trauma wasn't minimized, but this was a step forward for both their futures.

Oh, the perils of being nineteen! So many emotions, such a dizzying age . . .

She held out her hands, raised her arms with palms toward the brilliant stars above, and spun in clockwise circles. Turning and turning in steady, controlled spins, she tried to escape the weight of the last few months. She closed her eyes then increased her speed—faster and faster—as her arms fanned around her. She let the atmosphere carry her stresses, her shame, her uncertainty. She spun until she felt weightless, as if in this freedom of movement she could be lifted off the ground and join the night above.

When she finally slowed enough to open her eyes, her world was a blend of blurred sights. Though she couldn't see the neighborhood clearly, she looked again toward the sky. There, high above, her gaze met twinkling stars, reminders that even in darkness, there was light.

Chapter Twenty-Four

WINDS OF UNCERTAINTY had blown Alec back to Mallory, with Jesse in tow. Now, she had to decide what move to make.

If any.

Mallory was used to commanding a classroom, not negotiating late night apologies and their aftereffects.

She couldn't control Jesse or attempt to put herself in his shoes. Sure, she had been his age once, but she couldn't pretend to fully understand him. And she didn't need to do so. What she could understand and control was her own personal reaction.

Mallory could choose to move forward, not forgetting what had happened, but also not letting the past define her. She was meant to teach, and she was ready to be back in a classroom.

She had Dean Vanguard's email to share with Paige and Everett when they returned from ArtsFest. After hearing the news, both high-fived her success and told her how proud they were of her for staying the course. She really had found her professional purpose again.

Paige's words were especially sincere. "I am glad you will get back to doing what you love."

"Me too." Mallory knew in her heart that teaching college was where she needed to be.

But there was one more college surprise to share—the late evening driveway visitors of Jesse and Alec.

Everett's defenses rose as Mallory explained. "So they came in the dark?"

"They drove the whole way through from Santa Fe." Mallory knew the route well. "I don't think they intended to see me outside. But"—she jabbed Paige back with her own words—"I'm a gypsy, right?"

"Gypsies don't stand on residential driveways."

"This gypsy does." Mallory pointed her two thumbs playfully against her chest.

Everett kept them on track. "So, was this Alec's doing?"

Mallory had wondered that. "I suspect he offered to drive him." They listened with sympathetic ears to Mallory's appraisal of the reunion as well as Jesse's apology. "Ultimately, it doesn't matter to me whose idea it was to drive here. What matters is the result."

"Which is?" Paige prompted.

"That Jesse made things right. I'm not going to forget what he did. I can't." Situations like that with students didn't just evaporate from memory. "But one thing I have learned about life from my years of teaching is that it's a contact sport, not a spectator one. It's messy and emotional and sometimes not anything like we plan."

Paige and Everett voiced their agreement. "We can relate to that on more levels than one." Then Paige added, "So, gypsy, professor, or whatever you are, are you happy with

Jesse's apology?"

Mallory didn't feel it was her place to judge that. Instead, she circumvented the question with the truth of what she knew. "I'm happy that I have the strength to navigate situations like this."

"Fair enough," Paige conceded. "But what about Alec?" Ultimately, she wanted to know how Mallory felt about him.

She thought carefully before answering, sorting through her conflicting emotions. Alec O'Donnell had been an anchor when she needed it, and this spring semester had been her time to regroup. Now, she was back on track and could see her future more clearly.

And she saw someone very special in it.

Alec had been a surprise to her all along. The journey she thought had led her to Texas and back again had actually been leading her not just to a place—but to him. He was a part of her journey, but now she saw him at the end of it all. "With Alec, I feel like there's a chance." She saw romantic possibilities with a clarity that had eluded her for months. Mallory knew what she wanted.

"A chance for what? Is that what you want?" Everett asked.

She wanted her job, which she had. But she wanted to share her life with someone special. Mallory was ready to open herself to love. "I want to let people in. I've been so blinded, so closed-off by what happened that I couldn't do that with Alec."

"Cut yourself some slack, Mal." Paige reminded her that both people had to be in the right place for a relationship to blossom. She reached her hand to Everett's and squeezed it as if sharing a private message.

Mallory understood relationships took two.

"But I'm not sure if he'll even have me." All of this was brand new territory. "I don't even know if he's interested in a relationship with me or if bringing Jesse here was just some kind of closure for him."

"There's only one way to find out," Everett insisted.

"But you don't have to do that tonight." Paige pointed to the clock, the hour nearing midnight. "Get some rest."

That was best, though the uncertainty of not knowing her future with Alec was going to make it hard to sleep. Even as she tossed and turned in bed, she must have picked up her phone a dozen times, wanting to call Alec. She stopped short of pushing the call through each time.

Mallory finally feel asleep with Bella curled in her bed and her phone next to her pillow.

Sunday morning, her mind buzzed in a fog of half-slumber. She turned her head toward a sound that woke her, thinking for a moment it was her alarm. But she hadn't set one. She peeked with one eye at her phone and saw Alec's name lighting up the screen. She stumbled through her sleep to answer his call. "Hello?"

"It's me." And just like that, his handsome Hollywood voice slid back into Mallory's ear and to her life.

Mallory smiled through Alec's wake-up message. He and Jesse had spent the night at the Park Plaza Hotel in the heart of Seguin. "Traveling here is becoming quite a routine for you."

"Two trips in three months," he agreed. "Does that qualify me for citizenship status yet?"

"Hardly." Mallory continued to be charmed by his ease of humor. "But I'm impressed."

"I'm the one who's impressed." Alec's voice took on a tone of seriousness. "You are the epitome of grace under pressure." He told Mallory about Jesse's high praise for her as a teacher, in spite of his blowup. He didn't excuse Jesse's behavior—if anything, he helped him own it—though he wasn't someone to give up on a family member. He shifted the conversation back to Mallory with a new level of honesty. "I haven't been able to get you out of my mind."

Here, here. She could second that.

"I don't just introduce anyone to family."

She cringed at the memory of running out on his reunion. "About that . . ."

"Don't apologize. You have no reason to." Mallory appreciated that. "I didn't understand everything, and I didn't want to push. That would have pushed you away, which is not what I wanted."

You and me both.

Then Alec paused just long enough for the heft of his next admission to sink in. "Pulling you closer is what I want, Mallory." He continued, "I want to try to make something work. On your terms, completely. Whatever that looks like, whatever pace you want to set. If you're willing to give a long-distance relationship a shot, then so am I."

"Now would be a good time to tell you something." Alec was honest with her, and now it was time for her to be honest with him.

"What's that?"

Mallory wished she could do this in person. But a phone call would have to be enough. "I'm coming back to Santa Fe. Permanently."

Alec's voice rose like someone whose racehorse pick had just crossed the finish line first. "Does that mean—"

"That's exactly what it means." Mallory understood his enthusiasm because she shared it. "I want to try to make something work with you too."

MIDMORNING, COURT STREET Coffee was brewing with excitement. And so was Mallory for seeing Alec.

Alec and Mallory agreed to meet at the coffee shop before he would have to get on the road back to Santa Fe. While Alec walked the block to Court Street, Jesse stayed back at Park Plaza Hotel.

Jesse was close, but Mallory still felt safe. So much had changed in several months' time, not the least of which was her own confidence.

The purpose of Alec and Jesse's whole there-and-back trip was to see Mallory, so Jesse could have an opportunity to make things right.

Alec was not intending to be involved, though he admitted he was more than thrilled to get to see Mallory, especially for this private meetup at the coffee shop. "I'm glad we get to spend a bit of time alone." They made their plans over the phone, and now less than an hour later, they were seeing each other face-to-face.

No student apology.

No family reunion in the background.

No moving boxes in their way.

Alec and Mallory greeted one another in the interior of the quaint shop with a long and satisfying hug. Mutual smiles and warmth transferred between them, and their status just felt right.

They uncoupled but stayed close as they faced the counter. As they studied the board to place their order, Mallory acknowledged the distance back to Santa Fe. "You have a long trip ahead of you."

"I'm getting used to the drive." He nudged her gaily on the shoulder. "And I always go slow through Eden."

So many memories. She turned to him with a smile, sealing the bit of flirtation. She would always remember Eden.

Seguin had been good to her too. Being here helped her realize where she fit. Though this town was a perfect match for Paige, Mallory's was Santa Fe.

"Are you going to stay here through the summer?"

"That depends." And it did, on lots of factors. Details were to be determined, "But I'll stay here through Paige's summer wedding."

"That's in June?"

"If she and Everett can last that long." Mallory looked again at the order board, musing on her drink choice as well as relationships. "They are so much in love."

"I'm sure it's going to be a beautiful celebration." Alec pulled Mallory toward him and held her in a loose but comfortable embrace. She liked the feel of him close. "What are you going to order?"

If Paige were here, she'd order a coffee. But Mallory preferred a different beverage, and she was unable to resist a pun. "I'm steeped with a thirst for strong tea."

Alec's chest rose and fell with his chuckling. "Clever with your words this morning, Professor."

"Just glad you're someone who appreciates it." She squeezed his arm as he responded with a kiss atop her head. They shared so much.

In turn, they each placed their orders. Then, after Alec paid, they took their mugs and sat together at a table.

Close but not crowded.

Comfortable but not forced.

"Shall we toast with these?" Alec gestured to their mugs.

"Sure." Mallory raised hers. "Do you have an idea?"

Alec met her mug in the air. "I sure do." He looked at her with admiring eyes. "To the start of a beautiful relationship. You. Me. And that adorable cat."

Mallory's heart warmed at the mention of Bella, completely touched. "You hadn't forgotten?"

Alec raised an eyebrow. "A cat that slept closer to me for a night than her owner? Hardly forgettable, sweetheart."

Mallory grinned. "I'll drink to that." They clinked their drinkware in mutual celebration for what was beginning again between them. As Mallory took a sip of her tea, she eyed Alec over the rim of her mug. His gaze met hers, and with distance and challenges bridged between them, each knew they were staring into a future full of promise.

THANKS TO JOVANNA'S eagle eyes, Mallory was able to secure the one-bedroom rental down the street from her best friend, just blocks from the plaza. The home had all the comforts she had known in her apartment, with the added bonus of a bit of yard space.

It was a fresh start for Mallory in terms of residence, yet coming back to Santa Fe had been the best choice of all. She was renewed in her professional life, eager to get back into the classroom and make a difference for students who needed it after her sabbatical. She had even encouraged Jesse to consider a technical program, and he was applying for one at a trade school. He was getting his life back on track and realizing a poor decision had consequences but was not a death sentence.

Alec was glad to have her close, and they relished time together as their relationship grew. They enjoyed dinners, outdoor walks, and Mallory's favorite activity of all—Saturday shopping at the plaza.

"Ready?" she called to him as she grabbed her leather tote in one hand and her sunglasses in the other.

"If you are." Alec opened the gray, glass-inlay front door that was as pretty a part of the house as any of its other unique features. Mallory loved the wrought iron details of the frame and windows the best, bits of Santa Fe flair that made her smile. "Looks like it's shaping up to be a beautiful day." Warm sunshine bathed them as they stepped outside.

Mallory positioned her sunglasses into place before reaching for Alec's hand. He mirrored her movement, taking her hand in his and walking toward the plaza where jewelers and crafters of all variety showcased their wares every weekend. "Shopping for jewelry in my backyard is a dream."

"Actually, it's our reality." Alec squeezed her hand and flashed his Hollywood smile, both dimples lighting his face in shared excitement. "Looking for anything in particular today?"

They strolled past marketplace-style vendors who spread their handcrafted art atop richly woven tapestries of vibrant desert colors. Silversmiths displayed necklaces and bracelets strung with beading in every variance from flashy, sterling designs to polished, versatile patinas. Stamped patterns shone on rings adorned with turquoise, lapis, and larimar. Gems in a multitude of shades—from jaspers to jade and citrines to coral—added colorful choices that begged to be worn.

"I don't have anything like this." Mallory picked up a triple-strand bracelet accented with burnished sterling beads and a toggle closure. "I could stack it with these two bangles." She lifted her wrist to try it on.

Alec leaned close and helped her clasp it. "Not too heavy?"

Mallory rotated her wrist. Never one to sweat when it came to the weight of fashion, she apprised, "It's perfect."

Alec agreed and placed a single, sweet kiss against her

forehead. "Let it be my treat to you." Mallory was fully prepared to purchase it herself, but Alec insisted. "Consider it a coming home present."

Mallory liked the sound of that.

She lifted her heels and leaned into an embrace with Alec, which was as comforting as the scene around them. For after all the setbacks and turmoil of the past months, she was finally in the place that she needed to be.

Mallory had come home.

The End

The Texas Sisters Series

Book 1: *Finding True North*

Book 2: *Coming Home*

Available now at your favorite online retailer!

If you loved the Texas Sisters series, don't miss the

Texas BBQ Brothers

Book 1: On the Market

Book 2: Off the Market

Available now at your favorite online retailer!

About the Author

Audrey Wick is a full-time English professor at Blinn College in Texas. Her writing has appeared in college textbooks published by Cengage Learning and W. W. Norton as well as in *The Houston Chronicle, The Chicago Tribune, The Orlando Sentinel,* and various literary journals. Audrey believes the secret to happiness includes lifelong learning and good stories. But travel and coffee help. She has journeyed to over twenty countries—and sipped coffee at every one. Connect with her at audreywick.com and @WickWrites.

Thank you for reading

Coming Home

If you enjoyed this book, you can find more from all our great authors at TulePublishing.com, or from your favorite online retailer.

TULE
PUBLISHING

CPSIA information can be obtained
at www.ICGtesting.com
Printed in the USA
LVHW091549230919
631991LV00002B/447/P